The Book of Stanley

"Babiak has a keen eye for human foibles and our willful blindness of our own self-delusions." —*Edmonton Journal*

"Todd Babiak is my new favourite social satirist." —*Toronto Star*

"[A] mix of tenderness, kookiness, and high-spirited blasphemy . . . *The Book of Stanley* gives us a divinity for our noisy, coarse times." —*The Gazette*

"Babiak skewers all and sundry . . . with relentless good humour and keen wit. The strong cast of characters and sense of unpredictability will keep most readers plunging through the brief, almost capsule-like chapters." —*National Post*

The Garneau Block

"This novel is fast-paced, savvy, bursting with vivid characters. Satire that sucker punches everything sacred. Babiak comes out swinging." —Lisa Moore, author of *Caught*

"As only the best writers can, Todd Babiak has taken a small patch of turf and, through sparkling satire and a passionate eye, made it a world. A neighborhood in Edmonton is about to get a lot of honorary citizens." — Ian McGillis, author of *A Tourist's Guide to Glengarry*

"Mr. Babiak is blazing a trail—every city should have a story like this." — Alexander McCall Smith, author of *The No. 1 Ladies' Detective Agency*

"Babiak's language isn't lofty, but dense with keen observation— highlighting the beauty, kindness, cynicism, sense of humour and contradiction found in many Edmontonians, most Canadians and modern life in general." —*Ottawa Citizen*

THE SPIRITS UP

TODD BABIAK

McClelland & Stewart

McClelland & Stewart and colophon are registered trademarks of
Penguin Random House Canada Limited.

Library and Archives Canada Cataloguing in Publication data is available
upon request.

ISBN: 978-0-7710-9624-2
ebook ISBN: 978-0-7710-9630-3

This is a work of fiction. Names, characters, places, incidents either are the
product of the author's imagination or are used fictitiously. Any resemblance
to actual persons, living or dead, events or locales is entirely coincidental.

Book design by Emma Dolan
Cover art: Emma Dolan
Typeset in Fournier by M&S, Toronto
Printed in Canada

McClelland & Stewart,
a division of Penguin Random House Canada Limited,
a Penguin Random House Company
www.penguinrandomhouse.ca

1 2 3 4 5   25 24 23 22 21

Penguin
Random House
McCLELLAND & STEWART

THE SPIRITS UP

Only nine kids came that year, nearly all of them dressed as heroes. It was not a time for pretend scary. On any normal Halloween, two hundred little ghouls would stomp and shout on the front porch and at least twenty Belgravia parents would stand waiting for an invitation: beer, a glass of wine, the sort of whisky rich people were expected to keep. Hours later, when the network of motion lights popped on between the house and the garage, his first thought was for the peanut butter cups in orange wrappers, a hill of them in a blue bowl by the door. He should have left them outside. His staff worked from home now, so he couldn't even bring surplus candy into the office.

It was difficult to guess the time. The rain had stopped and the bedroom was cold. Benedict Ross touched his phone and the screen shone 3:07. The light popped on again, which usually meant a cat or a jackrabbit was moving through the yard, a coyote. Then he heard something, jiggles and scrapes. And a cuss word.

Why wasn't the dog barking? He remembered the dog was dead.

Benedict's hand scrambled across the bedside table, feeling for his glasses. He shoved the mug of chamomile tea and knocked his watch to the floor before giving up. Karen was a light sleeper. When he stood up out of bed in his blue pyjamas, the ones with the dancing giraffes, it felt colder than Halloween cold. He sneaked down the stairs, to the front door, and out into the darkness. The avenue in front of their home glistened in the witching hour. It was a phrase his mother had used when he was a teenager, and it remained with Benedict as he rounded the corner and down the path toward the backyard. It was icy, so icy on his bare feet it shocked him into the realization of his dreamy foolishness: no shoes, no glasses, no parka.

The Halloween rain had frozen on the paving stones, on the grass, and on the double-car garage. He expected to see nothing. He wanted to be back in bed. Yet there it was: a blur in a black hoodie working on the garage door. Benedict had run track in high school and university, a good solitary sport, and he jogged every morning until a few years ago when his knees betrayed him. He could run. He did run. The police helicopter was overhead, en route to a more dangerous criminal, and it obscured the slap of his bare feet on the ice. There was a shout of warning in him, but it remained in his chest with fear for his girls cloaked in the fog of sleep. It wasn't until he was ten feet from the man at the garage door that he had any thought about what might actually happen. He had miscalculated on the ice. He was running too fast.

Benedict slammed into the thief and his mouth clonked into the back of his head. He caught the thief as they fell back together. Blood popped in Benedict's mouth, he slipped, he stumbled, and the man fell on top of him.

This was not a heavy thief. This was a bird, a bird man, who flailed and softly gurgled. When Benedict shoved the little man off, his hands plunged into warmth and wet. And what else? A wide, thin, cool piece of metal. The motion sensor clicked and the floodlights popped on and Benedict saw blood on his hands. The metal was half inside the man. As Benedict slipped out from underneath him on the crispy grass, the thing fell out: a pry bar.

Benedict screamed and scrambled to his hands and knees. This was not a man. It was a young woman, a girl, with big cheeks and small eyes. She continued to move as though she were in another place. One of the dogs Benedict had grown up with was a Yorkshire terrier. When he held the dog over a full bath, she would swim in the air. The woman in the backyard tried to swim on her back in slow motion, in the dark and then the light, the dark and the light. She mumbled to herself.

The woman wore a bomber jacket over a sweater. Benedict checked her wound. The pry bar had plunged into her flesh above the waist of her jeans. She smelled of campfire and alcohol. Her teeth were bad. The woman shone.

She shone and shook and stared at him. He had to call an ambulance but he did not want to leave the woman alone so he shouted for help until their bedroom light turned on and his wife lifted the blinds.

ONE

The first blizzard of the year arrived in the middle of the night. Poppy usually loved blizzards, the sound of a chaotic wind slashing the old house. A storm made her feel cozy and safe in her bed, and it meant a proper layer of fresh snow in the morning. But it wasn't the wind that woke her up on the thirtieth of November. It was a scream, a cry, a howl in the hall.

Poppy slept with her door open, which also made her feel cozy and safe. The hall was long and dark with only two small windows at each end. She wasn't really looking but from her bed she thought she saw someone, some *thing* in the dark hall. The front and back doors were locked, like always. It could have been her mom, but why would she howl in the middle of the night? Her dad might have encouraged her mom to make a sound like that, through hallway sex activities Poppy did not want to imagine, but her parents hardly spoke to each other. And they were always so tired.

A few weeks earlier, a kid at school had tested positive for the virus and everyone had to go home right after lunch. Daphne did not greet her with a bark, when she opened the door, because Daphne was gone. Before Poppy could announce she was home, she heard her mom speaking on the phone, in the bath. Poppy listened at the door.

" . . . how it would actually go. And what's the reward for all this anyway, half a failing business? I mean, he doesn't hit me. He doesn't cheat on me or betray me in any way I could credibly . . . What can the settlement be if his only marital crime is neglect? I feel invisible. I'm a phantom wife. Is that enough?"

Every day since, every hour, Poppy heard her mother's echoey voice through the bathroom door. *I'm a phantom.* She tried to forget it, to forget the howl in the hall, but now it was cold in her room. She leaned out of bed and checked that the heating vent was warm. It was hot. The faint smell of burned dust, a smell she loved, lingered about the floor. This was a different sort of cold, the sort no heater could undo.

It had been a howl of sorrow.

Sorrow. Maybe as Poppy came out of a nightmare she herself had howled in the cold, in the blizzard, in the night. But she didn't remember any nightmare. At the start of the school year, her best friend since she was six months old, Blaine, had ghosted her. Blaine didn't even give a reason. They had *written down* plans to go to the same university, in Montreal or Vancouver, and then marry husbands who are also best friends and then buy houses on the same block and go on holidays in Tahiti together. Then, with no warning or explanation, Blaine was gone from her life. Their whole families had gone to the mountains together, and the Okanagan and Tofino and Playa del Carmen. Well, not their whole families. Her dad didn't go on vacation. But everyone else, and Blaine's mom and her mom were best friends too—kind of. Then one day it was finished. In class and in the hall, Blaine would see Poppy and then look away, like she was a decoration or a substitute teacher.

When Poppy messaged her, asking to talk, Blaine never responded. Poppy continued to like all of Blaine's Instagram posts because she knew Blaine kept track but that was it, what remained of them. *I'm a phantom.*

Poppy tried to fall back to sleep in the cold. In wellness class in grade seven, the teacher had asked them to close their eyes and rid their minds of all thoughts and to focus only on their breathing. In and out, in and out. This was the best way to calm the mind and the heart, to ease into a meditative state or into sleep. In bed Poppy closed her eyes, but she could not rid the cold and the sound of the howling woman from her mind, her heart. It wasn't her mom and it certainly wasn't Charlotte.

If Charlotte did not feel normal feelings in the day, feelings like sorrow, why would she howl about them in the middle of the night? Besides, she knew Charlotte's voice as well as her own. She could call out to Charlotte, ask her to come. She would come. Her sad, crazy older sister did anything she asked; she would climb onto the roof and jump off into the snow. Poppy could call out to her mom and dad, to protect her. But she was afraid to do that too, even to speak, in case the sorrowful thing in the hall was hungry.

Her room shone. Automatic lights sensed motion on their property and sneaked around her blinds. The last time the room had lit up like this was Halloween. She had gone into her parents' bedroom, to tell them, but they were gone. The room was empty. She looked out their window and her parents were in the backyard. There was someone else with them. In the morning, when Poppy asked, her mom had said a drunk had passed out and needed attention.

Since Halloween, her strange parents were even stranger with one another. Her dad was the loneliest person in the world, always thinking of his machine. Poppy figured her father was lonely and distracted without ever feeling so. It was his choice. Maybe it was worse, this past month, because maybe he knew his wife was talking to lawyers about divorcing him. Poppy understood her mom's feelings, especially since Blaine had abandoned her. It was like her mom had lost something, a jewel or an amulet she needed to be her finest self again, the woman she used to be. Her mom could not find the jewel anywhere and had probably stopped looking.

It used to be Poppy's greatest fear that her parents would divorce. Lots of kids at school went from house to house, parent to parent, and dealt with stepmoms and stepdads, stepbrothers and stepsisters. Poppy could tell it bothered them but it was normal, at least. Their parents were normal. Their sisters were normal. It wasn't Poppy's greatest fear anymore, that her mom and dad would divorce. Her greatest fear was something like this: there is a monster in the house and only she can hear it howling and at any moment it will crawl into her bedroom and devour her.

TWO

Benedict spent hours on the chlorine-scented white tile of the downstairs bathroom floor waking intermittently to dry heave. When he felt well enough, at just after three in the morning, the witching hour, he crawled into the guest bed. By then the blizzard had calmed. New snow would make the whole city quiet for a few hours, a muffler against distant sirens. He calmed himself in the quiet, imagined the snow on the boughs of the evergreens. Then he heard the creak of the 1918 oak stairs. He thought it might be Poppy, his baby, thirteen now. It was entirely like her to hear him suffering in the basement and to press a cool cloth on his forehead in the middle of the night, to whisper-sing a song.

Only these were not footsteps. They were not paw steps. When Daphne, his finest and truest friend, came down the stairs, her long legs and toenails made for a clumsy and dissonant click-click-thump. Benedict never had friends, not the way other people had friends. But Daphne had been different, and in her absence everything was darker and more sombre, less surprising, especially now that the gloom of winter had settled in. Her clumsiness had become the metronome of his life and now she was gone.

Daphne was gone. His daughters and his wife were still in bed, two floors above. Pale streetlights reflected off the new snow and into the basement bedroom. The sound of the stairs passed and then a tall figure moved across the basement floor. It was shaped like an upright torpedo only soft, ancient, rotting.

"Karen?"

The figure stopped and turned to him, looked into the bedroom, though it did not seem to have a face. Or arms. It rose and hovered in the middle of the room. He wanted to convince himself the rotting thing was not there, but it was there and it wanted something. He was too afraid to ask a question of it because he did not want it to answer.

When he was not yet old enough for school, Benedict's mother had told him he could destroy a nightmare by thinking of pumpkin pie. This was before he contracted meningitis and nearly died in the Royal Alexandra Hospital, which sent his mother and his father into religion.

Despite the swirl of nausea that remained in him, Benedict closed his eyes and thought of pumpkin pie sweetened with maple syrup, warm but not hot, with whipped cream and lots of cinnamon.

When he opened his eyes, his wife stood over him: a long silhouette.

"Ben. Oh, look at you. Are you done throwing up?"

"I think so."

Karen sat on the edge of the bed, the frame an antique purchase on a trip to France. The carved walnut squeaked. She placed her hand on his forehead.

It had taken awhile, after meeting Karen all those years ago, to accept it was an ordinary part of love to reach out and touch each other as a thing in itself, for no other reason than to do it. "Careful. I could have the——."

"Oh, it isn't that. You don't even feel hot."

He put his own hand on hers. "I was feverish earlier."

"It's one of those twenty-four-hour things."

"Wash your hands anyway."

Neither of them spoke for a while. Normally she was the one to break the silence but that time passed, then more time. "You said my name pleadingly, like something was . . . 'Karen?'"

"I'm all right now."

She yawned. "Don't need anything?"

Benedict needed the Chinese to say yes in seven hours, to avoid bankruptcy and ruin. He needed to get warm. "Can you put another blanket on me?"

She did, and at great risk to her own health she kissed his forehead.

The floating torpedo was likely a smear of E. coli on a leaf of Chilean spinach at lunch. Illnesses come with fevers, and fevers inspire hallucinations. Wives become ghosts.

In considering all of this, out loud or in his head, Benedict fell asleep.

Benedict woke just after seven o'clock in the remaining darkness of the northern morning. His head throbbed and his throat burned. Upstairs, Mariah Carey sang "All I Want for Christmas Is You." The espresso machine hummed and hissed. Water sloshed through the pipes. Ritual and regularity comforted him his entire life, long before the diagnosis. Now morning sounds, with replicating seasonal variations, were medication to him.

Poppy, who used to say she wanted to be a triple threat when she grew up, sang and danced when she wasn't asking Karen about the location of her leggings. Her heavy feet thumped on the main floor. Outside, the snow was already beginning to melt into the eaves. Winter was hardly winter anymore.

It was November thirtieth, a Monday, the culmination of three disastrous years. The thought of his presentation to the Chinese investors in just a few hours inspired another blast of nausea. What he needed, as one Christmas song ended and another began—Dolly Parton—was for Daphne to hop on the bed and nibble his ear. He wondered why his overheated brain had not conjured a ghost of Daphne in the night.

On his way up the stairs he met his eldest daughter, Charlotte, who was already dressed for school in what she wore most days—a pair of black jeans and a black hoodie. She had never liked the sun and she had not been afflicted with acne, so her face was whiter than white, her eyes pale blue like his but big and deep-set like Karen's. Her hair was in a shifting state between blonde and brown, though her eyelashes were so long and so dark it seemed she wore mascara. But Charlotte would never wear mascara. There were reddish half moons under her eyes; she had been sleeping poorly for years. Though Charlotte never offered a word about it, not anymore, she suffered from Crohn's disease and its obscene cramps often struck in the middle of the night. And there were medical mysteries. They had tested her for Lyme disease, for lupus and other autoimmune disorders. Something inside Charlotte was slowly eating her up.

"Bad night?"

She reached up and rubbed her tired eyes, like a much younger child. She hardly spoke and when she did there was scant emotion in her voice and none in her facial expression. She stood perfectly straight and, at fifteen, was only an inch shorter than Benedict. He did not see himself in Charlotte, not exactly, but he recognized what people had said about him when he was her age—before he learned to fake most things. Together they had been inducted into a club that had not existed when he was fifteen: *the spectrum*.

"You were up a lot? In the bathroom?"

"Someone has broken into the garage." His eldest daughter was not great on transitions.

"No, Charlotte, that was Halloween."

"What was Halloween?"

Benedict took a few steps up the stairs, into the kitchen, to look out the back window. "Sorry, yes. You mean last night."

In the kitchen, Dolly Parton was doing "Hard Candy Christmas" and Poppy sang along with cinnamon oatmeal in her mouth. Every year Karen began playing what she called "winter music" in November. This time she had started earlier than ever, the morning after Halloween. Without asking Charlotte, Benedict knew she had not said anything to Karen or to Poppy about her abdominal pain or leg cramps or the hot stretching feeling over her skin or about the break-in, and he knew why. It was the only way to prevent what Charlotte most disliked: emotional chaos.

Benedict put on his boots and walked out to the garage. The phone was heavy in his pyjama pocket. There was a light wind, mild for this time of year. Wispy clouds in the southeast were beginning to turn orange and pink, the first hint of dawn. Wet snow plopped from the boughs of the massive elm in his backyard. He estimated the new snow would be gone by the weekend. While it was unscientific to make any leaps between daily weather and climate change, he imagined today's visitors from Shanghai via New York via San Francisco would mention the eerie warmth in this wind. Canada did not feel Canadian, which was good for nothing except his pitch.

There was a grey cat in the yard, hunkered under the treehouse where the snow could not fall. While Poppy had outgrown it as a play structure, Charlotte continued to use the shaded treehouse

on warm summer days as a quiet place to read—an escape pod.
Benedict and the cat watched one another. It was clean and well
fed. It came to Benedict for some loving, when he wished it a
good morning, and a little bell on its tidy, pink collar twinkled.
While he preferred dogs, Benedict respected cats. This one purred
as he caressed it. The softness of the cat and its friendly manner
washed the darkness away for a moment. Charlotte's pain, the
rotting ghost, the fate of his company, and this.

The bicycles and downhill skis and power tools were gone.
Benedict wandered the garage, which he kept in perfect order,
and determined the thieves had been clever enough to take only
what they could sell for more than one hundred dollars per item.
Everything old, like hockey sticks, or obscure, like snowshoes,
remained in its place. He pulled out his phone and took photographs. The passenger-side door of the Model X was open. The
Tesla was only three months old, so the entire garage smelled of
treated leather and off-gassing plastic. Benedict leaned inside to
open the glove compartment, to see if the thieves had stolen any
documents, and with his left hand he broke through a thin layer of
ice on the beige seat and into a cold puddle.

He took a few steps back, to look at and then to tentatively
smell his hand. For most of the year, Benedict had been more
aware than usual of what he touched. The virus had destroyed
people, businesses, industries, entire economies. Whatever was
on his hand, he wanted it off. Outside, in the light of the morning,
he washed it in the new snow and confirmed it was urine.

Bending was painful, from the night's exertions over the toilet: his head, his stomach, the muscles that held his eyes in place.
He deserved this. It should have been more than his hand. They
should have come to him in the night and dragged him out here.
But he feared for his family and he knew what the insurance company would ask of him, so he wiped his hands dry on his pyjama

bottoms and dialled 911. The woman who answered told him flatly that property theft did not count as an emergency, even when accompanied by urine on a car seat, and gave him another number to call. After pressing through several menu options and waiting on hold, Benedict spoke to an elderly sounding policeman who asked a number of reasonable questions and said they'd have a car come by today or tomorrow.

The policeman had faintly whistled his *S*s, as Benedict's grandfather had done. Aside from Daphne, there were two other ghosts he would have preferred his fever to summon. His grandparents with their unshakable eastern European accents, their secrets, and their violins would have comforted him. His phone rang. Normally his calls were from con artists on the Indian subcontinent pretending to be tax agents.

It was someone named Constable McCaw. The constable announced she was leaving the scene of another break-in nearby if he was free right now. When Benedict asked about the urine, she said it was something she saw, from time to time, in affluent neighbourhoods. He was lucky to get off with urine. "It's been a year. You live in Belgravia. There's folks out there with nothing, and nothing to lose. It's no excuse but they look at people with a lot and they get aggrieved," she said. "What kind of vehicle you got?"

"A Tesla."

"That's, what, a hundred Gs? For a car?"

The Model X was just under 140,000 dollars plus tax. "So, you're saying we weren't the only ones? They stole from others?"

Constable McCaw said she would be on her way soon and ended the call. It tore some of the malice away, knowing others had been chosen too.

"Daddy?" Poppy was ready for school, with a white cashmere scarf over a snug-fitting red jacket. She dressed like a big city magazine editor, entirely unlike her older sister. In her white leather gloved hands, a blue mug. "I made you a coffee."

Benedict felt too fragile to drink anything. His first instinct was to tell her to bring it back inside because he would not need it, but he knew that was an ungracious thing to do so he took the mug from Poppy and placed it among the spiderwebs and rusted washers and gum wrappers on the windowsill, the one part of the garage he forgot to clean. "Thank you, darling."

"What happened, Daddy?"

"Well. People broke in, took some things."

Poppy breathed deeply. "They took my bike."

"All our bikes, the skis and snowboards, tools."

Her eyes were already wet with tears. "You love tools. First you were up all night, sick, and now this. I'm so sorry. And today is a big day at work, isn't it?"

"How did you know?"

"I heard you talking to Mom." Poppy hugged him, her tears wet on his neck. "Whatever it is, I know you can do it. You can *do it*, Daddy."

Benedict kept his urine hand locked in a fist so he would not touch her jacket. Her freshly washed hair smelled of warm herbs.

"Did the robbers get in the house?" Poppy spoke into his shoulder.

"No."

She stepped out of the hug and dabbed her eyes with a tissue. "Did they *try*?"

"The house was locked."

"But they got in the garage, Daddy. It was locked too." She whispered, "I heard something strange in the night, something awful."

His throat was sore from dry heaving. "I'm sure they wouldn't be interested in . . . Thieves just want what they can sell."

"There's this thing. Sex slavery. You break into a house, you steal a girl, you give her fentanyl, and you charge money for men to . . . you know."

Benedict lacked the capacity to think about it, and he instead assured Poppy he would never allow anyone to break into their home. If thieves did break in, he would be ready for them. She would get a new bicycle and a new snowboard from the insurance company, and she need not concern herself with his stolen power tools.

"I don't need any of that stuff, Dad. They're wants, not needs."

Benedict squeezed her arm with his non-urine hand, his way of ending a conversation with her.

Poppy didn't walk away. "You're sick. You got robbed. Your business is . . . I don't know."

Benedict had not spoken to her about the business in a year, maybe two. For a while Poppy had been proud, with so many questions. She had done an assignment on him for science class, with pictures cut out from newspapers and business magazines. Now it was a dark and growing thing between them, between them all.

When Poppy was gone, Benedict opened the main garage door so Constable McCaw would know how to find him in the back lane. He began to shovel the wet snow from the concrete pad and stopped midway to bend over and not faint. For years, homeless people had come into his quiet neighbourhood south of the university to sleep in sheds and heated garages. When the virus hit, they made lean-tos and temporary villages in the empty lots and in the park by the farmers' market because shelters were closed to them. Now and then, Benedict found used needles in his own backyard. Some of his neighbours—professors and lawyers and doctors and business owners—had written letters to the newspaper blaming it all on safe injection sites, the lack of enforcement on the light-rail transit system, and the policies of the mayor, councillor, or political party in charge when the pandemic hit, not to mention the World Health Organization and China and the spectre of communism. His phone hummed with a new text from his business partner, Marie-Claude Abboud. He was supposed to be in the office already, to go over today's presentation with her.

Is everything okay, Ben?

Nothing was okay and she knew it. Poppy knew it. Benedict was so deeply ashamed of how not okay everything had become, and how it had affected Marie-Claude, he could hardly muster the strength to respond.

Perfect. On my way.

THREE

Karen Sjöblad had never once purchased a magazine at the supermarket checkout. When she was a child, her mother had whispered judgments about people who bought trashy magazines with the rest of their poison: sugary drinks, potato chips, bulk-baked doughnuts, white bread, and jumbo packs of cheap ground meat. These people never looked around to see if anyone watched them and whispered judgments. They just *chose*, with perfect freedom. Karen had always admired that freedom even as she denied it to herself and did everything in her power to teach her daughters to pass on their grandmother's wisdom: it was the difference between success and failure, mental health and misery, designer jeans and pyjama bottoms.

Then her husband had attacked a woman in the backyard on Halloween night, the perfect culmination of months and months of horror. All the rules she had followed, all the sacrifices and healthy choices she had made, they were ultimately in preparation for a test that would not come. Karen had never been a believer, but if she had ever held a kernel of *maybe, just maybe* in her heart, for the Nordic god of her ancestors, it had recently departed. It turned out no one answered prayers. There was no spiritual protection, no reward. She had been so, so good, so self-denying and careful, waiting for everything good people deserve, while the naughty and the shameless bought private islands and second homes in the desert and potato chips. Someday and maybe soon, she would just die with a breathing tube down her throat—having never eaten a supermarket doughnut.

Two weeks after the gory disaster of Halloween, while she was loading organic chickpeas and yogurt and fresh kale, low-sugar granola and Chilean blueberries and a tube of all-natural toothpaste onto the Save-on-Foods conveyor, something changed. The cover of *Chatelaine* had a photograph of the prime minister's wife, who had beaten the virus, and a teaser about Christmas baking secrets. Below that, on the shameful bottom of the magazine cover: "Can an affair be *healthy*?"

It was a monumentally stupid question. If Karen had learned anything from movies, television series, and book-club novels in the past twenty years, it was that having an affair ruined everything. It was the relationship equivalent of sugary drinks, potato chips, and bulk-baked doughnuts.

Then again, clever, clever *Chatelaine*. What was left to ruin?

Karen pulled out her Visa card and put it away. Same with the Mastercard. There was a bit of room on the American Express, maybe $1,100. It had a smell, the money panic, this largely silent struggle. A cloak of debt had fallen over them and it was getting heavier and darker and smellier and harder to breathe underneath it every day.

"Find everything you needed?" The cashier, a stout woman in her thirties with a name tag that said Linda, had neck tattoos of tropical flowers. She started packing the cloth bags. Linda's face mask had pink cranes on it, flying over a mountainous landscape.

Freedom.

It was a whisper in the Save-on-Foods, over "Hey Sis, It's Christmas" by RuPaul. They played RuPaul in Save-on-Foods now. Karen turned around, to check if anyone was watching and judging. The people in line behind her were on their phones. She pulled the *Chatelaine* from the rack and slapped it on the conveyor belt, between the yogurt and the blueberries.

Linda the cashier looked up. Her eyebrows were painted on, ending with sassy upward swoops. While Karen did not have neck tattoos, and she was not buying a twenty-four of Mountain Dew or a package of cigarettes, she and Linda the cashier seemed to share something, that who-gives-a-fuck quality that leads one to purchase a supermarket checkout magazine.

The concrete of the parking lot, ripped up by the wild swings between hot and cold and covered in a layer of grime, made it difficult to shove the cart from the front door of the supermarket to the car. Empty bags of potato chips, Tim Hortons cups, and beer cans collected against the wall of the boarded-up Vietnamese restaurant and the police station. The cloud was low so it was grey and dark even at midafternoon, but the too-early Christmas trees in front of the Save-on-Foods and the decorations at the liquor depot did their job. They restored Karen to the finest days of her childhood, her delight when the best-before dates of milk and orange juice reached into glorious December. The nights before Christmas in her warm and elegant home in Edgemont with its creamy white carpets and twelve-foot fir, Swedish-designed stockings and her mother's collection of *tomte* Santas, the view out the picture window of the Rocky Mountains.

She loaded the bags into the back of the Tesla they could no longer afford, sat in the driver's seat, and paused before she pressed the deliciously designed ignition button. She opened the magazine.

One day soon, the credit cards would be full and the banks would grow weary of their excuses, the goodwill of the pandemic recovery would fade entirely, and the fine people at Tesla Financing would seize their asset. And before any of their loans were called in, the police would knock on their front door of an early frosty morning and charge them both with murder.

On page forty-seven of the *Chatelaine* Christmas issue, a photograph of a frustratingly young creamy-skinned model in a negligee lay on an unmade bed. Who was she supposed to be married to? The Tesla guy? In the parking lot, two men and an underdressed woman gathered up shopping carts and pushed them toward the building. Each cart was worth a dollar. All this work, in the cold wind, for a dollar. This year had been hard on everyone, but it seemed extra punishing for people who relied on shelters and food banks and libraries and emergency rooms, people who couldn't receive relief cheques from the government because they didn't have social insurance numbers or addresses. Despite all the billions in aid, the poor looked poorer, and there were more of them.

The truth: Karen was exponentially poorer than these men and women hunched over shopping carts in the dismal parking lot. When last she calculated it, she and Benedict owed more than $600,000 to banks and credit card companies, on top of their $840,000 mortgage. Her design business had gone into near-complete hibernation. Benedict hadn't drawn a salary from his company, Kutisi, in almost three years. They had depleted their retirement savings accounts to zero. There had been plenty of government assistance in the early days of the virus but Benedict had just plowed it back into Kutisi—his employees, his machine.

So a million and a half in debt, yet here she was in a leased Tesla with a few bags of organic food. The actual poor people in the parking lot were slamming carts into one another for one dollar coins. Net worth: one dollar, two, three, four.

There were thirty-two dollars in her wallet. Karen stepped out of the car and handed all of it to the woman, who smelled sweetly of alcohol and really should have been wearing a proper jacket and a face mask. She gave the woman a full mini-package of tissues as well, because her nose was running.

"Holy shit, thanks," said the woman, as the two men hurried over.

"You keep that for yourself."

"It don't work that way."

Karen returned to the Tesla, locked the door, and opened the magazine to the article about affairs. They had been through a shared trauma, she and the indigent men and women of the parking lot, the people who huddled in tent cities and lit fires to warm themselves in abandoned buildings. She had lost friends. She had lost hope. On social media, her first name had become a global synonym for *loud, privileged, racist, middle-aged white lady*. She was entitled to a bit of unusual behaviour.

It turns out a psychologist in Toronto had done her Ph.D. dissertation on how, for some Karens, a carefully managed love affair was a jolt of spiritual adrenaline that will not only power her toward a happy retirement, it will *save her marriage*. There were quotations from anonymous women in their forties and fifties who had pulled it off, adventurers who now felt sexy and mysterious and desired.

When she was finished reading the article, Karen tore it out of the magazine. She tore off the cover and the table of contents as well, and balled them up and stuffed them in her pocket for recycling.

For the next two weeks, as winter settled in, Karen Sjöblad felt things she had not felt since university. When the fears arrived—of prison and bankruptcy, of public humiliation, of the rampaging virus—she turned to Christmas music and to her yoga instructor. It made no sense that yoga classes and schools were still open but they were, so they all felt obliged to go because everyone else was going. At the end of a Bikram class, where she was one of the oldest women in the dimly lit, patchouli-scented room, her instructor, Jak Miller, Jak without a *C*, took her aside and said there was *something sensual* about her.

Something sensual!

Twenty-nine-year-old Jak without a *C*, who claimed he had never in his life used deodorant, was coming to her home at a quarter after noon to give her a private lesson. At the end of class one day a year earlier, Jak had announced that deodorant interfered with something primeval and true, like an unearned standing ovation or the way neckties and fake laughs interfered with who we really are.

Karen could practically smell him over the cinnamon oatmeal. But her husband had been throwing up all night. Charlotte's Crohn's was on fire and she belonged in bed. A gang of vengeful crooks was riding their bicycles north across the bridge in the morning darkness. As much as she had been anticipating November thirtieth, she was terrified and ashamed and concerned for her mental health. It had been messing with her sleep and her stomach. She would wait until midmorning to send Jak a cancellation text. A twenty-nine-year-old yoga instructor couldn't possibly be awake at this hour. Until then, Karen would dream a little more. In these dreams, it was difficult not to revert to a scenario where she was also twenty-nine. Or better yet twenty-two, her pre-baby body, when men flirted with her all the time and she dismissed them because she was married to a handsome young genius and she was morally opposed to extramarital affairs.

Nearly every hour this past month, she had checked the local news sites to see what had happened to the Halloween woman. She checked again. Nothing. Perhaps it was a stealth attack, silence as the authorities gather evidence and sneak closer and closer. If the woman's friends had not been the ones to come in the night to take her treasure, it had been the police, running a sting operation.

In the kitchen, Poppy was singing along to the Taylor Swift song about a Christmas tree farm being inside her heart. Karen had nine playlists of holiday jams, organized according to mood: the holly jolly, the contemporary pop, the churchy, the crooner, the worldbeat, the olde tyme English, the hip hop, the classical, and variations on "O Holy Night." She was more than ever an atheist but the specificity of the song, the purity of the faith that had inspired it, culminating in the key change and the lines "Fall on your knees / O hear the angel voices" was the only thing powerful enough to wipe everything away.

When Taylor Swift was finished in the kitchen, Karen put on the children's choir version of "O Holy Night." She waited for the invitation to fall on her knees. Now that the day of her private yoga lesson had arrived, and everyone in the house was sick and thieves were stealing their stuff, the song brought actual tears to her eyes. The thought of betraying Benedict and the girls made her cry, and she had *already* betrayed them in her heart by imagining the thing. And anyway: ha! It's one thing to say there was something sensual about a woman in her forties and it's another to assume a private yoga lesson is anything more than a private yoga lesson.

She closed her eyes and pretended to fall on her knees, with the toaster about to pop.

"Mom?" Poppy had started packing the lunch Karen had made her, adding two chocolate chip granola bars and a package of tamari-flavoured seaweed. "You okay?"

"Of course, sweetheart."

"Are you crying?"

"I yawned. It makes me tear up."

Poppy dropped everything on the counter and thumped across the kitchen to embrace her. "Don't fret. Daddy says the insurance will replace everything they took. And they can't get in here no matter what, Dad said, and if they did . . . "

When she reached around her, Poppy felt like a football player. This had been happening for a couple of years, her transition from a thin girl to a not-thin girl, and Karen did not know what to say to her about it. She knew it upset Poppy, that it felt to her like a sinister but unstoppable force. There had been tearful nights in front of mirrors, and kids had posted cruel comments on her Instagram even though bullying and body-shaming weren't supposed to happen anymore. She encouraged Poppy to join a soccer team and invited her to go on mother-daughter runs back when they had Daphne, but Poppy never once felt like it. She mostly felt like spending time with her phone. As they hugged, Karen looked at a photograph of her two girls on the opposite wall, Charlotte, three, and Poppy, one, in Florence. They had flown in business class! Unimaginable now. Karen did not want her big, kind, powerful daughter to release her but then she did.

"Thank you, Poppy."

At the other end of the kitchen, at the back window, Charlotte stood silently with her arms crossed over her shapeless grey parka, watching her father do whatever one did when one was robbed.

"Charlotte?"

"Yes, Mom?" She responded without looking away.

"Are you sure you feel good enough to go to school?"

"I do. Thank you."

They had tried everything to help Charlotte's symptoms: anti-inflammatories, elimination diets, opiates, herbal remedies, acupuncture, and preposterous visits to experts in Phoenix and Minneapolis. In the end, Charlotte decided to take care of it herself by researching Crohn's and meeting with a specialist at the university who found her so intelligent, she asked Charlotte to be an unofficial fifteen-year-old part of her clinical team. The bigger issue with Charlotte was her mind, the impenetrable quality of whatever counted as happiness for her.

A policewoman had arrived, and the lights on her squad car flashed shamefully against the snow. Why didn't she turn them off? The lights jolted Karen into the realization that it might not be about last night's break-in. Maybe it was the sting operation. They would dig up the backyard, find DNA. Poppy looked at her reflection in the back window and turned sideways, sighed. "I look like an orca in this."

"Honey. You look beautiful in this. In everything. Now, you two better get going."

Charlotte led the way to the front foyer. She had removed the Canada Goose label from her parka with a seam ripper. Karen loved that she had done it. What Karen did not love was when someone suggested Charlotte *didn't care* about her appearance. Nothing so simple could govern Charlotte's heart. The grade ten English teacher, Ms. Felician, had asked to see Karen in early October. While Ms. Felician could see no reason to give Charlotte anything less than an A, there was something missing in the way she read—in "her emotional architecture." Charlotte could explain why *To Kill a Mockingbird* was called *To Kill a Mockingbird*, with an elevated vocabulary, but she treated metaphors like mathematical equations and seemed to have no interest in what it *felt like* to be Scout Finch, Boo Radley, or Tom Robinson. Had they explored whether or not she was on the spectrum?

Ms. Felician had not read her own paperwork. In the over-lit classroom, at four thirty in the afternoon, Karen had wavered between crying, laughing, and screaming.

Once she had ensured the girls had lunches and books and binders in their backpacks, that their masks were properly fitted,

Karen kissed them and told them she loved them and that she was proud of them. She watched her daughters walk in the slush: Charlotte with perfect determination and Poppy with a slight slouch, clearly explaining something to her older sister. Of the two, Charlotte was the natural beauty. If she washed her hair regularly or dressed in clothes that fit her long limbs, if she didn't stare so much, if her posture weren't so perfect, if she could address herself to a sport without treating it like a physics problem, she could be what Karen had wanted to be in school and what Poppy longed to be: a star. But . . .

Karen's phone hummed. On the screen was Benedict's business partner, Marie-Claude. Her profile photo was a few years old, before the Bell's palsy had manufactured an unfortunate, permanent droop on the left side of the poor rich woman's face.

"Good morning, Marie-Claude."

"Karen. How are you?"

"It's winter in Canada."

"Is the Christmas tree up?"

"We're a little late this year, maybe the weekend. So. Today's the big day! How are you feeling?"

In the early 1980s, shortly after the great slump, Marie-Claude was fired from her job as a petroleum engineer. Instead of moving to Oman to start a new career, she bought a local oil services company in receivership, Aarhus Energy. As the industry, and prices, slowly recovered, her company grew and prospered. She was a rare female CEO in a field dominated by men. She sold Aarhus in 2014, at the height of the market, and read about Benedict and his idea in an in-flight magazine after he had won an award for inventors. Within a week she had invested twenty-four million dollars for 49 per cent of Kutisi. Since then, it had not made a dime. Benedict and his flawed invention had destroyed Marie-Claude. There was a dark, oozing beast of regret and pain between them.

Today was the last day of Kutisi, the final hours of a multiyear, slow-motion financial disaster.

"Well." Marie-Claude released something like a chuckle. "More importantly, how is Benedict feeling?"

"He was up all night, sick. Then we woke up to a garage break-in."

"Oh my goodness, no!"

Karen watched the police car drive away. Benedict exited the garage in his pyjamas, a mug in his hand, his head down. He lowered himself to the snow, to pet a cat.

"But he's feeling much better. He'll be in soon."

"I'd encourage him to stay in bed, if today weren't today. The investors got an exemption to come, which wasn't easy, and—"

"You can do it, Marie-Claude." Karen could hardly bear speaking to her. "Break a leg."

"Of course." She sounded exhausted, all of her seventy-two years. "Thank you, Karen."

Marie-Claude ended the call as Benedict thumped his boots on the front porch. Daphne was no longer there to bark, though Karen still prepared herself for it. Benedict walked into the kitchen without a word. Before the girls were born, before Kutisi, Karen found comfort in Benedict's silence, in his obsessions, in his ambitions. Thanks to her friends, and that era of childlessness, she had never felt alone. Then they moved here, to his hometown, for a grant from the university and economic development incentives, and even though it was only an hour and a half away from Vancouver on the plane, it might as well have been thirty.

Benedict was pale and walked slower than usual but there would be no legitimate reason to break off her engagement with the yoga teacher. While it made regular human sense that Benedict would crawl into bed, it would take more than nausea to keep him from work. Benedict did not understand holidays or evenings out with people who could not help or invest in his business. His hours had been especially long this year, as they ran out of Marie-Claude's money.

All day every day, and many nights, Benedict tinkered with his invention in the downtown warehouse. When he was not with his machine, it was obvious he wanted to be with his machine. Benedict would sneak away from family movie nights and dinner parties to poke and stare at it. The pandemic slowdown had not slowed him down. It had removed social obstacles: meetings, in-person complications with his staff, weekends, errands.

Karen had not even seen the thing in person. When anyone asked her about Kutisi, she struggled to answer, even though she had designed the logo. It was a miraculously safe, efficient, and powerful small-scale nuclear energy plant. It was even attractive, designed by a famous New Yorker with fancy sunglasses who lived on a hill near Avignon. *Kutisi* was a variation on the word for *box* in Uzbek.

Why Uzbek?

I don't know.

So it's like a generator?

Not exactly, no. More like a mini power plant. I mean, the boxes do generate electricity.

Benedict's a genius, so he knows generators were invented a long time ago, right?

Ha.

Ha, ha, ha.

It had always been her job to suggest date nights, to try new restaurants, but the virus had interrupted that rhythm. *Chatelaine* had confirmed it: this was what the end of a marriage felt like. Before the virus hit, she had scrolled through Instagram and Facebook twenty times a day to see her friends on ski trips or in Mexico, at their children's recitals and competitions, and clicked the heart button even though it was never, ever what she felt.

But since that day two weeks ago in the parking lot of Save-on-Foods, there were episodes of wonder and lust. A flock of tiny blue hummingbirds would come to life inside her at the thought of her yoga teacher. She felt twenty years younger and prettier, more articulate, more confident in her talents, better at stretching. She was kinder and more patient with the girls, more understanding of Benedict and his struggles. She watched the Christmas movies on Netflix and they hummed with truth. When everything crashed for the Ross-Sjöblads, and that day was coming soon, by the police or by the bank, they would get through the court case and declare bankruptcy and divorce and she would take the girls back to Vancouver: eat, pray, poverty.

"I Saw Mommy Kissing Santa Claus" by the Jackson 5 was playing. Benedict's forehead scrunched in puzzlement. It was hard to be angry with him, to feel hurt by him, as he did not have a malicious cell in his body. But even when he was in the same room, Benedict was gone.

"How was that?"

He stood in front of the kitchen sink to wash his hands. "The policewoman said we got caught up in a spree. But I don't understand."

"Understand what?"

"For what the thieves took, there was so much effort. Wouldn't it be easier to get a job? Then the risk wouldn't be there, of capture and punishment."

"There are no jobs. And some people don't fear punishment. The lucky few." She sipped her coffee. "What if it was her, or her friends?"

He turned, licked his lips, and looked at his feet.

"If it was her, Ben, that means . . . "

"Yes."

Karen wanted to pour a bit of Irish cream into her coffee. "Marie-Claude phoned. She was worried about you."

"I'm late. She texted."

"She understands why, now."

Benedict took a step toward her, which was unusual. He spoke as though he did not want to be overheard. "I was so sick last night I thought I saw a ghost."

"What? What kind of ghost?"

He was on the verge of revealing something, a secret, and it was a thrill to her. He shook his head, shook it away. "When I saw it I called you, and there you were."

Karen had forgotten. Benedict had called out to her in the night and she had gone to him. She had placed her hand on his forehead. She had kissed him there. Here was an excuse to cancel her yoga lesson with Jak after all, to ease out of this exquisite panic. She could be an asymptomatic carrier. "You have some pink in your cheeks now."

Benedict walked toward the stairs.

"I'll call the insurance company at nine. Benny? Do I need anything for that? I'll just go through our file cabinet. Oh, and I'm having a yoga lesson here today."

Jackson 5 ended and "Last Christmas" began, one of her favourites. She had been on a sea-kayaking trip with the girls a few years earlier when George Michael had died. Benedict had stayed home alone for Christmas, as it was a crucial moment for Kutisi that ended up being entirely not crucial. It wasn't until the following December that she heard the news and at first she didn't believe it. They were too close in age; if George Michael could die, anything was possible. The data from the pandemic had shoved it in her face. With every advancing day, we weaken.

The end had begun.

FOUR

Charlotte walked slightly ahead of Poppy with her chin up and her shoulders back, as if the Queen of Town was about to bestow an honour upon her. They went to different schools, for now, but when Charlotte was in grade twelve, Poppy would be in grade ten. That is when everything would change. Through the older sibling gossip network, and Instagram and Snapchat, Poppy knew what people said about Charlotte. It would profoundly affect her own high school prospects.

Oh, you're Charlotte's *sister.*

There were a bunch of boys at the high school who were in love with Charlotte. Not normal boys, obviously. Charlotte was pretty. That wasn't even the right word for it, even though the whole thing was wasted on her because she didn't care one iota. Charlotte could be a model if she put a bit of foundation under her eyes and didn't walk so weird. If Poppy could keep her own brain, she would definitely swap bodies with her sister. Oh, she could do amazing things with that face, those eyes and lashes of Charlotte's, and if her legs were like that, she would wear spring dresses all year.

The girls were vicious. They made fun of Charlotte, the way she sat in class and answered questions. She was a terrible know-it-all, but not because she wanted to show off or even prove anything to the teachers. She just *knew it all*, and she had no idea how to be cool about it or even why being cool about it would be remotely important. When a teacher asked a question and Charlotte knew the answer, she put up her hand. One afternoon in the treehouse, Poppy had tried to explain how crucial it is to *not* answer all the questions, to stay quiet and detached from all of that.

Every year, Poppy walked into class on the first day with a reputation. Teachers assumed she was brilliant and different, like Charlotte, exhausting and disruptive and clueless about her own effect on the class. Poppy *was* a good student, but she worked even harder on being a good girl, a good person, the best she could fashion, so the teachers who expected her to be an absolute alien found someone else. Her parents saw her this way too, and her drama and dance instructors over the years, her friends' moms. Blaine's mom. At least Blaine's mom used to see her this way.

They had to cross 109th Street, and there was a button to trigger the walk signal. It took forever, after you touched it, because the city didn't give a shit about people who walked, only people who drove. Poppy pressed the button and then, thirty seconds later, she hit it again. Charlotte looked down at Poppy's hand.

"I know." Poppy put the offending hand back in her pocket. "I know it doesn't make a difference. I know we just have to wait. It just makes me feel good."

Charlotte looked at her. "Why?"

"It feels like I'm doing something. I'm fighting the stupidity of the stupid fucking thing that makes us wait and wait just so the fat accountants can get downtown on time."

"Fat?"

"Sorry, Char. Not actually fat. Just . . . forget it."

Yesterday afternoon, when she was waiting for Charlotte outside her school, two boys she knew from gym class, boys who weren't in any of her academic subjects, stood by a big metal garbage bin and vaped. One of them was named Farts McCann. He had a real name, David or something, but since an incident in grade three everyone called him Farts. The boys didn't bother wearing masks because no one enforced it, not even the supervisor who was supposed to enforce it. The supervisor, Mr. Kernick, was looking at his phone with his glasses up on his toque. Charlotte was walking toward the school like always, stiff and tall and a bit too precise, like she was afraid of stepping on something slippery.

"Oh my God." The mist from Farts McCann's vape pen smelled like peaches. "She is *such* a tard."

Poppy hated all variants of the word retard. She hated that she had to smell fake peach, the sweet exhalation of death. They were losers who would end up doing something loserific with their lives, and she did not want to care about what they thought but . . . Poppy did care. She hated that she cared, that she wanted a boy named Farts to like her. Poppy walked around the garbage bin to the other side of a yellow school bus, where she whistled to Charlotte. When she was sure Charlotte had seen her, Poppy turned the other way and waited by a pile of snow that had been scraped from the ice rink.

The vaping boys would not see her with Charlotte.

Poppy could not count the number of times she had walked several paces behind her sister so no one cool would see them together. Poppy wanted to believe Charlotte was oblivious to this, and to all matters of social hierarchy. Poppy wanted to believe it to protect herself from the truth: that Charlotte understood everything.

One time in the summer, when the lockdown wasn't so strict, they were all in the car together on Whyte Avenue. They stopped at the lights and there was a group of cute skateboarder boys by the Starbucks. Poppy was about to duck but Charlotte put out a hand to stop her. Charlotte ducked. She hid herself so Poppy would not be ashamed. Whenever Poppy thought about this and what it meant about her and about Charlotte, she tried to push the thought away by thinking of the lyrics to "Yesterday."

If Poppy were to ask Charlotte to wear different clothes, to walk in a more relaxed way, to be cool in class, Charlotte would do all of it. Not because it made any sense to her. Much of it would make her uncomfortable.

If Poppy said, "Please do it for me," that would be enough.

None of the boys with crushes on her, none of the Farts McCanns who called her a retard, and none of the girls who pretended to ignore Charlotte knew she was sick, though if you actually looked you could see there was something wrong with her that had nothing at all to do with her place on the spectrum. It had always been bad, with her tummy, but it was getting worse. She didn't really sleep. Whenever Mom tried to sympathize in some gooey way, Charlotte dismissed it. She didn't want sympathy or popularity or Christmas presents or boys or friends or money or decent clothes or attention or holidays in Mexico or a new iPhone.

The light finally changed and they crossed 109th Street.

"Did you sleep well?" Charlotte continued to look straight ahead. Whyte Avenue was safest when there were a lot of people around, shopping and going to restaurants and cafés and bars. During the pandemic, it was just about deserted. The only people on it were crazy. So they walked down University Avenue. It took a moment for Poppy to understand what Charlotte had asked. She didn't ask questions like this, about a good night's sleep or the weather or current events. It was not at all normal to chit-chat with Charlotte on the way to school. If they talked about something, it was always Poppy who brought it up, usually something she could not figure out. Charlotte's brain was just faster than hers, faster than anyone's, and she could solve any problem that was not about emotions.

"I guess so. It was kind of a strange night. How about you?"

Charlotte lifted her upper lip, as though they had passed a sewer grate. "Strange night. Yes."

"Did you hear the thieves?"

"No."

"Or see them?"

"No."

"What was strange about the night, Char? For you, I mean?"

They were passing a nursing home built with bricks. Old buildings built with bricks were beautiful, but there was something about the newer ones. Poppy suspected the buildings weren't built with bricks at all. The perfectly smooth bricks were just glued on the outer layer of a wooden building, a slightly fancier version of vinyl siding that cannot hide the essential boringness of the design. In a career quiz at school, it came out that Poppy could be an architect. She feared the test was right, though what she really wanted was to be on stage.

It took a long time for Charlotte to respond, and in that quiet time she walked faster. "I think I had a fever and hallucinated. But I am overtired."

"What did you hallucinate?"

They were nearly at the corner where they separated. There was a way to walk a bit farther together, if they wanted, but Poppy had long ago decided she wanted to walk the last couple of blocks without her sister. She was not a good person. She just pretended to be a good person and the only one who knew the miserable truth was Charlotte.

"Come on, Char. What was it? I heard someone howling in the halls or maybe in one of the bedrooms. Crying out in pain.

I thought maybe it was you or Mom, it was a woman, but it didn't sound like you or Mom. It sounded like—"

"Stop." Charlotte turned away from her and started walking south to her school. "It's not real."

Poppy followed her. "What's not real? What did you hallucinate?"

Charlotte sped up. "A ghost."

"What did it look like?"

"It was not real so there is no point discussing it. Tonight I'll go to bed earlier and take anti-inflammatories."

Poppy stopped and watched Charlotte walk away. It was almost like her sister was afraid.

FIVE

The ghost followed Benedict at a distance as he walked through the university campus, its old trees and rocks and sculptures splattered with melting snow and populated now only by bunnies and masked janitors. His ghost moved past the empty restaurants and cafés, north across the bridge, and through the legislative grounds, its evergreens lit up for Christmas. Every time he stopped and turned, his ghost stopped. It had grown in size and turned white in the sunshine.

Downtown sidewalks were covered in brown pudding. A few business men in brogues and business women in heels walked daintily from one bare spot to the other, but most of them worked at home these days. Day labourers, new ones from the oil crash and quiet veterans of misfortune, tromped in boots and sneakers. Benedict hurried past the bookstore and the soup shop, the optician, the massage parlour, and all the restaurants on the ground floors of the concrete office towers, some open yet all deserted. In front of a shop with fancy second-hand clothing, Benedict stopped and turned. The ghost hovered in the middle of the sidewalk and Benedict's fellow travellers walked around it. They did not acknowledge the ghost but they did not walk through it either. He was imagining the thing, after a largely sleepless night of illness and panic, but what was he imagining? The people of downtown treated the ghost like a beggar, actively pretending it was not there.

By the time he arrived at 104th Street, his feet were soaked and cold. The downtown business association had put up blue LED Christmas decorations all over the street of pretend warehouses. A woman from London had designed it and it looked like a woman from London had designed it.

The offices of Kutisi were on the fourth floor of a pretend warehouse, the podium of a condominium tower. A few of the warehouses on the street were original but the rest, over the course of the twentieth century, had been torn down and the land developed as parking lots. Then in the early 2000s the non-parking-lot economy began to improve. Now there were entire blocks of pretend warehouses, inspired by the originals, with glass towers full of two bedroom condominiums rising from the back.

"Well, aren't you . . . " Ginny, the Kutisi office manager, was originally from Birmingham, Alabama, and to Benedict she sounded—and looked—straight out of the movies. This was her first day in the office in months, and for the occasion of their final pitch she wore a bright red dress with matching lipstick. Ginny's husband, a vice-dean of business at the university, was twenty years older than her and did not like that she worked for Kutisi. He was an oil man, originally from Houston, and believed—like other leaders in the province—that Benedict and Marie-Claude were out to destroy traditional sectors of the resource economy like coal, the oil sands, and natural gas. This was not remotely difficult for Benedict because he *did* want to destroy traditional sectors of the resource economy, but Marie-Claude had lost several lifelong friends. She had lost board positions that had meant a lot to her.

It was no great secret that Kutisi had not met its potential, and when Marie-Claude cajoled Benedict to join the Anglo-Saxon men of oil in traditional dress at Chamber of Commerce luncheons and energy conference events in Houston and Toronto and Calgary, they enjoyed asking how his little start-up was going. *How's that valuation? Getting close to an IPO, Ben? Haven't heard much.*

Ginny was trying to think up a compliment. She dished them out to just about everyone, but Benedict knew there wasn't anything to say, not this morning. He could feel the bloodlessness in his cheeks and neck, and his pants were wet halfway to his knees. Had he buttoned his coat improperly? Yes, yes, he had.

Instead of waiting any longer, he thanked Ginny and gave her some tips on what to do when the investors arrived.

"Y'all can do it," she shouted after him, as he made his way through the security door to the warehouse. "I know you can." Despite the warmth and enthusiasm in Ginny's voice, Benedict could tell she did not believe it.

No one did.

His footsteps on the wooden floor echoed through the pretend warehouse. Every workstation was tidy. A man who had grown up in Cambodia, with a wispy moustache, who was here on one of the economic recovery work co-op packages, was decorating a Christmas tree in the corner. His contract had finished months ago, but he couldn't go back home in the middle of the health crisis. Marie-Claude had decided they would continue paying him, though there was nothing for him to do. There was little for any of them to do, their fourteen staff working from home—down from a height of thirty-seven. A few of his staff members had emailed in the past week, asking if the rumours were true. Would they be shutting down in January? Should they be looking for new jobs?

Benedict had forwarded the notes to Marie-Claude, who always knew what to say. She wrote a memo to all staff, realistic but reassuring.

In semiretirement, Marie-Claude did not like to work any more than two days a week. Before the pandemic she had commuted between Canada, Palm Springs, and Puerto Vallarta to balance golf and her investments. When she was at Kutisi, everything felt better to Benedict, more possible. There were no offices, as Marie-Claude felt it was best to have a flat structure, but there was a conference room separated from the main workspace by a glass wall. Presently the sliding door was closed and Marie-Claude sat at the long table with her hands clasped before her, her shoulders hunched in what seemed, from the other side of the glass, to be prayer. Benedict did not have to say anything; Marie-Claude seemed to feel it when he arrived. She reached back and slid the door open. "Oh, Benedict."

"Yes. I look awful. Sorry, I'm still a bit sick."

"It's not—"

"No, no. Totally different symptoms. But I'll keep my distance anyway." Benedict put his backpack and jacket on a chair, squirted some sanitizer in his hands, and rubbed them. "Could you make the presentation? I have it on a memory stick. You've seen me do it several times."

Benedict could not see if Marie-Claude smiled but she carried lightness in her green eyes. She wore a dark blue dress with a white scarf, and a bit of makeup. From a distance it would be difficult to guess her age—anywhere from fifty to sixty-five. No one would think seventy-two. The slight droop in her face, from Bell's palsy, was hidden by her elegant black mask. "So it's the same presentation?"

"Yes."

"The one you always do."

"Yes."

"Ben, I've been thinking. It should be different today."

"Because I failed every other time."

She stood up and approached him, a bit too close. "We've not said it out loud, have we? That this is our last chance? I'm sorry but there's . . . no more money." She pointed to the other side of the glass, to where the employees would be on a normal day. "The kids know it."

Benedict turned. The ghost hovered in between the two long deserted tables where, this time a year ago, twenty people sat and stared at screens. He remembered where he had seen the ghost before. Marie-Claude cleared her throat.

"I can't put together a new presentation this late. They'll be here soon."

Marie-Claude sighed. "I'm afraid I'll have to insist."

"Insist?"

She slammed her tiny fist on the desk and then lifted both hands, in surrender, and wiped the desk as though she had soiled it with her anger. "This is your baby, but come on, Ben. I've put everything into this. Everything."

What did she want him to say, or do? He said nothing. He leaned on the leather back of a chair and looked out on the street. On a normal day, at this hour, young people from Kutisi and businesses like Kutisi, software and artificial intelligence and video game developers, moved from café to café. Now it was just a single car, something red in the slush.

"You know what Kutisi is capable of. What it needs. You know why they should invest. You know *why*. Just forget the damn slides and say it."

"But—"

"I'm furious with you, Ben. I've lost everything, and we've proven so many awful, awful men right. I don't sleep well. But at any moment I could have left. I could have found a way to exit with a bit of capital. But I knew, I still know, we can do this. *You* can. Don't tell them what we already have. Don't tell them what we still need to figure out. They've done some diligence or they wouldn't be coming to town. The Americans, the Chinese, they're not like us. It's okay to go a bit fake. Think of it as a show."

"Fake?" Benedict turned to her. The ghost was just outside the window now, staring without eyes.

"Not fake, sorry." Marie-Claude drew a cup of coffee from the urn delivered by the Melbournians below them on 104th Street. They did not like the idea of serving brewed *Canadian church coffee* but they paid their bills through catering and takeaway now. "Don't deviate from the science. Just be more . . . aspirational. Pitch it the way you pitched me, way back when, on the purity of the idea. Can I pour you one?"

Benedict was still not ready to eat or drink anything. His ghost would not go away no matter how many times he closed his eyes and thought of pumpkin pie. He turned away from his ghost and processed it, what Marie-Claude had said about going fake. The last time she was asked to make a speech, for a group of executives in Toronto, Benedict went with her to court other possible investors. On stage, in public, in front of strangers, enemies, Marie-Claude spoke of the emptiness that came with selling Aarhus Energy, the sudden lack of purpose. She had always been too busy to carry on a proper romantic relationship, let alone start a family. After some largely meaningless travel, taking photographs of places she felt she had already seen, because of other photographs, she discovered a spiritual hole in her heart. She did some work on her family tree and found a balance of Islam, Judaism, and Christianity in her Lebanese blood. This had not led her to choose from among them. She chose all three, in a mash-up of her own devising, and sought a way to bring her increasing concern for the future of the planet in line with what she knew best: business. This had led her to Kutisi. Benedict could not believe it, her candour, how vulnerable and uncertain and *searching* she had shown herself to be.

"If not fake, what?"

"You lured me with hope, Benedict. So many people died this year. The world's burning down and we all know it, that the *real virus* will never have a vaccine." She pointed down at empty 104th Street. "We've just been through the biggest shock in economic history. Why follow rules of business etiquette? Why pretend anyone is really in charge of what comes next?" Marie-Claude placed her coffee mug on the conference room table and took his hands in hers. No one outside his family had touched him in nine months and it was both a terrible jolt and such a comfort, he wanted to sit down and stay like this for a long time. It was against all the rules to touch, to touch a seventy-year-old woman, but her hands were cool and surprisingly soft, like carrots that had been in the fridge too long. "Kutisi will work. All we need is a bit more talent, time, and money. And when we get there, Benedict, what will it feel like?"

"Feel like?"

Marie-Claude released his hands and lowered herself back into the chair. "Sit with me a moment."

"If you want me to make a different presentation, I should get to work. Also you should sanitize your hands, after touching me. There's some hand sanitizer in—"

"Please."

Benedict sat.

"Have you ever prayed?"

"Please sanitize your hands. I won't be able to proceed with anything until you do."

She sanitized her hands and the smell of ethanol filled the room, smell of the year. "Now. Have you prayed?"

"My parents had me pray, when they joined the church." He looked up and his ghost was still there. *Go away.* "But of my own accord: no."

"I know you're not a believer in any ordinary way but sometimes—"

"No."

"Can we try, together?"

"No."

"Let's pray."

What he did know of prayer was that it could not absolve him of his regrets or his fears or his weakness, of what he had done. But he had learned long ago to live by the rules of superstition. His father had been red-green colour-blind. They had not reconfigured the traffic lights for him. Benedict's failure to bring his idea to reality had shredded Marie-Claude's net worth so he owed her this.

"Close your eyes, please," she said.

"I can do it with my eyes open."

"Let's imagine the investors of Sinotechnika around this table. They're looking up at you, to you, listening, and they are deeply moved. They believe as you believe. You *believe*, Benedict, as I do, that we're in the middle phase of a slow-motion disaster that will make a killer virus feel like a tickle in the throat of humanity. Only Kutisi can stop it, and there's still time."

He hated it when Marie-Claude said things like this, when anyone did. The pressure hurt his stomach. He wouldn't say it.

Marie-Claude did not know what he knew about Kutisi.

"Why else are we doing this? Why are all those sweet kids at home, at their computers, designing supply chains for you? Believe! Each Kutisi box will consume depleted uranium and waste plutonium and create fifty megawatt hours per year. Believe! It will create a massive reduction in both cost and emissions worldwide. Believe! It can withstand the worst that weather or earthquakes can throw at us and human error is *not an issue*, not anymore. It's cheap, it's safe, and it will allow us to cleanly electrify the world overnight. Urgent action. Three hundred coal-fired power plants under construction in India and China can stop now. Not in 2030. Now! Do you believe?"

"But the rules around . . . "

"Do you believe? Benedict, if you do not believe, I cannot believe and we might as well cancel this meeting right now. Let's phone the car service and tell them to turn around, fire up the Learjet, and fly back to San Francisco."

"No."

"Then what in the Tennessee fuck are we *doing here*?" She slammed the desk again. "Today there can be no equivocation, no compromises." Now Marie-Claude took a breath and spoke just above a whisper. "*Can* you believe?"

Benedict turned to his ghost again.

"Believe!"

He closed his eyes. He watched the video in his mind of a Kutisi box at full capacity. One humming in every community in the world, a shiny pod in big cities, in the jungle, in snowy mountains. Orchestral music is playing. There are drone shots: China, India, Indiana.

"Do you believe?"

He nodded as he nodded in church, when he was nine.

"Your invention works. It works, Ben. We just need these assholes to understand."

He saw engineers in high-visibility vests and hard hats, with tablet computers, in hot places and mountain places, people of all colours—like front covers of Jehovah's Witness brochures.

"All of it, these feelings and these images, see them and smell them and taste them. It has already happened. We are there. This is what we want our friends at Sinotechnika to see and smell and taste today. Yes? We are in the business of *faith*. Do not let a crepuscule of doubt or cynicism enter your heart or your mind today. I know this is not easy for you but for the next few hours this is your mission, our mission. And there is not a set of slides on the planet that will do it. Only you can do it, Ben. I smoked for thirty years. My lungs are garbage. I'm in the highest risk category, after nurses. I should be home in my pyjamas but *I am here*, on this miserable, mucky horse's ass of a day, because I know you will succeed."

Then all Benedict could hear was Marie-Claude breathing through her nose, another car on 104th Street below, and the faint music from *A Charlie Brown Christmas* on the other side of the glass. Was the music actually playing?

"Can you hear that?"

"Hear what?"

"The music." He wanted to ask if she saw the ghost too but Benedict knew the answer. "A jazz trio. Piano and . . . "

Marie-Claude took his hand again. "You're just terrified, in your way, aren't you?"

He was terrified.

"Accept it in your heart, Ben, the fear, and wash it away with a flood of belief. Believe it has already happened. It's here. Feel that feeling, make it manifest."

It embarrassed him that Marie-Claude was saying these things, that she really did believe. He had to tell her. He had a moral and legal obligation . . .

The phone rang and he jumped. Marie-Claude pressed the speaker button.

Ginny spoke in an elevated manner. "Our esteemed guests from California and China have arrived."

SIX

K aren decided the safest way for her yoga teacher to come into the house was through the front door. Belgravia was an inner-city neighbourhood just south of the university, so there were always students and lecturers, nurses and patients parking and walking. Their brick house was old, on the historic register, and it was part of walking tours. It was not like she lived in the distant treeless suburbs, where someone might notice and whisper about a man with cascading, mouse-brown dreadlocks. In the morning hours after her daughters and Benedict left, Karen loaded the dishwasher, and tidied the front entry. November was a mess of three alternating seasons' worth of footwear—from flip-flops to snow boots. Then she had a bath with her razor. Karen knew the dating young women of today were expected to have Brazilian wax jobs, or at least to shave it all off, but she couldn't bring herself to do it. Instead, she watched a YouTube video about sculpting. The presenter, a woman in her early twenties named Laine, kept calling her female viewers, "you guys."

Karen chose option three for her pubic hair, which Laine called
the old school.

When she was finished in the bath, Karen stood naked in front
of the steamed mirror and tried to seem sexy: the old school. Jesus
Christ, she was deluded. Jak Miller was not going to see her
naked! He was a yoga teacher, here to help her through a couple
of advanced poses that had troubled her. It was on the studio's
promotional cards: private lessons, eighty dollars per hour. Did
all of the women he visited sculpt their pubic hair and tidy up their
foyers? All the crazy hags of her generation? All the Karens?

She grabbed her phone to send him a text and cancel, began
typing the words. Then she erased them, laid out her dark blue mat
on the Persian rug, and switched the Christmas music to Chopin.
To kill time and to stop obsessing about him and hating herself, she
went into their bank accounts to budget for Christmas presents.
There was a little over $9,000 in chequing, but together their three
lines of credit were just under $650,000. The cards were a blood-
bath, and they still owed $842,000 on the mortgage. She was not
sure what the house was worth anymore. It had been well over
$1.2 million, but things had started to stink in the real estate market
even before oil cratered and the pandemic arrived.

From the couch Karen watched the sidewalk. Jak was sensitive
to chemicals so perfumes were not allowed in the yoga studio.
After her bath she had applied a few gentle dabs of pure sandal-
wood oil and then wiped it off with a damp cloth, so she might have
the faintest, sexiest hint of the forests of Nepal about her.

The thought of being naked with a man in his twenties who
could do the splits, a thought which had lit her up for weeks, now
filled her with terror. During her pregnancies her belly skin had
stretched, and at forty-three it was soft and a bit loose and there
was not a sit-up in human invention that could do a thing about it.
She had not been intimate with a man other than Benedict since

1999, and as much as she had imagined it now that Jak was actually on his way, it calmed her to think they would simply work on tough yoga moves.

She was forty-three! Karen could die any given day from the virus and in her final moments she did not want to look back and think, *Fuck, that was it?* She googled the mental health help line and just about pressed the call button, to beg someone to talk her down.

When he was one minute late, Karen was relieved. He had forgotten. At two minutes after the hour, Karen was about to send a passive-aggressive text to him about how she must have mixed up the dates. And there he was, moving down the sidewalk with his slightly bouncy walk, a bright yellow yoga mat popping out of his backpack. His face mask had daisies on it. Her stomach went so queasy she feared Benedict's virus—*the* virus?—might have passed to her. She screamed out loud.

Keep walking, right past the house, Jak Miller. She was ten years too old for this feeling. Her eyes went wet and she ordered herself to *fucking stop it*, held her breath a moment. Jak knocked on the door the way her father had knocked on doors; he made a little song of it. *Shave and a haircut / two bits.* Her father had always pretended to be happy, though Karen came to understand he was sad, worse than sad. The sound of that knock was the sound of secrets and hopelessness.

Karen had lowered the blinds and half closed the curtains in the living room, so there was just enough light to see how beautiful she was but not enough to see how old she was. She opened the door and backed into the living room, an instinct the pandemic had honed in her. It still felt dangerous and wrong to welcome any human being into the house, let alone her yoga teacher.

"Wow, sweet house." He kicked off his fur-lined Birkenstocks. There was a bit of snow on his bare feet, which were otherwise filthy. And, she could see for the first time, exceedingly warty. "I love these old houses."

Karen sneaked around him, now that he was in the living room, and locked the door. "We like it." Oh, why did she say that? It was something an old person would say, the least clever thing in the world, like buying your decor at Costco, those huge letters that say HOPE or DREAM, like waving a giant flag: "I am married with two children and I belong to a book club!" She had never said it before, *We like it*. Had she heard the line in a movie or read it in a book? Some boring idiot maybe said it? Not even the villain. Some unimaginative, chubby, bald guy eating too many chicken wings with his three pints of light beer. Perhaps there was a way to undo this. Yes. "It's a good party house."

"Party house?" said Jak.

Karen thought she'd be okay killing herself now. "Would you like a glass of water?"

"You got distilled or artesanal?"

It was hard to keep track of what progressive people felt about bottled water. Last she heard, it was like clear-cutting old-growth forests for wood chips. Was it cool again? And what was artesanal water? Was there a difference between artesanal and artisanal? She was afraid to ask, and now that Jak was in the living room, she had a solid view of his warty feet.

"Just 'cause . . . we're all taking so many pharmaceuticals and they show up in our urine and then we flush it all into the same system we recycle into tap water."

"Does it help to boil it?"

"No."

"Because I could make us herbal tea."

"You know what, let's just practice, Karen." He pulled off his backpack and slid his yellow yoga mat out of it.

This was an absolute relief: like learning she didn't get a job she desperately wanted, because it would have been a hard job doing things she did not know how to do. She slipped off her socks and joined him on the centre of the Persian rug. Her Chopin playlist had eased into Erik Satie. She wore her most flattering leggings, the ones that made her bum seem the highest and tightest, and a black merino T-shirt.

"Unless you want to . . . take me on a tour of your house."

This hit her so hard she could only respond by stuttering and pointing up and down and then toward the kitchen. A tour? What house?

"Just breathe," he said.

She did. She put her energy into her feet and cleared her head for a moment. Jak did not want a tour. Jak wanted what Karen had hoped he wanted, but now that Jak clearly wanted it Karen was not at all sure she wanted him to want it. What did she want? She had wanted *something*, had longed for it for weeks. At the base of the private lesson she imagined was a feeling that Jak had understood her, that he could heal and forgive her. Her doubts, her worries about money and her age and dying, the dumb movies and *Archie* comics she could not help but adore, her relationship with the Toronto Blue Jays, Johnny and Jeanette Sjöblad and the bloody secrets of Halloween night. But Jak was not who she thought he was, a poet who would get her sense of humour, a man of the spirit who could read from the look on her face across the room exactly what she was thinking, her mysteries. Now that he was in the house she shared with her daughters, close enough to smell, in the grey light of winter, Karen accepted that Jak did not understand her. He did not want to understand her. He wanted to fuck her. But why? She knew there were all sorts of fetishes out there, including the *older woman*, the mom. Her mouth felt like she had just guzzled a cup of sand. Karen was now entirely sure she did not want this. It was enough that Jak had come in. Perhaps she could get him out without touching him or allowing him to touch anything, and then she could bleach his wart juice out of the floors. Feigning illness was the way to do it. "Well. I could show you upstairs. It has historic details."

"What's up there, Karen?"

"Four bedrooms. A bathroom. We use one of the bedrooms as an office, but that's the layout, and there's also—"

"Karen. Shh. Just take me."

She did not entirely trust her legs to carry her, so she held onto the oak banister. There was no point talking anymore. Jak was different at Belgravia Bikram: more searching and curious, a monkish man. Karen had mistaken his manner in the yoga studio for divinity.

The bedroom at the end of the hall was the master. She pointed in there, in case he wanted to look in, and she let him know that it was the largest bedroom in the house but in the tradition of prairie architecture at the end of the First World War there was no ensuite. In fact, there wasn't even a bathroom up here originally. They had to find the right contractor because it wasn't an easy plumbing challenge. Jak looked at her in a practiced manner. He wanted Karen to know he was not listening to a word she said. He was only *looking at her*. She was about to claim a bladder infection when Jak put his hands on Karen's face and kissed her.

The blast of touch, after months of the pandemic, was violent. She wanted it to stop. Benedict was gentle, almost a closed-mouth kisser, while Jak was aggressive about it and wet. He made noises and darted his tongue around in her mouth like he had lost something in there. A layer of blond stubble rubbed against her chin as he moved and pushed. His breath had a hint of Indian food about it. She did not want Jak to shove her on the bed so she stepped away from it and pulled away.

Karen was about to ask him to leave when he bent over and, in an attempt at sexiness, removed his pants and underwear. And there it was, *there he was*. Karen felt silly for sculpting. How, she wondered, do men come to believe that being naked from the waist down, standing up, with a shirt on, could be anything but an atrocity?

In all her time in his yoga studio, Karen had never noticed the warts on his feet. The floors were sweaty in the studio, all the time, and now all she could think of was sweat and wart juice on her floor and whatever it was in Jak's hair to keep it from frizzing and of course his penis. His hair had felt sticky, like corn syrup, and smelled like a five-year-old farm boy's scalp. On the other side of him she spotted a photo of Charlotte and Poppy on a carousel in Aix-en-Provence. From afar she had always imagined herself loving Aix-en-Provence: the climate, the architecture, Cézanne's hometown. But it was dreary and a bit dirty on the day they arrived, and there were posters for the Front National all over the place. Despite it being a university city, everyone looked stupid and carried bags from the Gap and L'Occitane en Provence—fake mall Provence in actual Provence.

So many people were stupid, cruel and selfish and aggrieved, given to conspiracy theories and nonsense. And now all she could do, as a *Karen*, was listen. No matter what she wanted to say, it was better unsaid. Her people had said plenty, thanks so much. How would her Scandinavian daughters, future Karens, make their way in a world that had heard enough from them? She needed to arm her blonde babies, somehow, to be ambitious in a different way. Hold on. Was it racist to think these thoughts? Yet instead of figuring this out, in a time of fear and scarcity, she had invited a warty-footed yoga teacher into her house, into her *bedroom*, to do something she had not done since she was younger than Jak.

He fell back on her bed. Their bed. His wang lay shyly in his unsculpted pubic hair like a snail recently emerged from its shell. Jak pointed at it as though it were a plate of delicious food he had just assembled from local ingredients.

Karen wanted him out of the house immediately but she could not rouse the courage to order him. She sat on the corner of the bed and prepared to tell him about her bladder infection when she went cold, the whole bedroom went cold, deep cold even though Karen had turned up the heat to replicate Bikram conditions and the fantasy feeling of the studio. "Baby, It's Cold Outside" was one of her favourite Christmas songs. She knew all the words, the woman's and the man's, and sometimes when she was alone she sang it to herself, and she thought of it now. But the cold was not outside. It was in her bedroom and it was getting worse. Then a shadow moved past the open bedroom door.

Jak had misunderstood her decision to sit on the bed and slid toward her.

"Just wait a second," she said. "Don't move."

"Why?"

Karen was looking away from him, into the hallway. Had Benedict come home? Or one of the girls?

"Ben?"

Jak rolled like an armed commando off the bed, under the window.

"Char?" she said. "Poppy?"

There was no answer and the house was silent. But also not silent. There was a low hum.

"Jak, you hear that?"

He whispered, "Hear what? Is Ben your husband? Is he a gun guy? What the absolute fuck? We didn't do anything. We barely even kissed. Tell him this is yoga!"

In the silence again it was an ancient hum, older than electricity. Karen stood up off the bed, to discover its source. Her sexiest leggings seemed ridiculous now so she put on her silk kimono, a Christmas gift she had chosen for herself on a trip to Japan with her girlfriends back in her early thirties, when she still had girlfriends.

"Where are you going?"

What would she say to Benedict? There was no defence.

"Hey. Hey you." He seemed to have forgotten her name. She wanted to rinse Jak's sour curry saliva off her face but first she had to know. "Hey. Where you going?"

It was as cold in the hallway as it had been in the bedroom. Colder. And the hum was deeper. She walked to the other end of the hall. Near the stairs it got warmer and the hum faded. She felt better with each step, more philosophical about the thing she had just done. After all these weeks, months—years—of feeling ignored and alone, of aging into invisibility.

The doors into the girls' bedrooms and Benedict's office were closed.

"Charlotte?"

Her oldest daughter never spoke unless she had to speak, so Karen called her name again. Maybe she was sicker than usual. Maybe the day Karen had long feared had come and Charlotte had decided she could not take it anymore. She would lock herself in her bedroom and make it go away. No. With each step in this direction, it got colder and Karen was more frightened. Of what? Of the shame of being discovered? Yes. And something else, a deeper and more sinister shame that crackled in her guts and in her bones.

"Poppy?" It grew colder.

"Benny? Are you home?"

She opened Poppy's door and looked in. Her comforter was half on her bed and half on the floor, and her stuffed chicken, sasquatch, and bunny were strewn about with weeks' worth of discarded clothes, some clean but most dirty. On her desk there were novels about teen life, a lot of makeup drying out in left-open containers, and some drawings. It was too dark to make out what they were. The bedroom smelled of scented candles, possibly vanilla. It was warmer than the hall.

If Poppy had come home stricken by her father's illness to see a man with dreadlocks seemingly eating Karen's face, it would make for the worst mother-daughter conversation imaginable.

"Pop? You hiding in here?"

Karen returned to the long hall, dark at midday. The old floors creaked. Their cleaners, two women from Bacolod who came every fortnight, did not dust the floorboards or the wainscotting. There were cobwebs along the groove between the red walls and white ceiling, both in need of a new coat of paint. Benedict's office had a desk between two walls of built-in bookshelves, with moulding and the intricate woodwork of a century ago. The house's first owner was a judge who had moved here from Montreal. He had donated a lot of money to the law faculty, so hallowed things at the university were named after him. At one time, it was the only building in the neighbourhood. Its name in the historic register was Finster House. This was Finster's office. Benedict rarely spent time in this room. He rarely spent time at home. The room felt lonely and smelled pleasingly of dusty books. "Ben?"

Charlotte's room was at the back, across the hall from the master bedroom. As she passed, Karen looked in to see Jak peeking up from the far end of the bed. The source of the cold hum, the shadow, was on Charlotte's side.

"Dude." Jak was in near-complete darkness now, as though hours had passed and it was already late afternoon. "Dude, what is going on? Is there a window open in here?"

Karen put her hand on Charlotte's doorknob. It was cold.

"Wait," said Jak. "Don't leave me, man."

Karen knocked before she opened the door, and cold air that smelled far older and far lonelier than any book rushed into her and she backed away, confused and dizzy.

Unlike any other fifteen-year-old girl Karen had encountered, her fifteen-year-old girl had designed her bedroom like a miniature laboratory: a long, white table with beakers and pipettes and tools of science Karen did not understand. In earlier, more hopeful, and prosperous times for their family, Benedict had organized an industrial circulation system that brought fresh air into the room and sent whatever foulness their daughter had schemed into the northern winds.

"Charlotte, darling? Are you here?"

The laboratory half of the cold bedroom was in perfect order, and so was what Karen could see of the bed. But she was not alone in the room, and she could tell the other presence was not Charlotte.

Even so: "Char?"

Karen did not want to see who had broken into their house. Though she was sure she had locked the doors, someone had come inside. It calmed her somewhat that she was not alone, that Jak would come running.

She bent forward to see wool pants in a shade of grey, street maniac grey. "Hello?" Her voice shook and already there were tears in it. "I'm going to call the police!" There were two brass candleholders, a long one and a medium one. Karen had placed them in here as decorations long ago, to inject something like beauty into the starkness of her daughter's life. She grabbed them both as she stepped forward and called her lover—whatever he was. "Jak!"

The ancient, rotten smell intensified and so did her dizziness as she took one more step into the room. Karen prepared to scream at the vagrant who had broken into the house, to bat him in the face with a brass candleholder, but she could not speak when she saw him. He was a tall and stooped man, bald on top with messy grey hair on the sides, wearing a shirt and tie under a brown cardigan. A dead man with spoiled-milk skin and a slouch of misery. She knew this slouch so well. *Shave and a haircut / Two bits.* It was Johnny Sjöblad, her father, gone these twenty years.

He stood next to Charlotte's bed, his pants touching his grand-daughter's white pillowcase. He coughed and slowly turned to her and his eyes, what remained of them, carried the family shame so deeply Karen could not stand before him. She collapsed into the wall as he continued to cough.

"Daddy, no." Karen felt as though she had been hit on the head. Either she had closed her eyes or everything had gone momentarily darker than dark, as though they had entered and departed an eclipse.

Her father was gone.

From across the hall, a scream. Jak screamed. The heater was on, and warm air blew. She was not at all sure how much time had passed. Karen tried to right herself and fell into the bedpost at the foot of the bed and then she tripped on her own ankles and crashed to the hardwood floor. It smelled like a regular bedroom now. Without any strong warning from her body, she threw up.

There was a man in her house. She would be discovered and despised. First she crawled out of Charlotte's bedroom. She would return with a roll of paper towel and some cleaner, a little garbage bin. In the hall she climbed to her feet using the dusty, dark wain-scotting. "I'm coming," she said, exhausted.

In her own bedroom the comforter was messed up. The heat was back on in here too. Jak was no longer hiding at the side of the bed.

Karen called out for him again and held the banister on her way down the stairs. Everything was as she had left it. She was obviously being shellacked by Benedict's virus. It hit her stom-ach and her mind at the same time. Her fever had spiked and she was delirious.

"Jak?"

He was not on the main floor. The bag was gone and so was the yoga mat but his wet Birkenstock sandals were still in the foyer. Karen turned on every light in the basement and checked every room, and Jak was not here either. Years of playing hide-and-seek with Poppy had been instructive. She knew every corner where a person could be. Back on the main floor, she checked all the hiding places and did the same thing upstairs. She brought the cleaning products from the laundry room into Charlotte's bedroom and took care of what she had done on the floor and then she cried for a while. There was a hint of old cigarette smoke. In the months after her father died, in the aftershock of all his betrayals, Karen had thought of him constantly—hating him, loving him, smelling the residue of his cigarettes, wishing she could go back in time to save him and her mother, herself.

Karen turned her holiday music playlist loud, washed the sheets and duvet cover from her bedroom and from Charlotte's bedroom. She mopped the floor, every spot Jak's grotesque feet had touched. She showered. She sang along to "Fairytale of New York" five times in a row and poured herself a glass of Pinot Gris. It would be their last Christmas in this house, their last Christmas as a united family, and she had been sleeping poorly, that's all. A virus in a time of viruses. They had been robbed. Trauma works in unexpected ways! Winter was here and she had been deprived of light, of vitamin D, of purchasing power. None of it had happened.

There was really only one thing to do, to defend herself: put up the fucking Christmas tree.

SEVEN

The decorations were in the basement, in what they called the rec room. The pot lights had burned out in there and neither Karen nor Benedict had bothered to replace them. It was a damp and cool spidery place. In the northernmost major city on the continent, it was already nighttime at four in the afternoon. Wine had helped. Wine always helped, but still the image of her father and the heartsick unreality of Jak Miller's visit were as fresh as the bloody pry bar that had been haunting her since Halloween night. She stared into the dark hollow where they kept all of their seasonal antidotes and felt a presence there. "Hello?"

She pulled the Christmas tree from the web-strewn place in the corner. Karen hated artificial trees but this was the one that used to go up in their basement in Edgemont, *her* tree. The proper one, the white spruce, was always upstairs. Her father decorated it with a ladder. When he disappeared and they had to give up the house to pay some tiny percentage of his debts, the plastic tree, her tree, was the only tree. Her mother died and the six-foot miracle of moulded

plastic carried the childhood she most longed for, her true childhood, before she knew. And for Benedict, an artificial tree from
1989 made the most sense: nothing had to be cut down and the
plastic was already in the ecosystem. Last year she had sprayed
organic silver fir essential oil on the fake branches to manufacture
a hug of nostalgia.

It was not a heavy box but it was awkward to drag up the stairs.
A third of the way up, she heard the ping of her phone over Nat
King Cole. *Chestnuts roasting on an open fire.* She crawled over the
busted Sears box and ran up the stairs, hoping it was Jak. It was
Poppy, advising her they would stop at Starbucks on the way home.
Did she want anything? An eggnog latte? Karen did not want a
latte and she did not want her daughter, who was struggling with
her weight, to spend six dollars on five hundred gooey calories
either. Midway through each of the responses she crafted, she
erased the words. In the end, she simply wrote, "Nice thought but
no thank you."

She gulped what remained of the Pinot Gris in her glass, slid her
phone into her back pocket, and walked back down the stairs. The
tree box was not where she left it, and it had not slid down. The box
wasn't there at all. Karen stood at the bottom of the stairs. "Dad?"

The only answer she could hear was Nat King Cole singing
in the kitchen. Karen walked back across the basement floor and
looked into the rec room. She used the flashlight on her phone to
illuminate the space. There it was in its place in the corner. A large
dollhouse, two boxes of stuffed animals, Lego scenes, and other toys
and games Charlotte had always found irrelevant and Poppy had
outgrown were shoved against the back wall next to the Christmas
tree along with boxes of children's books Karen could not bring
herself to donate or trade.

No intruder squatted there in the spiderwebs.

Karen sat on the floor. She was sure she had pulled out the

Christmas tree, had lugged it halfway up the stairs, but the Pinot Gris had fogged her up. She had imagined it, like she had imagined her dead father upstairs in Charlotte's room. She concentrated on the dollhouse, on the beautiful books she had read to the girls. When they were forced to move to some boiled meat apartment building in the welfare part of New Westminster, there would be a reckoning. She did everything she could to slow it down, *to live in the present tense*, but her girls were nearly grown and this secret shrine to their childhood was essential. Maybe a storage facility? The Nat King Cole album ended and the house was silent apart from the mechanical groan of the furnace.

If only Daphne had not died. The dog had understood things Karen was too smart, or too dumb, to see. It smelled like ancient mould in the rec room, the kind that ruins lungs and causes cancer. Not even a ghost could be happy in there.

Still. "Hello? Daddy?"

Karen turned off her phone's flashlight and with her first few steps she walked calmly across the basement floor. Then she ran. Upstairs she asked Siri to play her Christmas Cheer playlist, loud, poured herself another glass of Pinot Gris, and sat on the couch nearest the front window, where there was still daylight. She had a fever or something. It was just an old house.

This Pinot Gris from Alsace, in its long skinny bottle, was just the right amount of sweet. She wished she could call someone to talk about the wine but she had lost her only real friend in the city. Next to the fireplace there was an atmospheric photograph of Benedict and Marie-Claude on the cover of *Report on Business* magazine from about five years ago. The photographer thought it would be cool to have them both in black turtlenecks like Steve Jobs because it was the "disruptors" issue. Karen was embarrassed for them but she had paid to have it mounted and framed for Benedict's office. Poppy had wanted it in the living room.

———

Karen had been just as proud of her own father, Johnny Sjöblad, a petroleum engineer and then a vice-president of exploration with Royal Dutch Shell. In the late 1970s he bought the new estate home in Edgemont and a condominium on the water in Osoyoos. He made it through the dark days of oil in the 1980s when so many others lost their jobs and their homes. Karen was an only child and her mother, Jeanette, a former Miss Alberta from windy Lethbridge, served on community boards and led fundraising efforts for sick children and research into Alzheimer's, which had taken her own father. Jeanette was in the *Herald* a lot and on local television promoting charitable events. Karen and her mother both wore designer jeans and sweaters, and had magnificently golden tans in the summertime. Karen went to private school and spent much of her free time at the Glencoe Club, swimming and golfing with the other children of the executive class. She got a candy-apple-red Volkswagen Cabriolet for her sixteenth birthday.

When everything ended for Johnny Sjöblad, and so publicly, Karen looked back and saw her entire childhood differently. It had been years since she had thought of her father's last weeks in the Edgemont house. His final day was Christmas and that earth-tone outfit was what he had worn as he pretended to be happy, to be hopeful, to see his way out of the hole he had dug for them. Karen had not understood. She believed him that final Christmas, thought he could do anything. Though she had read the articles about his Ponzi scheme in the *Herald* and the *Globe and Mail*, she knew the real story. Her father's take, contrary to the journalism: risks are risky! And then he was gone, and she decided to think about an earlier version of Johnny Sjöblad, the loud and funny man at dinner parties in Calgary and on vacation in the Canadian desert—diving awkwardly into Osoyoos Lake.

When her father disappeared and did not come back, when they declared him dead and gone, they sold the house and the condo and the bankruptcy court allowed the grand and elegant Jeanette Sjöblad just enough of her husband's pension for a dark little suite in one of the new car suburbs in the southeast, preposterously named Bonavista Downs. She died of a stroke in 2015 but it was really of loneliness, abandoned by the aging socialites who had been her friends.

Karen's own oldest and finest friends in Calgary, the few who had remained with her through everything, had been hoping oil would prevail. It would have to prevail. The world would need it for another hundred years and it would pay for their own estate homes and German SUVs and Hawaiian condos. When Benedict and Marie-Claude had first announced Kutisi, it was another social disaster for Karen. Her Facebook feed was filled with sarcastic congratulations by the last of her petroleum pals. If Kutisi succeeded in its ultimate mission, the energy finance towers, branch plants of American and European companies, would empty out. Kutisi would own the next phase of electrification. The oil sands and the industrial parks where the blue-collar men of her generation, who dropped out of school in grade eleven, earned $200,000 a year slinging mud and operating dump trucks would become ghost towns. The earth would reclaim them. When the oil prices had really crashed, back in February and March, Karen's final three friends from high school stopped speaking to her entirely.

Poppy's Christmas list was on the coffee table. Karen turned on the lamp in the corner to read it again. The list contained thousands of dollars' worth of wishes: $1,200 to support two girls' high school educations in Kenya, $650 to help build a school in Bangladesh, five UNICEF vaccine super-packs, reusable dignity pads for young menstruating girls in the developing world, and thousands of water purification tablets. Karen decided to buy everything Poppy wanted

on credit. It did not amount to much when you're—let's be
honest—several hundred thousand under water.

Back in August, Poppy's best friend since playschool, Blaine,
had dumped her. Blaine's mother, Melissa, who happened to be
Karen's best friend in town, had orchestrated the end of the girls'
relationship. She felt Poppy and Blaine had become too close. They
had built a force field around themselves, which prevented other
fabulous girls from getting to know Blaine. In grade six, a mean
boy had accused them of being lesbians. Besides, and please don't
take this the wrong way, *Poppy was not motivated? The way Blaine
was motivated?* She was not a talented pianist or a ranked athlete.
Melissa wanted *excellence?* for her daughter, and that meant sur-
rounding her with the most excellent girls.

It's, like, all about the peer group?

Melissa delivered her rationale for the breakup over afternoon
tea in the Glenora mansion her husband, Ray, had inherited from
his grandparents. She added a shortlist of Poppy's bad behaviour
going back several years. None of it was terribly bad. In all Poppy's
years of school and after-school activities, Karen had never once
heard a report of poor behaviour on Poppy's part. Quite the contrary: Poppy was sweet and trusting, the kindest person Karen had
ever known, so kind she saw little of her own motivations in her.
Teachers and camp counsellors and dance instructors loved Poppy.
Check out her goddamn Christmas list, *Melissa.*

Ray came from a wealthy oil family. Last Christmas, his parents bought matching Rolex watches for Ray, Melissa, and Blaine.
Blaine, a thirteen-year-old girl, wore a nine-thousand-dollar watch
to school.

Blech! Karen and Melissa had gone on spa holidays together.
Absent Benedict, they had eaten breakfasts and dinners as families.
It had been odd between them, the last few months, but Karen had
been so shocked at the presentation in the Glenora mansion, she'd

nearly laughed out loud. She could list, if she were inclined, twenty barbaric things Blaine had done over the years. They were kids! They were in the mistake-making business!

The failure of Kutisi, the news of which had begun to travel through the business community, was surely another factor. Melissa seemed to smell what was coming: bankruptcy proceedings and schadenfreude.

Karen had steamed and gritted her way through too many nights, thinking about what she ought to have said to Melissa, over tea, in her mansion. In typical adolescent fashion, Blaine had been cruel and mocking. Karen and Melissa had stayed in touch for a week or so after the afternoon tea, and Karen had made the mistake of telling Melissa that Poppy had been crying in the evenings about the way Blaine had been treating her. The next day, Blaine announced in social studies class that Poppy had been bawling herself to sleep every night.

Then Halloween night happened, which had moved Karen from fury and sleeplessness into sneak-attack crying fits. Melissa had been the only person in the city she could confide in but that was ruined, and with her own mother dead Karen had no one. Truly, no one. She was no longer in a book club and she was ten years older, at least, than everyone in her yoga class. When Karen did online meetings, it tended to be with a client or a potential client, the sort of meeting where the end of the hour would arrive with a silent gong. Then the computer would go quiet, quiet, quiet.

She had spoken to a few divorce lawyers but there was no real need. On the digital billboards along the freeways, there were advertisements for consultancies that offered pleasantly negotiated settlements; all they had to split up was debt. She had kept what remained of her mother's estate in a separate bank account. It could be the down payment for a miserable little place in the Vancouver equivalent of Bonavista Downs for her and the girls.

Now the light had gone entirely. Christmas songs were not jolly enough to protect her anymore. For the first time since moving into Finster House, it felt like these walls did not want her. This was not just a century-old thing they ate and slept in. It was not passive. It listened, it worked, it felt. It knew what she had done upstairs with Jak. She laughed out loud. Her virus, whatever it was that had inspired her to hallucinate, and these new thoughts . . . the wine and Christmas would have to drown it out.

She opened her laptop and searched Halloween, stabbing, attack, Belgravia, and anything else she could think of, *sexual assault*, and hit news. Nothing. Nothing yet.

The girls always walked home together. At the end of her day, Charlotte would wait on the far side of the football field adjacent to the junior high school. Charlotte's unfashionable taste in clothes and her odd manner sometimes embarrassed Poppy, though Poppy would never say it out loud. Even so, Charlotte knew it, so she created some distance to spare her little sister any brand risk. If they did not stop at Starbucks, they would occasionally stop at La Boule, a French bakery and pastry shop in Old Strathcona, and Poppy would buy *pain au chocolat* or a custard tart. Karen had quietly schemed with Charlotte to avoid La Boule by giving Poppy a different sort of distraction; they now took an extra ten minutes, through the Queen Alexandra neighbourhood, where a popular group of boys skateboarded in the summer and played shinny in the winter. Still, Poppy found her way to dairy and sugar at Starbucks. Karen hated herself so much for thinking about it, she finished her glass of wine.

It was agonizing to wait for the girls in the dark. The house seemed to breathe with judgment and malevolence and Karen had nothing to do but feel scared, poor, lonesome, middle-aged, and drunk. Any moment her dead father could walk down the stairs. Or up the stairs, if he lurked in the basement. She wanted to put on some Christmas cartoons and decorate the tree but she was too scared to go down and get it alone. Karen searched her phone for another Christmas playlist, to find songs she did not know, and played *Jim Henson's Emmet Otter's Jug-Band Christmas*.

Karen refilled her glass of wine, not all the way. Just a final splash. She wanted to pull the warm bed linens from the dryer and make the bed and crawl into it, to wake up when it was all over, the divorce, the bankruptcy, the holiday season, the move to the coast. But she could not stand up from the couch, the only lighted place in the house. She could already see the dreary condominium in New West, no Langley, with industrial carpet, old appliances, and a wood-grain ceiling fan, a fifty-minute drive from downtown, the girls lying on squeaky IKEA bunkbeds in their shared bedroom. She could smell the frying onions and soup in the hallway, hear the crying babies, the shouts of domestic misery.

On a decorating show Karen learned about a thing in northern Europe, maybe Denmark, called hygge. She had been particularly moved by the bit about light in the dark seasons. She lived in the darkest big city in America, dark like Edinburgh and Copenhagen. In December it made candles and soft lamps and warm colours extra cozy. If Charlotte had her way, their ceilings would be packed with bright fluorescence. There were lamps in her bedroom but she never turned them on. Charlotte needed powerful light to build and design impossible things in her room, small engineering marvels that Benedict applauded and Karen only ever pretended to understand. Charlotte had wired the house so anything could happen by speaking into a bulbous speaker in the kitchen or by tapping an app she had created for her iPhone, and she had done it so ingeniously—in conversation with Apple— that the company had sent a local representative to explore and take notes. They had given her a new phone and a MacBook for her time and her ideas.

The door finally opened and the dog did not bark, and immediately Karen felt so much better she fast-walked into the foyer to hug Poppy and wink at Charlotte. Long ago they realized that Charlotte *would* hug but that it made her uncomfortable. In fifteen years she had never once initiated a hug or any other bodily contact. The shadows under her eyes seemed darker than ever.

"Sweetheart, are you feeling okay?"

"Yes."

"Really? You look pale."

"Her Crohn's is flaring up." Poppy did not have an eggnog latte. "And she hardly slept last night. She doesn't want you to know because she doesn't want you to worry. Why are you sitting in the dark?"

Charlotte was already halfway across the living room floor, on her way to the kitchen.

"Out of ten?" said Karen.

"Fatigue is at six." Charlotte washed her hands. "I could still concentrate at school."

Karen was never worried about Charlotte's performance at school. She could write the textbooks. "Any bleeding? Pain?"

"Seven out of ten. I think I had a fever last night, and I'll likely have one tonight. But it isn't severe." She drew a glass of water.

"Girls. How about we put up the Christmas tree?"

Poppy quick-clapped her hands. "One thing. Instead of *The Grinch*, could we watch *Love Actually* while we put it up?"

It was one of the great Christmas mysteries: how did a crap movie like *Love Actually* become a classic? Karen still had a quarter of a glass of wine. She filled it up. The bottle was nearly gone. What the hell? It's Christmas. She tried to remember if *Love Actually* was dirty. It was a bit dirty. She had certainly watched dirtier things by the time she was thirteen. In grade six, at a sleepover, she had watched *Debbie Does Dallas*.

If Poppy didn't want to watch cartoons anymore, what was next? "Let's stick with the tradition, okay?"

The wine was a bit acidic. She had wanted to ask Charlotte something but it was gone now, in the mists of Pinot Gris. She needed to sit. What would they do for dinner? Eggs. Eggs and something. She asked them to go down and bring up the tree, and then she waited in the kitchen with her eyes closed, hoping. Why was her father in Charlotte's room? Why did Charlotte have to suffer? Did he live in the rec room? A few minutes later they were up with it, and a few minutes after that all of the boxes of decorations were upstairs too. Karen set up her laptop to stream *How the Grinch Stole Christmas!* while she plugged the three parts of her plastic tree together.

Poppy opened the box with the lights. "Charlotte saw a ghost."

"What, now? Downstairs?"

For the second time since coming home, Charlotte looked deeply and flatly into her sister's eyes. Poppy was the one person with whom she made eye contact without being asked or forcing herself. It was unusual for Charlotte to appear angry, but this was close. "No, I didn't."

"You told me you . . . "

"I told you I had a fever. I hallucinated, that is all."

Karen wanted to put her hand on Charlotte's hand, to comfort her, but it would only be to comfort herself. When was the last time she had washed her own hands? "A ghost? Who was it?"

Charlotte shook her head. "There are no ghosts. It was in my mind."

Was it your grandfather? Karen did not ask because she did not really want to know. How could two people have the same hallucination? Charlotte had never met her grandfather but there were photographs of him in the house, from the pre-digital era, in frames and albums. She started to ask Charlotte if she wanted to talk about the ghost but the two—three? four?—glasses of pre-dinner wine had ruined her oratorical skills. She stuttered and slurred. Karen was about to try again when a large black suv pulled in front of the house. Poppy stood up when she spotted it.

"Daddy's home early. And he has—what?—Dad has flowers." Poppy went to the door, to greet him. "Flowers for you, Mom."

Karen had tried to conceal it from them, that she and Benedict were having economic and marital trouble. It had not worked. Poppy often tried to get them to go on dates, to hold hands during family movie night, to book a romantic holiday.

There was a flushed look about Benedict as he walked into the living room arm-in-arm with Poppy. Now they would both have to disinfect. Poppy was smiling. Benedict was almost smiling. Cool, moist air came in with them. Benedict presented Karen with a bouquet of flowers, wrapped in brown paper and a ribbon from The Artworks—her favourite shop. The top two buttons of his shirt were undone and his tie hung around his neck like a thin scarf. There was a moment in 1990 or so when her father was off on his own, running his investment fund, driving an actual Maserati, that he looked like this, with an almost-smile like the one Benedict wore. Like that particular day was the best day of his life.

"What's this for?" Karen unwrapped the thick brown paper, revealing an ornate bouquet in Christmas reds and greens. She could not remember the last time her husband had bought her flowers, just for the sake of buying her flowers. "Wow."

Benedict took one end of the string of lights from the box of decorations. Poppy took the other end, and together they untangled them.

"The presentation?" said Charlotte.

"Darlings, we're not poor anymore."

"Wait. What?" Poppy dropped her end of the lights. "We were poor?"

EIGHT

On the first of December, a day after Benedict's performance in the pretend warehouse on 104th Street, Marie-Claude worked with Sinotechnika's chief investment officer, Jessica Wolfe, to craft a press release. Benedict and the CEO of Sinotechnika were quoted, talking about how Kutisi would allow every region in the world currently operating on fossil-fuel power to stop—in months, not years. Each impossibly clever modular generator would create 100 megawatt hours, with zero emissions and virtually no safety risks, thanks to its largely passive operation. There was no need for huge infrastructure upgrades to make it all happen, as Kutisi could plug into existing grids. You want to bury it in underground bunkers in seismically active places or areas with terrorism? Bury it! Cities and states on the verge of modernizing their current grids could shave billions off their budgets. Any neighbourhood in the world could switch to Kutisi—and soon. As property owners added microrenewables over time, solar and geothermal, they could plug it all into the elegant and discreet little power plant on the corner. Kutisi generated, stored, and delivered power.

> *"The world doesn't have to phase out slowly," says Zheng Lau, chief executive officer of Sinotechnika. "Not anymore. We can stop talking about 2040 or 2050 as targets. There hasn't been much good news this year but we're here to tell the world that once we begin manufacturing, we can implement Kutisi, globally, in months. This is the climate change equivalent of a mass vaccination campaign. I don't want to sound hyperbolic but Kutisi can save the planet, and that's why we're so excited to have embarked on this journey with Benedict, Marie-Claude, and their team."*

The national newspaper ran a front-page story because technology giants rarely launch in Canada and almost never receive significant foreign investment. They were on the front page of the *New York Times* business section, below the fold. And they were all over the internet. Benedict and Marie-Claude were part of a new class of entrepreneurs who had found a way to generate massive value while also being environmental warriors. Mr. Zheng spoke at the Zoom press conference, which attracted over eight hundred journalists. In his photograph in the *Globe and Mail*, handsome Mr. Zheng stood in front of a coal-fired power plant in Trona, California. Benedict and Marie-Claude posed in Alberta's industrial heartland at dusk, with plumes of smoke billowing from oil refineries and hydrocarbon processors.

For the rest of the week, Benedict and Marie-Claude had to hire three lawyers and two full-time HR consultants to oversee new complications. They had received hundreds of requests to meet with venture capitalists and private equity firms now that Sinotechnika had invested. Over three hundred engineers from around the world had sent CVs. Representatives from the European Union and the United Nations wanted to visit the factory. Sino-technika put them in touch with a public-relations firm in New York to handle doubters in the press. Both energy journalists and retired CEOs of legacy power operators found different ways to call Kutisi a ridiculous fantasy. Elon Musk tweeted that if it wasn't a fairy tale, he would buy it. Terrorism experts predicted catastrophes. Everyone who hated nuclear power *really* hated Kutisi. But the PR strategy was working. Positive stories were beating negative stories ten to one, no surprise in a year when the oceans were heating up 40 per cent faster than climate scientists had predicted. A columnist in the *Wall Street Journal* speculated that if its claims were true, this little Canadian start-up could be a multibillion dollar company by 2024.

Eighteen million dollars had already transferred to Kutisi from Sinotechnika. The day Benedict transferred money into their joint account, paying off his shareholder loan to Kutisi and retroactively paying his salary and bonuses, Karen booked a weekend getaway at a spa on Vancouver Island for January, just the two of them.

Benedict spent his December evenings alone in the Kutisi factory, a few blocks north of the warehouse in an old car dealership. His private workshop was in the former painting bay, separated from the rest of the factory by two walls and a kitchen. It had a dis-carded couch from their basement and he had bought a patio table and a chair from IKEA so he could sit and work in front of his Kutisi with a computer and a notepad.

On the night of the seventh, Benedict sat on the cracked leather couch and streamed *A Charlie Brown Christmas*. It was one of the few holiday specials his parents had allowed him to watch. He had removed the silver front plate from his Kutisi and his tools lay in perfect order in a semicircle on the concrete floor. The ghost hovered next to him, twice as large as the first night he saw it, watching him watch an animated television show.

Benedict's parents had not grown up in religious families. His father became an engineer, his mother a pharmacist. When he was in elementary school Benedict contracted bacterial meningitis, it turned nasty, and for nearly a week he was in intensive care. His young parents were frantic, sleepless and helpless, and at the peak of his illness—when the British doctor warned them to brace for the worst—the chaplain at the Royal Alexandra Hospital asked to meet with them in a lamp-lit room one floor below Benedict's hospital bed. His mother at first refused, because she thought it meant he was dying. Why else would a priest, or whatever you call them, want to chat in the semidarkness? The hospital was tricking them into signing away his organs. Benedict's father had found the idea of meeting with the hospital chaplain silly, embarrassing even. If his mother had been agnostic, his father had been a genuine atheist, hostile toward believers who tended, over history, to get in the way of human advancement in support of fiction and fear.

The chaplain, whose name was Roddy, had them sit in matching brown easy chairs that had lost their padding in the 1960s, and for nearly an hour he listened to them, their anger and desperation. And then he asked, gently and charmingly, if either of them had thought to pray.

Neither of them had thought to pray. To whom? To the army of prokaryotic microorganisms feasting on their son's brain and spinal cord? They desperately needed to sleep. Chaplain Roddy was such a warm and winning man, white-haired and tiny, maybe five-foot-two, so small his feet did not touch the floor when he sat in his easy chair. Neither of them had the energy to walk out or even say no when he suggested they hold hands and close their eyes and ask something of God.

Both of his parents had been to dinners at the homes of believers, where someone would say grace. They would daydream while God, who clearly had nothing to do with the turkey and the stuffing and the cheap sparkling wine, was thanked for providing it. But that night in the Royal Alexandra Hospital was not like grace at Aunt Ida's place. His parents *did* have something to ask, and nothing in the world was more important. Roddy did not lead them in any operatic manner. He whispered for them to close their eyes and break through frustration and fury to simply and purely love little Benedict with every cell in their bodies. Love him and imagine him doing what he most enjoyed, what made him *him*, when he absolutely shimmered: playing hockey or running or vrooming Hot Wheels cars around the track. Both his parents had nearly laughed, holding Chaplain Roddy's tiny warm hands, at the idea of Benedict with Hot Wheels. His current favourite thing was building a giant Rube Goldberg machine in his bedroom with household items and a bunch of Erector sets.

Benedict never really believed what came next, and he noticed that when they told their story as missionaries, his parents added details with each telling. They made it more dramatic.

"Our little boy, all that mattered in the world, was on the verge of death."

"Just upstairs."

"We knew why Chaplain Roddy was there, or thought we knew."

"His body. Our little boy!"

"We didn't think he'd make it through the night."

"No one did. Not a doctor in the hospital, and certainly not Chaplain Roddy. Wonderful little man."

"If by some miracle he did pull through, he was meant to have brain damage or paralysis."

As they prayed before tiny Chaplain Roddy, without speaking a word aloud, Benedict's parents individually heard and felt the beneficence and power of God. The light from that dim lamp exploded orange inside the room and filled them with what they did not have: faith. Their son was special, a magic boy. If they believed in Christ the Redeemer, His Wishes and Theirs would become one and all the glory and power of the universe would move into their son and the infection in him would be overwhelmed.

How had both of them, separately and silently, received this message? When Benedict asked this, his parents always looked at one another with dreamy smiles. "Benny, miracles are miraculous."

And so it was that at 11:19 p.m. little Benedict woke out of his fever with a headache and asked for a glass of water.

Once Benedict was old enough to understand this rebirth story, he thought only about the glory and power of antibiotics. In time, he argued with his parents. Their conversion had nothing to do with Chaplain Roddy and prayer. It was Sir Alexander Fleming.

In his teens Benedict went in one direction and they went in another, leading to the Assembly of God on the south side of the city. They took sabbaticals from their jobs, the summer he graduated from high school, and joined a mission in rural Angola. Three months into their mission they died of dysentery—probably shigella. Two men in sweaters from the Assembly of God came by to tell him on a Saturday in late October, a week before his eighteenth birthday. When he asked them to go away without leading a prayer session, they asked—at the door—if they had been remembered in his parents' will. Benedict did not know the answer. Seized now with grief and with terror, he went to the filing cabinet where they kept their papers and learned they had left everything but fifty thousand dollars—for his education—to the church. Even their insurance policy had been directed to the Assembly of God.

While he never agreed with his parents' turn toward spirituality, he respected them, even their decision to give his inheritance to
the Assembly of God. Their faith was absolute. Every crepuscule
in their bodies believed in the gospels, and they were absolutely
certain Jesus Christ himself had chosen to save their boy's life
when he was dying of meningitis.

After his parents' transformation, a television had remained in
his childhood home but they strictly controlled his viewing. At
school he could not participate in conversations about *The Cosby
Show* or *Cheers* or *ALF*, and Super Bowl Sunday and the Stanley
Cup Finals were irrelevant distractions from God's teachings. They
did have a VCR so they could watch *The Greatest Story Ever Told*
and *A Man for All Seasons* and *Tender Mercies*. There was a Christian
fundraising show on most mornings and on Sunday afternoons after
visiting the Assembly of God and going for hamburgers and onion
rings at Red Robin, they would watch American preachers in their
big, beautiful megachurches.

There were few shows he was allowed to watch that other kids
watched, so *How the Grinch Stole Christmas!*, about a conversion
miracle, and anti-commercialism *Peanuts* specials were like foun-
dational documents. *A Charlie Brown Christmas* was his mother's
favourite, as it contained actual scripture in the form of an on-stage
speech by Linus: "For behold, I bring you tidings of great joy,
which shall be to all people."

Benedict owned the soundtrack, on cassette. He had seen the
special so many times as a child, he could recite the lines. While it
had been on in the background, as Karen loved it and played it
for the girls, Benedict had not watched *A Charlie Brown Christmas*
since he was eighteen—the year his parents died in Angola. The
way he remembered it, there were ghosts in the show. It held the
secret of his condition, woeful nostalgia for a time when someone
else was in charge. Someone would save him. In the warehouse he

watched it all the way through, and when he got to the end the
gloomy children and the dog sang a carol, but there was no ghost.
The ghost was something else.

Through the legislature grounds lit up for Christmas, across the
great black bridge, the ghost followed him at its usual distance.
Poppy was still up, baking cookies with a Kutisi-branded apron.
She looked directly at him when he entered the kitchen and even
though her hands were white with flour, his daughter hugged him.
"Daddy. You look sad."

"I'm not."

"You should be happy. Everyone's talking about you. We talked
about Kutisi in *science class*. My teacher knows who you are."

"Oh?"

"And kids are like, 'That guy's your dad?' There's something
about their faces too, when they say it, something different from
ever before. They're like . . . I don't know. Anyway. I'm a Ross.
I'm . . . "

Benedict had to look away from her, as her eyes were welling up.

"I was so proud." Poppy moved in front of him, so he couldn't
look away. "You work so hard, and you never boast about it or
complain or anything. I am so lucky to be your daughter."

Benedict did not know what to do or say. "Well . . . "

"My daddy!" She hugged him and kissed him on the cheek and
turned back to the oven.

Kate and Anna McGarrigle sang "Seven Joys of Mary," a more
obscure and therefore strange Christmas song. With "Silent Night"
and all the other ones he heard all the time, Benedict tended to forget how they were all about the virgin birth of a Jewish person two
thousand years ago. "Seven Joys of Mary" sounded like it was sung
in a church. Their kitchen was a church. His parents would have

known and loved this one, as they turned away from the actual fun and popular bits of Christmas to remind themselves and everyone else that the story of Christ is the story of torture and sacrifice—not dolled-up pagan rituals. Karen sat on the couch with her phone, scrolling through something. Instagram, he assumed. She sipped from her glass of wine. The day after the deal with Sinotechnika was in the news and therefore real, Karen ordered a box of her favourite white Burgundy, a Puligny-Montrachet by Domaine Leflaive. Each bottle, as Benedict understood it, was a little over $150.

As he passed through the living room, Karen did not look up. She had seemed so much happier in the past week, with her wine. Clients had begun calling her again, and she was often busy at her two computer screens. Benedict put his boots back on and the thousand-dollar parka Karen had just bought him.

He carried his heavy silver flashlight into the backyard. The snow had almost completely melted and there was a freshness in the air that only a Canadian in December would find pleasant: wet leaves, thawing dog shit, stagnant pools. Around the back of the house Benedict shone his light on the newly revealed grass next to the garage. In the periphery of the flashlight's beam there were two little eyes, the grey cat, who approached him with a mew. He bent down and petted it. The cat softly purred, spun around, and arched its back to get maximum pleasure from the attention. Its little bell, on its clean pink collar, tinkled pleasingly. With his other hand, Benedict shone his light on the ground where it had happened and the trail from there back to the little garage door, the trail of blood.

"Well?" Karen was lit from behind, by the chandelier in the kitchen. She carried her glass of white Burgundy. "Find anything?"

"I thought since the snow is melting . . . "

"What happens to evidence?" She wore a lopsided hat and his black wool overcoat. On her feet, his tennis shoes. "DNA would still be there if they knew where to look." Karen took a sip of her wine.

"Obviously they don't. It's been more than a month now. On those *csi* shows they say . . . "

They had discussed it so often, in the two sleepless weeks after Halloween, there was nothing new to say. Karen had made all possible points about what she had learned on television and then she had made it almost all the way through an ebook from a college course called *Techniques for Crime Scene Investigations*.

"Where did the cat come from?"

Benedict put his face close to it, to see if it might give him a kiss like Daphne. He missed dog kisses. Its whiskers rubbed against his cheek but the cat did not lick him. "I don't know. One morning, the night of the break-in, the night I was sick, the cat was just here."

"Look on its collar. Does it have a name?"

He shone his light on the cat and it squinted. On the silver tag in the shape of a heart it said Steve. "Steve."

"Steve?" said Karen.

"Steve."

Together they walked around to the front of the house. Karen touched his arm. "It was her, her and her friends, who broke into the garage. They have their revenge, their drug money. It's over." Nothing felt over, and Karen did not sound convinced. "I can hardly believe it, Ben. Your very last meeting with an investor and *boom*. I was preparing myself for total humiliation."

Benedict was CEO of a company that was officially worth $200 million, based on Sinotechnika's valuation, but had already grown significantly since last Thursday.

"Shit, it's so nice out. I'll be a bit crestfallen when you and Marie-Claude stop climate change. Anyway, you should give yourself a moment to celebrate. Your whole adult life . . . "

He scanned the neighbourhood from the front terrace of their old house as Karen outlined his achievements. A woman walked her dog through the pale yellow of the decorative streetlights and waved as she passed. It took effort for Benedict to raise his hand. There was no one and nothing else on the avenue. Their Christmas tree was not the only one lit in the neighbourhood anymore. Nearly every house had a tree in the front window and more holiday delight: blow-up Santas and Grinches, menorahs, dirty blobs that were once snowmen.

With her hand on the doorhandle Karen looked at him, waiting for a response.

"Sorry," he said. "What?"

She sighed and opened the door to warmth and gingerbread, no barking. The Christmas tree twinkled. A Diana Ross cover of "Wonderful Christmastime" was playing in the kitchen, where Poppy sang along and danced on her tiptoes.

"I said you won't believe who asked me for coffee today."

Benedict had trouble with this sort of thing. "I won't?"

"Nope. Melissa."

He had nearly forgotten about Melissa, even though she had sent an earthquake of agony and confusion through Karen and Poppy. "Did you go?"

"Yeah. But she didn't even say sorry. It was so weird. It's like we're supposed to be best friends again. She wants to get Blaine and Poppy together too."

It made him tired and sick to think of it. "Why?"

Karen pointed to him. "You, I guess. You showed up in the news as the saviour of the climate crisis . . . "

His stomach clenched. "Some say I'm a fraud and a charlatan."

"I haven't read anything like that. *All* Melissa thinks about is status. When it seemed we were nobodies, that Kutisi was dying—sorry—Blaine wasn't allowed to hang with Poppy anymore. But now . . . "

Once Karen was finished talking about Melissa, and whether or not they should *get back together*, just because Poppy and Blaine were so well matched as friends, and it's all about the peer group, she pressed her finger to her lips to shut up about it and led him into the kitchen.

"It smells great in here, Popsy."

The modified HomePod interrupted Diana Ross with a gentle alarm. Poppy applauded and put on oven mitts, pulled out the cookies. The heat from the oven was too much, as Benedict was already sweating. Karen and Poppy discussed the cookies, and bedtime, and brushing teeth, and then Poppy kissed them both on the cheeks and went upstairs.

When they were alone again, Karen moved the hot cookies around on the baking sheet to be sure they weren't sticking. She poured a bit more wine into her glass and offered some to Benedict, who declined. She smelled it and swirled it, moaned with pleasure, then sipped. "I was thinking: should we move? Get a bigger house a couple of blocks west on Saskatchewan Drive? There's a few for sale, all under three million, with amazing views. You could sell some shares, right? Did you spend all the money Kutisi gave us?"

"But—"

"We could keep this one and rent it out to professors or something."

He moved into the living room and Karen followed him, continued to argue for a new house. "It's a long time to live without a wine cellar. I never know where to put it in this drafty old barn."

They went up to tuck the girls in. This was a simple process with Charlotte, who preferred not to be hugged or kissed, though she had grown comfortable saying, "I love you," when the lights were out. She was in wrenching pain again, eight out of ten, she said. It came in waves. She winced as Benedict backed out of the room, after hiding it from them. The ghost hovered on the stairs. Benedict was no brain scientist but it seemed wrong, psychologically wrong. If the ghost was a manifestation of his childhood confusion and floating guilt from Halloween night, if he had figured it out, why was it still here? What was the point?

Poppy asked him to make sure the doors were locked. When Benedict hugged her, she said she had been having nightmares.

"What are they about?" Karen stood behind him, with her fragrant glass of wine.

"I don't know. It's stupid."

"Stop eating before bed, sweetie."

The smell of the cookies hit him at the top of the stairs and the ghost disappeared. They were still too hot to eat. He pulled some cheese out of the fridge, cut it up, and paired it with a few of those Raincoast crackers with dates and nuts that cost seven dollars a box. For months the Raincoast crackers and organic hazelnut butter and exotic fresh fruit imported from the southern hemisphere, boutique olive oils and vinegars, farmers' market sausages and gouda, local sourdough for eight and a half dollars a loaf, health food supplements to treat ailments that seemed invented, and avocados—so many avocados—had kept him from calm. Every month they went deeper and deeper into debt, and the prospect of rescue had seemed as distant as a tropical vacation.

In the end, Benedict could not help himself. He ate a cookie too early and it burned his mouth. From behind, Karen hugged him as he drank cold water to soothe his tongue. Her breath was sour from the wine. "They're sweetened with maple syrup instead of refined sugar."

The bottle of organic maple syrup was on the counter. The sticker on it said $43.86. "Whew," said Benedict.

There was a little television in the bathroom. While they brushed their teeth they watched a *Saturday Night Live* holiday special. Tonto, Tarzan, and Frankenstein's monster sang "Deck the Halls."

"That's racist, I think." Karen spoke with her toothbrush in her mouth. "I can't tell anymore. Is Jon Lovitz allowed to play Tonto? I know it's from the eighties, but even *broadcasting* it now."

Benedict spat into the sink.

In the 1930s, Karen's paternal grandfather was part of the messy national socialism movement in Sweden. They were a wealthy family with aristocratic roots and it was acceptable in her grandfather's peer group to support Hitler. Just before the Second World War began, they swapped out the swastika for a patriotic bushel of wheat, and Sweden remained officially neutral, but he and his friends in banking agreed to quietly launder gold for the Nazis—gold that had surely come from Norwegian Jews who had been transported to gas chambers. The war itself was a time of great comfort for the Sjöblad family. It wasn't until 1943, the year after her father's birth, that Swedish sentiment began to change. The country finally agreed to accept Jewish asylum-seekers. It became uncomfortable for her grandparents, as people who had been perfectly agreeable for ten years slowly and then quickly shunned them. The Sjöblads were no longer invited to the finest parties, and at the symphony on weekends former friends avoided eye contact. They moved to Canada, first to Toronto and then, in 1950, they followed the oil to Alberta where no one ever asked what they had done during the war. Johnny Sjöblad learned to call the leaders of Swedish society, who had turned on his parents, hypocrites. The same people who ignored them at the theatre had spent multiple evenings in their rooms in Östermalm, drinking aquavit. Karen did not consider her grandparents Nazis and took their side as her father had done. Revisionist history! They had been strict and sullen people who lived in a big house in Bragg Creek that smelled of roasted meat. There was a gorgeous view of the Rocky Mountains from the living room but they almost never went outside. It was like they were afraid of something out there, that some monster from the past could one night roar out of the mountains and forests and murder them in their sleep.

All the mythology in Benedict's own family was about Jesus. He was an ethnically rootless person, a white Canadian mongrel. When he spit in the AncestryDNA tube, a Christmas gift a couple of years earlier, it came back as he expected. The only hint of the exotic came from a hunk of Jewishness on his father's side, which jibed not at all with his own thoughts about bacon. When he discovered that 17 per cent, he did not tell Karen about it.

In bed, Karen looked at real estate sites on her phone and talked about the houses she particularly liked on Saskatchewan Drive. One was just under four million but in any other city it would be ten. Thanks, oil crash. The houses along Saskatchewan Drive had massive lots and views of the conifers and the river at the base of the valley, the orange and pink sunsets of winter. She had always wanted a topiary garden. If Kutisi became a multi-billion dollar company, like everyone was saying, they would be multibillionaires. Maybe she could open an art gallery here or in Palm Springs, where Marie-Claude lived, because when there wasn't a pandemic on there were two or three direct flights a day. They could buy a house in California, for when winter really came at them. It might be lovelier to have a place in Puerto Vallarta but it's a lot farther and every now and then a gangster gets his head chopped off in a municipal plaza.

"As parents, maybe we should try to protect the girls from that sort of thing," she said.

Benedict flipped through an issue of *The Economist*. The officials from the European Union, who wanted to engage Kutisi to power an experimental community in Poland, would arrive January fourth. They would demand a tour of the factory. They would want to see a Kutisi box humming and glowing as advertised. The online version of *The Economist* had published an opinion piece from a German physicist who was sure she would be proven right about Kutisi: it did not work and could not work. Benedict tried to do what Marie-Claude had taught him to do, to dismiss the jealous protectors of the status quo, to see and smell his perfect future. Only Marie-Claude did not know what he knew.

The only light in the bedroom now was from Karen's phone. With it he could see a part of the ghost in the hallway. Benedict was the only one who could see his ghost and it did not exist, so he did not indulge the part of himself that wanted to protect his family. He closed his eyes and thought of pumpkin pie with allspice and ginger, and when he opened them the thing was gone.

"Karen?"

"Yeah?"

"Show me your favourite house on the Drive."

NINE

Poppy and Blaine, Blaine and Poppy, PB, BP. For years other girls who couldn't break into the perfect box that was their best-friend-forever-hood had made jokes about them that weren't really jokes. But it was true. No one could enter, not really.

Poppy had a few neighbourhood pals and so did Blaine. They had different hobbies. Poppy liked drama and singing and Blaine was into speed skating and rhythmic gymnastics, two sports her parents chose according to an article they found online that showed the easiest paths to the winter and summer Olympics. But when Poppy and Blaine arrived at school in the morning, ate lunch, chose school options, partnered up for assignments, and planned for the weekend, it was always about each other. Every week they tried to persuade their moms to organize dinners together and trips to the mountains because their moms were best friends too.

The dark days began with questions about Kutisi. Blaine wanted to know if it was going well because her dad had heard it wasn't going well. He was in the business of knowing these sorts of things

for the government. At first it seemed Blaine was worried for
Poppy and her family, but then it seemed like something else. And
stuff got really weird. There was a pastry shop on the walk home,
and whenever Blaine came over after school they stopped for *pain
au chocolat* or these amazing Portuguese custard things. When it
was cold outside, the windows of the place steamed up and you
could smell it from almost a block away. One day in September,
when Poppy suggested they stop, Blaine poked her in the side and
said something no friend should say: "Maybe you should watch it
with the pastries. You're chubbin' it up."

Chubbin'!

Every week, it seemed, there was another lecture or lesson at
school about the dangers of bullying. This wasn't bullying, exactly.
Your best friend can't *bully* you. But it wasn't nice. Poppy thought
about it a lot, chubbin' it up, especially when she was alone in bed.
What could she do? She began to eat less. It was hard to sleep for
a while, especially since Blaine had started to spend more and more
time with this other girl, Aoife, from her speed-skating team. Aoife
was one of the tallest girls in eighth grade, with blonde hair and
purple braces and—Poppy had to admit it—the sort of laugh that
made you want to laugh, even if you didn't know what was funny.

Blaine never said anything cruel, apart from that one day on the
walk home. But then, without any warning or a talk, Blaine forgot
she existed. Was it about Kutisi? Was it about her weight? She and
her mom whispered about it sometimes, about how lucky they were
to be "the normal ones," but Charlotte and her dad didn't seem to
care what people thought about them or said about them. What
was good about normal feelings anyway? All of the anxiety in the
Ross-Sjöblad house about the weirdness of her dad and Charlotte
rested in the hearts of Poppy and her mom. There were other kids,
other friends, but no one like Blaine. Blaine *got* her. In the early
days of the eighth grade, Poppy began to feel she had to carry all of

it alone: the weirdness, whatever was going on with her dad's company, her mom's sadness. And this new thing, the way Poppy looked in front of a mirror.

If her mom knew she was skipping breakfast, she would freak out and take her to a clinic, so Poppy had to be devious. The morning radio was always on, the CBC show, and her mom talked to it—outraged about whatever. Poppy would eat a few spoonfuls. Then, when her mom was focused on making lunches, she would sneak into the kitchen behind her and dump the majority of her cereal and milk into the compost. It helped if her mom was really furious about the news, as it drew her focus away. Lunch was easy. Poppy would eat a couple of sliced carrots and pepper, and throw away the soup or pasta—as badly as she wanted it. She absolutely hated herself for doing it, because she loved her mom so much and there was a bit of her mom in the lentil soup, in the pasta primavera, in the organic macaroni and cheese.

But she wanted Blaine back and she couldn't just *ask*.

When it got really bad, she was honest with her mom about what Blaine had said and how it felt, and then her mom said something to Melissa—Blaine's mom. Then everything at school went to shit. Melissa told Blaine and then Blaine told Aoife that Poppy had been *crying* about the end of their friendship, crying about her dad's garbage company and being fat. All Aoife had to do was tell a couple of kids and then, ten minutes later, everyone in school knew. No one bullied Poppy, not in any outward way like in the books and movies, but they looked at her differently. They laughed at her. A couple of the boys passed her in the hall mock-crying.

Was that bullying? Maybe it was.

Poppy decided this was why everything changed at the end of November. First the howling in the hallway on the night some asshole broke into the garage and stole her bike. There was already snow on the ground so it didn't matter too much apart from *what it meant*: that anyone could steal anything from them and there wasn't a single effing thing the police could do about it. Also, deep in her heart, Poppy only pretended to love her bike, and bike-riding, and pedestrian infrastructure, and climate action, because she knew it pleased her mom. She would much prefer a car ride to school every morning.

Ever since things ended with Blaine, Poppy had trouble falling asleep. She couldn't get her mind off it. Then she cut her caloric intake by half or more. She was scared of the howling and the break-in and what Charlotte had said about a ghost. That day, when she got home from school, she and her mom did one of their favourite things together. They put up the Christmas tree and watched *The Grinch*. Her dad came home and announced they were rich.

It didn't help. That night, she lay awake worried about everything. What if the woman howled again? Poppy looked at her phone, even though it wasn't allowed in her room. It was 2:14 and she hadn't slept. The house was quiet but somehow Poppy knew it wouldn't be for long. Something was coming. A cough, and another one, a woman's serious cough. Poppy called out for her mom and for Charlotte, but neither of them answered. She got up and tiptoed into the hall. She peeked into her parents' room and both of them were in there, calm and quiet, her dad lightly snoring. Then Charlotte's room, where it smelled a bit like hard-boiled egg farts because her sister had been experimenting with something gross that evening, as usual. Or it was just farts. Charlotte's tummy was really bad, worse than ever; she seemed to be getting skinnier every day, and Poppy was so aware of her sister's pain she wasn't as jealous about her legs. Charlotte was sleeping too. It had definitely been a woman's cough, and everyone was asleep, and then she opened the door into her dad's office.

It wasn't her dad's office anymore. It was a small bedroom,

strewn with clothes and soiled tissues and bags, food containers, pizza boxes. There was a woman on a bed, an enormous woman, sitting on the edge and staring into a tissue. The covers had fallen on the messy floor beside her. It smelled like hot, sweet, cranberry jam that had gone off in the heat, but there was no heat. The room was as cold as outside, though the windows were shut. Light from the street shone on the woman, who was naked and slumped. Her head drooped forward and her blonde hair covered the side of her face. She coughed. Poppy had never seen a woman this big or hair this greasy. The word *obese* wasn't obese enough. Her first thought was how amazing it was that the human body could do this to itself. Only this wasn't amazing. It was easy. She understood exactly how this could happen and a part of her longed for it. Was this a nightmare? This was not even a room in her house and this coughing stranger was not in her family.

Poppy wanted to go back to bed but every time she turned away the room reconstituted itself in front of her. She would turn away, only to arrive at the same place. There was no escape. It made her dizzy, all this spinning and the sweet acidic smell of the woman's body. Poppy felt both sorry for the woman and so ashamed.

In the corner of the bedroom, on a bedside table, there was a small Christmas tree. It looked like some of their bird decorations were on it. Their Ross-Sjöblad family star was on top. Different lights though.

The woman turned to Poppy and threw her tissue on the floor and shouted something, though she had been in the middle of the cough and it was unintelligible. She shouted it again. "Who the fuck are you?"

Poppy was too afraid to speak.

"You're not the nurse. I called the nurse. Aliya. Where the fuck is Aliya? Who are you?"

"I'm—"

"If you're the nurse, get in here. This hurts. Right here it hurts. Bring the cream."

Poppy wanted to tell the woman she was in the wrong house. She was not the nurse, she did not know Aliya, and she could not help. Every time Poppy tried to get away she was here again. What cream? "I'm not . . ."

"You're not what? Get the fuck over here."

Poppy did not want to move, to walk toward the woman, but she did. The food containers, made from something she did not recognize, squished and broke under her feet, and beneath the clothes there were other clothes, other things. Under all of it there must be a proper floor, probably covered in carpet, but in the dim light she could not see if there were any points of separation between the piles of clothes and the garbage. The tree lights were on: soft red ones that seemed to float without wires. It was the colour she would choose, if she had to choose. From this side of the bed, she could not tell if the tree was real or fake but it was beautiful, the only beautiful thing in the woman's room.

It was Poppy's job, she understood, to lift one of the layers of fat and rub where it had gone raw, where the water did not reach. Poppy saw all of it, the woman's whole world. She rarely left this room. The woman sat on a white stool when she showered and she didn't need help for that, not yet, but soon she would. Something had happened to Aliya. Perhaps she had given up. The woman had pushed everyone else, the people who loved her, out of her life the way Poppy sometimes felt like slamming a door. After a while if you slam all the doors and say all the mean things you can think to say, and you tell them never to come back, *even if you don't mean it*, they don't come back. And you're alone here until you die, with only one meaningful thing in your whole life, a little Christmas tree with the family star.

The smell was worse, close up. Poppy wanted the woman to

know that if she did not get up and move around and change her life, she would die soon. Her heart did not grow with the rest of her. It was not prepared for this. The woman was saying ugly things to her again but still the woman did not turn and look. It was dim in the room, with only the poor light from the street. Poppy could see the trees were different outside, a relief, and there was no snow.

"The cream, goddamn it! The cream!"

It was in a long tube on the dresser, next to some electronic equipment Poppy did not understand. The small things glowed with life, though they were not plugged in. What were they? One of them was something like a tablet, though there was no screen. She tapped it, reaching for the cream, and it flickered to life. There was a picture of the woman, younger and not as big as this, and of her own mom and dad. A bit older than they were now and far sadder, especially her dad. His eyes. He could not fake a smile the way she and her mom could. Charlotte was not in the picture. Where was Charlotte? Picture wasn't the right word for this thing. It was a mini version of them, made by light. A hologram? Charlotte? Poppy turned the screen away, the figures disappeared, and she prepared to touch the woman, to lift a flap of her skin because it was her duty. The woman's hair really needed a wash. It needed to be brushed. Finally, the woman stopped issuing orders for a moment and looked up, and she recognized Poppy. Poppy recognized her, or nearly did, and stepped back and dropped the cream, and the woman did not shout at her.

This was not right now. This was not her house, not her bedroom or her father's office. All of that was gone: the rooms, somehow her sister. Her beautiful sister would not come back if she told her to go away forever. Her sister would listen. Her sister would die. She has gotten rid of all of them and all Poppy has left is this.

The woman exhaled. "You."

———

When Poppy opened her eyes, ready to scream, it was not as cold and she was standing in her pyjamas in her father's office. To be sure it was a dream, she peeked in her sister's room again. Charlotte lay on her side, softly breathing, smelling like the sulphuric hot springs in the mountains. She tiptoed into her sister's bedroom.

Her sleepwalking dream of the obese woman in her father's office that was not his office had shaken something. Charlotte would only ever help and support her, if Poppy asked. She wished she had waited bravely there, right next to Farts McCann and the other idiot, for Charlotte to approach. She wished she had walked off with her sister with pride in her heart, love and pride for her brilliant and gorgeous but different sister, her sick sister. She might have called Farts McCann a piece of shit, or worse. Instead she had sneaked off like a coward and she had wanted to duck in the back of the car and she had chosen not to walk with her sister too close to her own school. And now, in Charlotte's bedroom, she vowed never to do it again, though she suspected in her weakness she would do it again.

Poppy had never read the Bible though there was a little red one on her bedside table, a gift from passing missionaries. She did not know how to pray, or to whom to pray. God? Jesus? Mary? If Mary, why Mary? Poppy felt like a moron but she tiptoed next to Charlotte's bed and lowered herself to her knees—how had her knees gotten so thick?—and clasped her hands and asked for forgiveness. From Charlotte, from her mom and dad, from God.

Then she lay in her own bed staring up at the white nothingness of her stippled ceiling and thought about her Christmas list. Whenever the image of that woman in her father's office entered her head, Poppy whispered to the darkness about educating the girls of East Africa.

TEN

Daphne the vizsla would have been an inferior guard dog in action, wagging her tail and licking any intruder's hand. Even so, her bark was loud and fierce. Every knock and doorbell, every outdoor footstep, every thump on the porch or deck, every tiptoe down the hall to pee in the night would launch her into action. The dog's instinct to alert the family was always stronger than Benedict's commands to shush her.

She would have barked on Halloween. Daphne would have barked tonight, when the sounds from his dream bled into the moment he opened his eyes. The power had gone out, so Benedict could not see his alarm clock. He wore a watch, a present from last Christmas, that monitored his vital signs, received texts, and captured his data for Apple. His watch said it was 3:58. The house was silent for a moment as he sat up. He prepared to lie down, relieved, when he heard it again: a faint animal shriek.

There was nothing in the bedroom to use as a weapon apart from a heavy chunk of Vancouver Island jade. He opened Poppy's door, then Charlotte's door, and both of them were sleeping. On the main floor, the front and back doors remained locked and the only breach-able windows were closed.

The power was on across the street, as his neighbours' Christmas lights shone. He would look at the breakers.

In the dark kitchen he hoped to hear nothing and go back to bed. Then he heard it but instead of a cry of distress it was a groan of pleasure, the sound of a hungry thing finally discovering food. Benedict wanted to call the police, to beg them to go down with their guns, but he knew they could not stop it.

He traded the jade for a butcher knife and held the silver flashlight in his left hand. "Is anyone there?"

Halfway down the stairs Benedict could see nothing when he shone the light. The basement living room was set up like a home theatre, with four reclining black leather chairs and cup holders the perfect distance from the fifty-five-inch flat screen television and speakers set into the ceiling and walls in just the right places. Charlotte had designed it after an extensive research process. They almost never watched a movie together because it was nearly impossible to find something all four of them could agree to watch. If it was not a documentary or at least a biographical feature about astronauts or physicists, Charlotte would happily retire to her bedroom laboratory. Karen would insist they compromise and find a movie everyone wanted to watch, and twenty or forty minutes later some or even all of them would give up, exhausted, and Karen and Poppy would watch *Pride and Prejudice* again.

Benedict walked down the remaining stairs. From somewhere, at four in the morning, inside or just outside the house, a child sang "The Little Drummer Boy." Or was it? He put the knife and flashlight between his legs and closed his eyes, covered his ears. The song was still there and the other sound, of a starving animal eating a wet dinner, was gone. He silently pleaded with himself for sanity. When he opened his eyes and scanned the room, he saw it before he could reach it with the full beam of his flashlight: the ghost hovered over something, seemed to present it to him.

"No," he said, or thought. His legs shook and no longer held him. Benedict crashed on his left knee and dropped the flashlight. By the time he retrieved it, his ghost was gone. He raised the knife and tried to scream at it to get out of the house and leave them alone, but again he could make no sound. He spun on his knees, because the phantom seemed to be everywhere at once. Then he crawled forward, to see what it had presented to him, and shone his flashlight on the sweet grey cat from the backyard, its stomach open. Steve.

Benedict ran up both flights of stairs with the butcher knife, to protect his girls and his wife, but the ghost was not up here: not in the bedrooms and not in his office. In the kitchen pantry he found gloves and a garbage bag and paper towel and the cleaning women's tray of disinfectants. As though he had ravaged the cat himself, Benedict resolved to hide and disinfect all evidence of the horror before morning. As he was halfway down the stairs, the power came back on and the electrical system popped and whirred. He turned on the lights with his elbow, though he did not want to see the dead cat under full LED.

And it was gone. All of it. There was no Steve, no trace of him, and no ghost. The furnace turned on with a low whomp and the scent of scorched dust filled the basement. Benedict looked around one last time, abandoned his cleaning products and supplies, and climbed up the stairs. He poured a glass of milk, looked out on the backyard where all of this began, and surveyed his land for Steve—the actual cat. He did not feel remotely sleepy so he sat in front of his laptop at the dining room table, with a piece of lemon cake, and googled reasons he might be seeing a ghost. It cheered him to learn he was not the first to seek out this information; there were enough people like him to warrant scientific responses to the question.

Reason one was a high fever, which explained the sighting on November thirtieth, but he did not currently have a temperature. While he had been sleeping poorly since Kutisi began its downward trend, and particularly since Halloween, Benedict could not honestly say he was delirious with insomnia—despite the fact that he was eating cake in the middle of the night. There might have been a rush of geomagnetic activity in the land around his house, but why would it suddenly affect him now? Stress was a possibility, as it could trigger a rush of hormones. Some psychologists wrote about a "sensed presence" that leads us to safety in times of intense perceived danger. The basement was not a dark alley or a war zone, but he was—at least intellectually—on the edge of despair.

A tumour. He might have a tumour in his brain. If he was honest with himself, Benedict did not feel like he had a tumour, and when he read more about the symptoms, few of them seemed right. He went online and booked an appointment with Medcan.

None of the articles from *Psychology Today* or Baylor College or NBC News had put forth the hypothesis his parents would be most comfortable with: the ghost was a messenger from God. Or—why not?—the devil. It did seem unlikely that his parents' God would reveal himself as a ghost, devouring a cat in his basement and offering to share.

His parents had always prayed with their hands together. When she did yoga at home, Karen closed her eyes and put her hands together at the end of her session, muttering to herself. Alone, at the kitchen table, he closed the laptop and pushed away the small plate of cake and put his hands together.

There was, as there had always been, a veil, a thick colourless curtain his mind could approach but not touch. It was there at the Assembly of God, back when his parents had made him go. Benedict had whispered to his mother and she had whispered back, out the side of her mouth, as they kneeled in the hard pews together.

I can't make it work, Mom.

Just accept Jesus Christ into your heart.

How?

Speak to him and he will come.

I did, last week and this week. He doesn't come. Mom: no one ever comes. My heart doesn't do that.

Close your eyes and feel him.

My eyes are closed.

Feel him.

I don't know what that means.

Just believe, Benny.

I can't.

You're not trying hard enough.

Benedict had tried so hard. He wanted to *just believe* more than anything when he was twelve years old. His parents and their friends and their children, who were supposed to be his friends, all of them believed. They closed their eyes and said the words before dinner; they cried and hooted in church when the spirit entered them. They loved Jesus in their hearts, which Benedict had taken literally. A man in a robe in a heart.

He went upstairs and into his daughters' rooms, to watch them sleep. "The Little Drummer Boy" was still softly playing somewhere and everywhere. If it was a tumour, and so advanced that it was inspiring hallucinations he could hear and see and smell, even taste at the back of his throat, Benedict did not have much time left with Poppy and Charlotte and Karen. He brushed the cake from his teeth and washed the smell of dead cat from his face and hands and went back to bed. The ghost was there when he closed his eyes.

ELEVEN

Just after seven, Charlotte walked gingerly down the stairs with a brown paper bag discoloured by evaporated water. Karen had stuffed the bag of fur-lined Birkenstocks at the back of the hall closet, under the spare iron. Until this moment, she had forgotten about Jak's abandoned sandals. Before Charlotte could ask the obvious question—*Whose are these?*—Karen had the answer.

"Oh, thank you, darling. I had forgotten about those."

Charlotte tilted her head. The orbits of her eyes were even darker this morning, dark like her hoodie, like something had been drained from her in the night. Karen shivered. She knew what had drained her daughter, though she did not understand. There was nothing she could do to stop it.

"Would you like to stay home today? I could take you to the doctor."

"No." Charlotte looked at the bag of sandals, contaminated by Jak's warts.

"I found those next to the garage." Karen took them from Charlotte. "You know, where homeless people sometimes leave things?" A tent, a bag of blankets, broken things ripped out of recycling bags that turned out to be . . . broken things. "I'll take them to Goodwill."

"They don't smell good. They're garbage."

"You think so? I suppose I could throw them out."

Charlotte seemed to have a question about them anyway—about why they were stuffed in the closet—but before she could speak, Poppy shouted from the foyer: "Let's *go*!"

The fifteenth of December dawned sunny but not warm just before nine. Hoarfrost gripped the boughs of the trees, impossibly white against the deep and serious blue of the sky. This was the kind of pretty blue sky that would kill you if you walked into the forest without a decent jacket. December was the only month of the year Karen did not resent winter because it helped her feel closer to the feelings of her childhood: "O Holy Night" and screw-in bulbs, the Grinch, Mickey Mouse playing Bob Cratchit, presents, the smell of Scotch tape while wrapping presents, mandarin oranges, turkey, snowmen, mulled wine and eggnog, the grand piano in the living room, even her parents' revolting Swedish traditions like head cheese and pork hocks.

Living without a care: blonde, pretty, tall, clever, rich.

The forecast leading up to Christmas Eve was unpleasant, another bout of snow, a proper blizzard, and a deeper cold. For years it had confounded and embarrassed her that the people of her blood had come all the way to America and had then lacked the imagination to live in a more pleasant climate or a more cosmopolitan city. They wanted to hide, to be sure no one recognized them from the war, so why not Texas or Arizona? Growing up in Calgary, fleeing to Vancouver, and returning here felt like a downgrade. She knew what her school chums on the West Coast and

Toronto thought of her, living in a place that was only ever in the national media because of oil, hockey, or knife-play.

It was a forgotten city and until ten days ago she was a forgotten woman.

Her Facebook account was full of messages now, from all those school chums and other people she hadn't heard from in years. Tech stories out of Canada were so rare they received more attention than they deserved, and it was only magnified in the prairies. People she had not spoken to in years were asking her for Zoom chats, inviting her to remote Christmas parties, seeking her attendance at online charity events. In the past week, Karen had been asked to join three book clubs and two volunteer boards. People wanted to hire her. Others were more aggressive, hinting at money problems she might solve for them. She didn't respond to much of it. It would add mystique to seem distant and hard to reach.

Karen had been awake since three in the morning, when she was awakened by the cold and drawn again into Charlotte's room. There he was in his Ralph Lauren cardigan, standing next to her bed. Her father watched Charlotte and after a while slowly turned to Karen. The streetlight sneaked into Charlotte's room from either side of her blinds, just enough to see the expression on her father's face, which sent her back in time to the moment she learned who he really was: a liar who did not think of her or his wife, who did not protect them, who thought only of himself, who pretended one last Christmas and disappeared.

"Daddy, where have you been?"

Johnny Sjöblad did not answer. His thin chest expanded as he inhaled and then sunk as he breathed rot into her daughter's bedroom. Karen approached her father, to remove him from here.

"Mom?" said Charlotte.

"Sweetie."

Her daughter rubbed her eyes. "What are you doing?"

"I wanted a hug. I know you don't like them but I was feeling . . . so much love for you."

"Mom, I'm a bit scared."

"Of what?"

"If you need to hug me."

Karen hugged her, quickly and lightly, and made her way back to her room where she lay awake until just after five, when Benedict's phone alarm went off. Since Halloween night, her brain reserved these early mornings for obsessing over the murder. What had Benedict really done to that young woman?

When he finally went downstairs, after his shower, Karen stopped pretending to sleep and looked at her phone. She used every possible search term to see, once more, if the Halloween woman had become news. When thoughts of her dead father in Charlotte's bedroom arrived, she pushed them away by logging into their bank account.

The numbers, the glorious delicious new numbers.

When the sun rose enough to shine into her kitchen, Karen made herself a coffee and answered work emails with work words. She showered and put on her second-skinniest jeans and a T-shirt, her floppy hipster toque from a bar in Madison, Wisconsin, and her white Canada Goose jacket. On her walk to Jak's yoga studio, with the bag of Birkenstocks, she tried to see the humour in all of this, to smile it away. She was still poor then, just a couple of weeks ago, in the middle of a crisis. The private yoga lesson was nothing more than a private lesson.

The yoga studio was in the basement of a vegan restaurant on the corner. A physically distanced class had just ended and several women and a few men walked up the stairs, looking hot and wrecked behind their masks. They smelled of armpit and patchouli. Only the ones who had immediately pulled out their phones had a flustered air about them. The virus was supposed to enlighten us, pull us out of our mediated lives and into something more human and authentic. It had not worked out.

At the bottom of the stairs it was quiet and moist and smelly on the periphery of the yoga studio. There was an old garage-sale credenza in the entrance, and a lit Christmas tree built with books about meditation and Eastern spirituality. Three women in tiny spandex shorts and sports bras, Jak's colleagues, stretched together on the laminate floor. They were not wearing masks. Eucalyptus-scented mist shot out of a black bulb, though it was powerless against the heavy glonk of morning sweat. Karen did not want to disturb the women so she placed the paper bag of furry Birkenstocks, lousy with wart juice, under the credenza.

"Heeeyy," one of the women whispered to her, from across the room. Now that marijuana was legal, all the yogis sounded high. "Can we help you?"

"Yeah, sorry. I was just . . . " Just what? Karen hadn't prepared to speak to anyone but Jak. She was not sure these women would understand her from a distance, behind her mask. "My daughters are teenagers, and I thought I might get them an intro yoga class for Christmas."

The woman walked over on her tiptoes and looked down at the brown paper bag. She had obviously seen Karen put it there. There was a sheen of sweat on her forehead and sticky curls along her hairline. "Oh right, of course. I can make a gift card for you. Or you can do it online: just hit the gift option and print it out. To keep it digital, you can have it emailed or texted to them or whatever."

"Oh cool." Karen made her way back toward the stairs. "Cool, cool, cool. All right, I'll do it online then."

"Um." The woman was looking really intently at the bag now, and then back to Karen, with her eyebrows furrowed. "Is that . . . "

"Oh, it was just sitting at the top of the stairs." Karen took a few steps up. "I thought I'd bring it down."

"In the restaurant?"

One of the other yoga instructors approached them and took the bag of smelly sandals from her colleague. Karen knew this one; she sometimes ran Jak's classes. "Karen, right?"

"Yeah. Bye."

"Wait, I think Jak would like to see you." She did a yoga version of shouting across the room to the remaining yogi, a tiny Black woman whose name was Fflur. In a loud whisper she asked Fflur to grab Jak.

Fflur was locally famous because she was probably the most beautiful woman in the city. If she had been taller than five-foot-four, she would have been on the covers of international magazines. She had eighty thousand Instagram followers. There were men who came to hot yoga just to be in the same room as Fflur.

It was terribly quiet for almost a minute. Karen was steaming in her rich-lady parka and wanted to leave, but the women were staring at her. What had Jak told them? He bounce-walked out from the back room in his Speedo and spotted her and stopped. Karen could tell by the looks on the women's faces that she had been a topic of conversation here at Belgravia Bikram. Whom else had he told? The women in the front entrance retreated back into the studio, and the assistant teacher handed the bag of Birkenstocks to Jak as though it were a package in a spy movie. More whispering ensued.

Jak arrived in the entrance and when the two of them were alone he looked back into the studio, perhaps to ensure his associates weren't watching and listening. Of course they were watching and listening. Jak only wore a mask when he had to wear one to avoid a fine. In his classes he made it clear he did not believe in vaccines or any other form of modern medicine, as it was run entirely by pharmaceutical companies and all they wanted was to keep us sick. He led Karen halfway up the stairs and sat down, patted the stair next to him. This way, the women in the studio could only see their feet. Jak really did have rank feet. Even in the soft orange yoga light she could see the warts. That said, he smelled amazing for a man covered in sweat—a bit of cinnamon, maybe a shot of vanilla?

"What are you doing here?"

She pointed at the bag of sandals.

"Yeah, Karen, you could have mailed them or something."

This freed her to apologize inauthentically and then to stand up and walk out of the yoga studio and vegan restaurant forever. "I'm sorry," Karen said and began to stand. Jak reached up and pulled her down by the sleeve of her white winter coat. This was not allowed, touching a woman without permission, not anymore, especially in a pandemic. But she sat back down anyway.

"Did you . . . Was it supposed to be a joke? Or do you believe in that stuff? Was that your husband?"

Karen didn't understand. Had Jak also seen her father in the house? "Was *who* my husband?"

"Who?" Jak laughed sarcastically and looked around, as though they were on the stage of a talk show. "You're asking who?"

"Sorry but yes. Who?"

"The Nazi! The man in the Nazi uniform who *shouted in German* at me."

"What?"

"You left the room after it got cold and I was hiding because you said someone was there. Yeah, a fucking *Nazi*. Your Nazi. He screamed at me to get out. I guess that's what he was screaming because I don't know German."

"I didn't . . . "

"You didn't what? The whole thing. Booking a private lesson, suckering me into going upstairs with you."

"Hey, wait a second. You were the one who—"

"I oughta call the cops."

"It wasn't real, Jak."

"What wasn't real?"

"The man you saw. It's the house. There's something wrong with our house."

"You figured it would be funny?"

"I had nothing to do with it. I promise."

"You figured I'll pretend to be into my Jew yoga teacher, lure him to my house, and have my Nazi husband shout at him."

"My husband was at work. He doesn't speak German. I didn't know you were Jewish."

"Look at me! Miller!"

Karen thought *Miller* meant one of Jak's ancestors milled things. Grains, now that she put her mind to it. And his only really notable features, besides his disconcertingly sexy body and unsexy warts, were the dreadlocks. Were white guy dreadlocks a Jewish thing? She was afraid to mention it because it might be racist. Karen had no idea anymore.

"Did the Nazi touch you?"

"What?"

"Some man shouted at you, in German." Karen slid as far away from him as she could, as his feet were right next to her boots. "Did he touch you, or did you touch him?"

"I just ran out of the fucking room, down the hall, down the stairs, and out the door. I ran barefoot, all the way here."

"I'm sorry."

"Why did you do that to me, Karen?"

"It wasn't me. It wasn't my husband. *It was the house.*"

The yoga teacher watched her for a moment, sighed, and stood up. He did not turn and say any final words to her, or even look back. Two of the women came into the entrance to look up at Karen, who continued to sit in the awful warmth that leaked out of the studio and up the stairs. She would never come back here.

Less than a block from Finster House, her phone blooped with a text, and another, and another. Karen fished it out of her pocket. They were from Melissa.

Happy Tuesday. Hey it's gorgeous out, right? Care for a run this morning? I could come to you.

Antoine would love the exercise.

I mean . . . if you're free.

Karen didn't answer the texts right away. Instead, she played a sombre Sting Christmas album and washed the morning dishes. She looked west over the white trees and the rooftops of Belgravia with her third coffee. When the wind wasn't hurting your face, and Christmas was coming, and Melissa was texting, and the Jak thing was finished, and yes Nazi ghosts but also white Burgundy, and there was plenty of money in the bank, and Kutisi was in the *New York Times*, this city wasn't so bad.

The final and tallest rooftops were those on Saskatchewan Drive. If they lived in one of those fine houses, she would see the big river snaking through the city, the prairie version of an ocean view.

She did not know any of the people on Saskatchewan Drive. Most of the global companies based here were privately owned, and their owners and executives tended to be discreet about their enormous wealth. There were plenty of Maseratis and Bentleys and Ferraris in the summertime, but the drivers were good-looking university students from mainland China—not any of the secretive homegrown multimillionaires.

Karen decided to ignore Melissa. Karen wanted Melissa to suffer, to feel minuscule and ridiculous, as she had felt. As she still felt, when she was honest with herself in the bath. Karen wanted to somehow *buy* Melissa and sell her to a North Korean glue factory. She opened the messages app and stared at it and felt strong enough to be weak.

A run would be amazing.

Forty-five minutes later, Karen and Melissa were running down the off-leash trails of Belgravia, toward the river. As usual, Karen was listening, but she had trouble concentrating. She focused on the screaming Nazi in her upstairs hallway, her lost father in Charlotte's room. But she knew how to fake it. Listening had been the foundation of their friendship: Melissa offered strong opinions, often about her volunteer initiatives, and outlined her grievances with those who stood in her way. This was all mysteriously charming. It often astounded Karen that her friend could be both self-deprecating and self-glorifying at once. Melissa was thin and tall and muscular and played in a women's soccer league twice a week. Her early forties ass held its structural integrity. Her second most important project, after the social and intellectual triumphs of her only child, Blaine, was Antoine, her English setter, a competitive show dog and occasional actor in local commercials and visiting third-tier Hollywood films that used Alberta as a stand-in for Rocky Mountain states and fantasy realms. Antoine, who had been in an Adam Sandler movie, trotted ahead, sniffing for squirrels.

"If you want to be the chair of the United Way, maybe don't use the word *tit* as your go-to pejorative, and while you're at it maybe stop looking at *my tits* when I'm talking. I mean, such as they are."

All the way down and all the way up the riverbank Melissa entertained Karen with her anecdotes, all she had missed. So much had happened since Melissa had decided to dump her and Poppy. Melissa was clever enough not to bring up the girls at all. The closest she came was to ask about "the family" during their cool-off walk. Regal Antoine had given up on squirrels and now carried a stick.

Karen said everyone was fine, Poppy was fine, and she did not say *despite what you did to her*. The thought of it now inspired some darkness on a bright late morning. Melissa had turned against Poppy not only because members of the business community were openly mocking Kutisi and her husband. It was also about the weight Poppy had gained. It was a different, subtler time to be cruel now that we had identified the dangers of social media. We were learning, as a people, to say it without saying it.

Near the top of the bank there was a steep section. Afterward, both of them took a moment to catch their breath. Then Melissa took Karen's hands in hers. "Can I say something?"

Melissa had said hundreds of things over the past hour and a half. Why would she need to ask? Why was she touching her hands? When had Melissa last washed or sanitized them? Karen vowed to wash her own hands before she touched her face. Her mother had often said a version of this, when Karen was in her late teens and early twenties: *Can I say something without you getting mad?* Right there, in the premise of the question, was a reason to get mad. And the *something* was always a provocation, an attack. "Of course."

"Blaine really misses Poppy. She feels . . . just miserable about everything that happened."

Everything that happened? Mistakes were made?

"Kids, right?" Melissa sighed and shook her head, as though it were all a great enigma. "It's best not to be too involved. I try not to be, anyway. But I think it was just . . . Blaine thought she and Poppy had grown too close. You know? And . . . "

Karen had a hard time concentrating on Melissa's monologue, which was a steaming pile of horseshit, because they were passing a house on Saskatchewan Drive that was still decorated for Halloween. It seemed dark and empty, unheated and unloved. This was one of the houses that was for sale online, $2.3 million. Melissa stopped to look at it while she stretched her calf muscles against an elm tree. "It looks haunted."

"You think?" Karen endeavoured to keep the bounce in her voice. "You ever been in a haunted house? A real haunted house?"

"As in, at a carnival or . . . "

"No, an actual house with actual ghosts in it."

Melissa finished her stretches before she responded. "This one time, in my redneck youth, my dad took us to an abandoned farmhouse outside town. We were on motorbikes. That's what I did in my youth. I rode motorbikes for fun, with the neighbourhood gimps. Luckily I met Luke, my oil-family prince, who saved me from all that. Anyway, we got to this house at dusk. It was summer. And there were *pentagrams* burned into the wall. Maybe it was just the pentagrams but I guess I felt a presence. It felt haunted for sure."

"You didn't see a ghost?"

"No, it was just a feeling. Why?"

Karen was desperate to tell her, to tell anyone. Melissa was a phoney, and she had chosen to hurt Poppy and lie about it, but it had been so long since Karen had a face-to-face conversation with someone who was neither an immediate family member nor a client. A bank of cloud was coming in from the west and the weak December sun turned it grey and pink. There was snow in that cloud. If she lived in this house, this finer haunted house, she could stand in the living room with a glass of wine and watch it come in.

"I'd like to see a ghost, I think." Melissa knelt down so Antoine could kiss her. Her platinum Rolex shone in the sun. Who wears a Rolex for a run in the river valley? "It would mean something comes after this—or could. I'm too healthy to die of the plague but I think about it. We all did, I guess. Do. Do. We don't have the vaccine yet."

They walked up Saskatchewan Drive and then turned right, toward the house where the ghost of her father had stood over Charlotte's bed, where a Nazi had ordered her secretly Jewish almost-lover out of her bedroom.

"How's Charlotte's health?" Melissa put her hand on the small of Karen's back, where it must have been damp. More unnecessary touching. "I think about her sometimes, how beautiful she is. Yet so . . . anyway."

Karen was on the verge of telling her former best friend in the city, best friend left anywhere, that Charlotte had removed the Canada Goose label from her parka. It was a path into her daughter's strange heart. It carried hope. She did not tell Melissa because it was too special. It was sacred. Melissa did not deserve to know.

"I've been thinking so much about you, the four of you, since the news came out. You were always so dismissive about Kutisi, pretending you didn't understand what Ben was on about. Like it wasn't going to work out. Then one day Ben's on the front of not just our paper but *all the papers*. And I'm like, 'Whaaat? I know that guy.' They're saying billions? Oh my God, my best friend the billionaire?"

Karen was lit from within. When she had decided to go on the run, she had decided to be open to forgiving Melissa if she sincerely apologized. Now that she was a block away from home, her principles didn't matter so much. Best friend for Christ's sake. An unexpected and entirely unwanted rush of feeling rose up in her face. Karen turned away from Melissa, to hide the tears in her eyes. The new clouds had moved in so quickly; the sun was gone. There were Christmas trees alight in front windows in the

middle of the day. She did not have to forgive Melissa. All she had
to do was invite her back in, figuratively and literally. There were
still plenty of bottles of her ridiculously tasty white Burgundy,
and of all people Melissa would understand what made it special.

They stopped on her front sidewalk. Antoine sat in his lordly
fashion on the cold grass. By next morning it would be covered in
snow again, which was only correct. Karen was just about to invite
her in when Melissa sighed. "Can I say something?"

Again?

"Ray hasn't been fired exactly but he's been suspended." Melissa
put air quotes around *suspended*. "They're using the virus to clean
out the bureaucracy, to bring in people just like them. If you didn't
join the Young Conservatives at fifteen, if you don't speak in tongues
every Sunday and own several guns, they don't want you in the
senior leadership. The whole system, in government, is about sus-
taining and nurturing the status quo. Ray is a disruptor. And I was
thinking . . . disruptors are better off in the private sector, in industries like tech, where it's all about ideas. Where it's all *about* change."

"Yeah." A police car was parked in front of her house.

"He's been looking for work but honestly, with the pandemic
and everything that's going on with all this—I'm sorry—radical
nonsense, it's just impossible to get a hearing. You have no idea
how hard it is to be a middle-aged white male today. I know, I know,
these fuckers built the world and they have some explaining to do,
generally, but Ray? He was born in the seventies. He didn't steal
anyone's land or swipe their kids from them or, I don't know, participate in the great Canadian slave trade of the eighteenth century.
You know who last had slaves in Canada? Yep, *the Natives*. How
noble is that? Anyway, sorry, sorry, sorry, white privilege. Oh God,
can you imagine what it'll be like for Blaine and Poppy? In university every class will be Being White Is Bad 101. God, my neck's
a disaster." Melissa reached up in a stretch and turned her head

slowly, side to side. "It's just, for Christ's sake, I'm the most progressive bitch out there and if you're losing *me* with the woe-is-me shit, you're losing everybody. I mean, what do they want us to do? Perform some ritual self-flagellation about how we're all racists at heart? Then we euthanize our white children and surrender our bank accounts to, what, the Assembly of First Nations and Black Lives Matter? I'm sorry but hard work matters. Sacrifice matters. Ambition and motivation matter. You know what I'm saying? I mean, of course you do. You're a motherfucking *Swedish* lady named Karen. They're coming for you and your blonde babies first."

Karen could not see into the police car because of the angle of the sun on the windshield. "Yeah, I don't know."

"And all our investments, Ray's parents' money, was in—you guessed it—oil and gas. Just to keep things going through the crisis, we had to sell a lot. You know, that old genius move, buy high and sell low? The house was paid for but we remortgaged it. The issue, now and going forward, is cash flow."

Karen took a step to the left, for a better look into the police car. There was someone in there.

"This might be crazy, Kare, and I would *never* want to jeopardize our friendship but . . . no. No, it's too crazy. Oh my God, it's crazy. I can't even believe I'm *saying* this."

There was a policewoman behind the steering wheel, her hair tucked into her dark blue hat.

"What?"

"Could you . . . Do you think Ray could get in on the, I don't know, ground floor of Kutisi? I mean, I only say it because he has a lot to offer. In a couple of the articles, it said Ben and his partner were on a bit of a hiring spree. And God, you know *Ray*. He hits his targets. He's a super-good leader. People-first all the way, and he's really innovative and committed to building resilience and collaboration in his teams. He's innovative as hell. You know Ray!"

Karen had been on holidays with him, and at innumerable dinner parties with him, but she only sort of knew Ray. She had forgotten Melissa was a bit of a left-wing white supremacist. A squirrel chirped at Antoine. The dog normally stared at Melissa, for the next command or declaration of love, but even he seemed to understand she had debased herself. Antoine looked at nearby shrubbery.

The policewoman exited the car. She carried a clipboard. "Excuse me. Are you Karen Sjöblad?"

Despite the low-level anxiety at seeing a police car in front of her house, Karen had been thinking of Ray, blandly handsome and mostly bald, proud of his barbecuing prowess and his ability to make a delicious mojito. Old money but Alberta old money. That is to say second-generation wealthy. Melissa's tirade about Indigenous and Black people getting all the sweet jobs and attention was straight out of one of Ray's half-drunk "I'm not a racist but" monologues. In sum, Ray was a grown-up frat boy with a really fancy pickup truck he didn't use to haul anything. So much of his middle-age personality and self-worth seemed to be wrapped up in mountain biking, barbecuing, mojitos, and hating the prime minister's cute socks. This had always confused Karen, especially as she bought into the mythology. And she wasn't alone. In better days, when Melissa and Ray hosted dinner parties, others— coached by Ray—would make similar exclamations, as though a mojito were something more mysterious than a mixture of lime juice, sugar, mint, ice, and booze. *Oh my God, these mojitos are amazing, Ray. You muddle the best mojitos in the world!*

Karen knew his job title because Melissa bragged about it so much. Ray was—or had been—executive director of strategic policy for the department of economic development. Even if Karen could sell this idea to Benedict, how would she do it?

Innovative and resilient? What policy *wasn't* strategic? Benedict didn't really laugh but if he did laugh, he would laugh at that.

Her anxiety passed immediately into panic. DNA analysis had led them to this prosperous corner of Belgravia. She had the right to remain silent. Did the police say that in Canada, or did that only happen on American television? Karen bent her knees slightly. Once, during a presentation to a client, she had fainted from standing with her knees locked. In moments of high stress, her fight-or-flight mechanism tended to malfunction. Every time Charlotte hurt herself or suffered from a really bad flare-up in her tummy, every time Poppy was in a dancing or singing competition, Karen would feel herself fading.

"Yes. I'm Karen." She remembered what she and Benedict had decided to say. They watched a scary movie, after trick-or-treating, locked the doors, and went to bed. It was always super-active on Halloween night, on years when the weather is good. The garage was spray-painted one time. Jack-o'-lanterns smashed on the front sidewalk almost every year. Someone had toilet-papered the apple tree in the front yard. But this year there were only nine kids and a massive surplus of peanut butter cups.

The policewoman looked at Melissa and Antoine. "I don't mean to interrupt but . . . "

"Oh. Right." Melissa pulled Antoine off the cool grass. "I'll text you?"

"Yeah."

"Hey, um. Forget what I said just there, okay? I was just, like . . . Ray would kill me if he knew I'd said all that to you. He'd never want to jeopardize the friendship we have, as families, together? You know Ray. He's like . . . "

Black socks, hamburgers, truck, four-thousand-dollar mountain bikes, white people, Rolex, mojitos. The executive director of something boring. What else *was* Ray? Karen was unable to process any of this, let alone respond, and sought something like refuge in the neutral menace of the policewoman's face. She was pretty, thirty or thirty-five, with a tiny nose and red hair.

Once Melissa and Antoine were gone, the policewoman smiled, introduced herself as Constable McCaw, and apologized again. "You didn't have to end your chat, or your run, or whatever. This might be really short."

"You want to come in?"

"We don't do that anymore unless we have to. Pandemic."

"Of course." *Don't touch your face.*

"Ms. Sjöblad, do you know Jak Miller?"

"He's my yoga teacher."

"We had a call from him today, suggesting you . . . your husband or another man dressed up as a Nazi and shouted anti-Semitic things at him."

Karen shifted and powered down her engine of worry. She had learned the story of her grandfather the Nazi when she was twelve or thirteen. The context was always that he was never a *proper* Nazi, as Sweden didn't have those. But still. One of Karen's various teenage fantasies was to have an easy-to-pronounce non-Swedish-Nazi surname like O'Brian and be a girl with red hair, a girl just like this policewoman. Nancy Drew but with a cool Irish accent, solving whodunits. "Yeah, I spoke to Jak this morning. I honestly don't know what he's talking about. The house wasn't locked that day, so I suppose a crazy person could have come in. Neither my husband nor anyone I know has a Nazi costume or even speaks German."

Constable McCaw nodded and made some notes on her clipboard. "He, Mr. Miller, said the man wasn't wearing a Halloween costume. It was a proper Nazi uniform."

Karen shook her head and shrugged. "I mean, how weird and awful."

"Can you tell me why Mr. Miller was here? The nature of your relationship?"

"Jak's my yoga teacher. Bikram yoga."

"The hot kind?"

"Yes."

Karen backed up a few steps and leaned against the brick foundation of the old house. It felt so good to be telling the absolute truth.

"Mr. Miller came over to . . . "

"To give me a private lesson. I don't know if it's kosher, with the pandemic and all, but this was back in late November."

Constable McCaw looked up from her clipboard, just long enough to make eye contact and evaluate the meaning of *private lesson*. Or kosher? Then she continued writing.

"It was, uh, an unusual day. Jak thought it was something it wasn't. He kissed me."

"In an . . . unwanted fashion?"

"The moment he realized it was unwanted, he stopped."

"Good boy," said the constable.

"I hope you can keep that part to yourself. Things are . . . were . . . anyway, I supplied no Nazis. I wouldn't know how to supply them."

The constable sighed. "Yep. This is an unusual one. November thirtieth, right?"

"Yes. Can we change the subject ever so slightly, Constable?"

"For the moment."

Karen told the constable about the garage break-in on the same day, November thirtieth. The constable listened and recalled that she had been the one to take the report. There had been a number of break-ins that night. Ross.

"We haven't heard a thing back from you guys, about whether or not you found our stuff or the people who took it."

"Yeah, there's a pretty efficient machine out there. Stealing things, reselling them. You might check the pawn shops and online marketplaces. If you see any of your stuff there, let us know. And please . . . if you remember anything about Nazis." Constable McCaw pulled out a thin card, moist from something else that had been in her pocket. A bit of food, maybe. Karen resisted an urge to smell it.

As the constable returned to her car, Karen called out to her. "What do you think happened? Honestly? With the Nazi?"

Constable McCaw didn't respond or even shrug. She looked back at Karen, who thought it must be something they learn in police school. Break down the accused by staring at them. She thought of how Benedict or Charlotte would react to such treatment. They could hold eye contact forever, in a neutral and probing manner, like big cats figuring out the weakness of the gazelles. If Karen held her own, before the young constable's psychological techniques, it was because she had grown accustomed to interacting—loving—those with abnormal social skills and cues. Her question about the break-in was what they call in detective novels a "fishing expedition." If Constable McCaw had heard anything about the Halloween woman, she would have "played her hand." What fun, to be Nancy Drew.

Back in the house, she washed her hands and traced Jak's route from the front door to her bedroom and washed and wiped everything three times, with chlorine bleach, even though she had already cleaned and it had been a long time since he had been here and all of his germs would be dead anyway. She threw her duvet cover and sheets in the wash again, with the heavy duty setting, and sat down with her laptop. There were plenty of articles about idiots harassing Muslims but no one had written anything about actual Nazis around here in a long time.

Karen poured a glass of white Burgundy and listened to the house. In all this worrying about Jak and Nazi phantoms, she had not taken a moment to appreciate all that had happened with Melissa. *People-first all the way, and he's really innovative and committed to building resilience and collaboration in his teams.*

Exquisite.

TWELVE

I t had been another night of very little sleep. His rotting ghost had hovered through the house and yard and sent a charge through him that had a smell and taste, like deeply burned marshmallows. Benedict could see it and feel it even when he was not looking.

The doctor at Medcan had ordered two brain scans and informed him, in her twenty-fifth-floor office overlooking the white valley, that there was nothing physically wrong with him. Against all his instincts Benedict told her he had been seeing things, and the doctor had blamed it on a miserable cycle of poor eating habits, stress, and sleeplessness. It all made perfect sense to her. The investment in Kutisi was monumental, the culmination of his life's work, and after years of what he called *crushing failure and humiliation*, it had arrived like a blinding light. "You don't feel worthy, do you?" she said.

Benedict admitted he did not.

Two cabinet ministers in the provincial government had worked for Marie-Claude back in the good and profitable days of Aarhus Energy. They granted Kutisi travel exemptions under a vague

clause in the pandemic legislation that dealt with "economic bene-
fits." There were rules foreigners had to follow, and on their way to
the airport Marie-Claude explained these rules to Benedict. The
government was concerned primarily with media and public criti-
cism over its handling of the public health crisis. News of fancy
people flying in and out while regular folks won't see Grandma at
Christmas was the main issue but it was less likely to be relevant
now that the virus was out of control and the government had
unofficially given up.

Jessica Wolfe was a tall woman with big, brown eyes. When
she entered the conference room they had booked at the airport,
decorated for Christmas, a perfume bomb went off. The American's
face mask was yellow with blue flowers and said Hermès in the
bottom right corner. Jessica had flown in from Amsterdam, on her
way home to San Francisco. Benedict wondered if she had smelled
this way the entire eight-hour flight.

His mother had worn perfume when he was little, before he
contracted meningitis and nearly died in the hospital. Then her
perfume disappeared with her gold and silver jewellery, her dia-
monds and opals. In his research on Protestantism, he discovered
John Calvin had made these sorts of demands on the people of
Geneva in 1541, outlawing jewellery and other ostentation and
adornment. The clever Swiss responded by putting their jewels in
their watches.

Until after they died, Benedict had understood that Leonard
and Clara Ross turned into Christians because of what had happened with the tiny man of God at the Royal Alexandra Hospital
on the day of their son's miraculous recovery. When he went
through their paperwork, looking for their insurance arrange-
ments, he had discovered something else. He had an older brother
named Mark who was born with severe autism and epilepsy and
something called fragile X syndrome. Benedict did not remember

a thing about Mark, but when he was two and Mark was five, his parents had given up trying to care for the boy and abandoned him into the foster care system. They received regular updates about Mark, visited him on occasion, and provided financial support. In a locked cabinet, Benedict discovered letters from exhausted and bruised foster parents who pleaded with Leonard and Clara to take Mark back, to see the wonder and delight in him. In 1986, when Mark was seventeen, he died of something called SUDEP—sudden unexpected death in epilepsy. It might have been his heart. It might have been his lungs. There was an invitation to attend Mark's funeral but Benedict could not tell, from any of the papers in the cabinet, if his parents had gone.

This was, to Benedict, a far more logical reason to become an evangelical Christian and a missionary in Angola. The saviour will wash your sins away. He will forgive you even when you cannot forgive yourself.

"Uh, Benedict? Hello?" Jessica Wolfe seemed on the verge of laughing, but not because anything was funny. Marie-Claude was looking at him too.

This was a familiar feeling. Someone had asked him a question, possibly twice, and he had been so focused on other matters he had not heard it. "I do apologize. Can you repeat that?"

Marie-Claude sighed. "Poor Benedict. He's been sleeping poorly."

After a short pause, Jessica Wolfe sat up in her chair. In front of her there was an apple-ginger kombucha and a gluten-free ball of something nutty. "We're not friends, Marie-Claude. Benedict. We're not even co-workers. I carry the weight of all the men and women and institutions who invested in us. If you're not sleeping well, Benedict, you might get sleeping pills. If you can't concentrate long enough to converse with me, I can't see you inspiring a team to deliver . . . "

Over the years, Kutisi had hired plenty of brilliant engineering graduates. Not one of them had been able to break the code. In their own ways, each of them had determined the only solution was to make the boxes bigger. They had competitors in Germany and China, even the U.S., who could already generate nuclear power—but not with waste. Why did it have to be waste? And why did the box have to be so small? Why did it have to be elegant?

It just *did*.

The ghost was in the hall of the airport administration building, waiting for him, and when he looked away for a moment it moved through a series of walls and hovered on the runway. It was the dead thief and she wanted something from him and he was on the edge of understanding it for the first time, here in the airport conference room, like an algorithm he could just about remember.

"Benedict." Jessica looked to Marie-Claude. "Have I lost him again?"

"No." Marie-Claude wanted this to be warm, to be funny. "He's with us. Aren't you, buddy?"

"Can I be frank?" Jessica touched the nutty food-ball. "You seem like a different person today, from the man who pitched us two and a half weeks ago."

"Just take a moment, Ben." Marie-Claude put her hands together, pleadingly. "She just wants to know *our plan* to take Kutisi to the world. Our scale-up strategy."

Benedict closed his eyes and when he opened them again the ghost was gone. "Rather than hire another thirty recent grads, Ms. Wolfe—"

"Jessica."

"Thank you. Jessica. Rather than immediately hiring thirty of them on permanent contracts, at one hundred thousand dollars a year, we're bringing in five of the best in the world, for a week. Later today, in fact. As consultants, with rock-solid NDAs."

"Why?"

Benedict did not want to reveal anything he did not have to reveal. "To help us with the scale-up."

"Five of the best *what* in the world?"

"Engineers. Physicists."

Jessica looked at Marie-Claude and back at Benedict. "What do engineers and physicists know about scaling an invention? It's already invented. Shouldn't we be recruiting, I don't know, salespeople and supply-chain experts? People who speak multiple languages? Lawyers to draft up contracts? Retired diplomats to—"

"We're close."

For an uncomfortably long time, Jessica watched him. Her hair was pulled back in an elaborate bun, like a ballet dancer. She removed her face mask. Her skin was preposterously clear, apart from a delicate constellation of freckles under each eye. From her bio Benedict knew she had lived and worked in Shanghai for eleven years. The bad air had not affected her. They were about the same age.

Just above a whisper, she said, "You didn't sell *close*."

Benedict returned to the day of the pitch. *Believe*. Jessica looked at him for so long he stood up and took a kombucha from the tray.

"Anyone want anything?"

Jessica typed something into her iPad. "These five wizards of scale: who are they and how much do they cost?"

Marie-Claude had all of this information, but instead of reading it out she told Jessica she would send it by email. Ultimately, the reason for Jessica's visit was more pedestrian. Where would they build Kutisi? Canadian officials could not compete with Americans in the manufacturing subsidy game, especially the juicy post-pandemic "Build Back Better" subsidies.

The ghost was outside now, on the tarmac, in the light snow. The land was flat here, flat forever in every direction, the plains, the prairies. Benedict imagined his grandfather the violin-maker arriving here from the Carpathian Mountains and looking around. It would have been terrifying, especially in the winter.

"Some places on the Eastern Seaboard where the virus came in hot, they'll kill babies if they have to, to bring a few hundred jobs to town." Jessica had already created a spreadsheet of her top cities. "Ten-year, twenty-year tax breaks, free buildings. North Carolina lost billions when they passed their idiotic bathroom law, and that was before the pandemic. New Jersey? Even Michigan. They'll do *anything* for advanced manufacturing. We're getting a lot of attention, and a lot of calls, am I right?"

"Correct," said Marie-Claude.

Benedict had already finished his kombucha. It was cold and sweet, though the fermented tea could not pull him all the way back from Halloween night, his dead brother, the truth in the painting bay of the factory. If Medcan was wrong and he was terribly sick in and about his brain, he might close his eyes and never wake up. All of this would become someone else's problem. He would not miss Jessica, or financial statements, or the circulation of reactor coolant flow.

The glow in the backyard.

"Benedict?" Marie-Claude lifted her own kombucha and tilted her head at him. "Do you have thoughts?"

I am a fraud and a charlatan. I cannot protect my family from the beast. I am a murderer. On the other side of the glass, in yet another conference-room meeting secured by cabinet ministers who did not have to follow their own rules, someone was playing orchestral Christmas music: "Es ist ein Ros entsprungen," his mother's favourite Christmas carol.

"About . . . "

"North Carolina," said Marie-Claude, with a quick glance at Jessica. "They're the leading bid right now. And the U.S. has long pulled away, on corporate tax. It makes sense."

"We're a Canadian company."

"You can maintain an office here, if you like. Perhaps it would qualify us for government grants, I don't know. Who cares, really?" Jessica looked around, appraisingly. Several venture capital and private equity firms from the U.S. had flown up, over the last few years, to look at Kutisi. Every one of the principals had seemed surprised by Canada. It wasn't as though they disliked the country. They tended to forget it existed. And when they were here, it felt even smaller and less consequential than they had imagined on the bilingual flight north. Jessica had not said a word about the relative Canadianness of Canada. "I suspect there aren't any real advantages to it, Benedict, apart from emotional ones. With the amount we'd be investing in a place like Raleigh-Durham or Princeton or Las Vegas, permanent residency for you and your family wouldn't be an issue." She gestured out the window at the flatness, land and light, at the flakes falling. "I mean, I don't imagine you're here for the top-shelf climate."

Marie-Claude did the thing she liked to do when she felt a meeting was over. She placed her palms on the table and stood up. "Can we order up some lunch, Jessica?"

"I have to get back to California. They'll serve lunch on the plane."

Now that the meeting was over, the two women, who had varied business experiences and global adventures, had plenty to talk about. They knew corporate jets well. Marie-Claude and Benedict escorted Jessica down to the departures terminal. Elvis sang "Blue Christmas" through the intercom system. Masks back on, they did not shake hands or hug or air-kiss. Benedict was delighted to be free of it all: when to reach out, how hard to squeeze, what cheek to pretend to kiss first. He had already smelled plenty of Jessica's perfume. Then she took a small, naughty step to him, so close he could see one of her eyelashes had detached and rested next to her nose. "For now I won't pretend to know what you mean by *close*, Benedict. You didn't sell *close*. You sold breakthrough. We fast-tracked our diligence because you absolutely convinced Mr. Zheng. It was brilliant. I hear pitches all day. I hear pitches for a living. Yours was very, very good."

"It was." Marie-Claude was muffled by her regular old black mask.

"I deal with . . . scientists and engineers all day. I can forgive behavioural nuance."

"That's it. Those are the words, right there." Marie-Claude lightly clapped her hands. "Benedict's got a fair dose of behavioural nuance in him."

"But we're not so far down the road that we can't cancel the whole thing and request the money back, with interest and a penalty. The contract gives us—"

"Hey, hey, hey." Marie-Claude stepped back. "Only if—"

"Only if you lied to us, Benedict. Here's what bugs me. I don't see the value in bringing wizards to town for a scale-up strategy. I'm making an appointment with one of my own wizards, the best of them, let's call him Gandalf, to come and take a look at everything. He won't like it, this close to Christmas, but that's how it's going to be. Is this agreeable to you? You can get him an exemption?"

"Of course," said Marie-Claude. "Anything. Just send Gandalf's name and details and the time of his arrival."

Benedict felt dizzy and nauseated. The massive terminal only had five or six people in it, and a tan dog, as one of the people was blind. There was a large artificial Christmas tree decorated with glass balls emblazoned with the names of airport staff members. The ghost hovered next to it. Benedict left the two women in the middle of the hall and approached it. Approached her. It struck him in the airport that he had allowed the thing to pursue him without ever asking what it—what she—wanted. Her eyes were there but not there. As he got closer to the thing, he tried to see the woman in it: the way she had looked and sounded that night as he crouched over her.

"Hey, buddy?"

He stopped. There was fear in Marie-Claude's voice.

"Ben? You want to come back here and say goodbye to Jess-ica?"

Behind him, he could hear them whispering to one another about him. He wanted them to go away for a little while so he could sort this out with the ghost.

"Benedict!" Marie-Claude's voice echoed through the terminal. In all their years of working together, he had never heard this tone. Frustration, confusion, anger. He turned away from the ghost for a moment to see Marie-Claude with her arms out, chuckling in a *this isn't funny* manner. His face was hot. A sheen of sweat popped and freshened his forehead. Marie-Claude waved him back. "He hasn't been getting much sleep," she said.

"You mentioned." Jessica sighed. "I should be going."

When he turned back to the ghost, it was gone. A couple of kids approached the Christmas tree and read the names on the glass balls aloud.

Rather than wait together for their arriving engineers—now Marie-Claude called them wizards too—she ordered him to go and get a few hours of sleep. Everything would be fine. The wizards would help them sort out a scale-up plan and they would be more than prepared for Gandalf, whenever he arrived. Representatives from the European Union, their first customers, would arrive in

January. All Benedict could do was nod, though Marie-Claude wanted more from him. She wanted reassurance.

It works. It works perfectly, partner. By this time next year, there will be thousands of them operating around the world.

Benedict took an Uber from the airport to the factory. There were five Kutisis on the main floor, for the arriving wizards to play with, plus his own box in the painting bay. He stopped at the refrigerator, opened the door, and stared at the healthy snacks the Kutisi HR director stocked: farmers' market carrots, grainy gluten-free lumps sweetened with coconut nectar, hard-boiled eggs, and organic cheese nuggets. All he really wanted was a peanut butter cup, but he had long run out of his Halloween stash.

Jessica Wolfe would demand what Kutisi had taken out of that first cheque, plus 15 per cent. There was an easy way out. His insurance policy was worth five million dollars, and thanks to mortgage insurance, the house and home equity line of credit would immediately be paid off. Even if Karen never worked another day, as long as she could find an investment vehicle that paid a few per cent she would live debt-free with a little more than $150,000 a year. They would not be rich but they would not be poor.

Of course, he would not want his wife and daughters to think he had suffered—physically or emotionally. Karen's own father had done it enviably. He had just disappeared. While Karen accepted Johnny Sjöblad was gone—there was a funeral—he carried a bit of magic. For a long time, he was around every corner. She had hoped for an email from Dubai or Luxembourg or Guangzhou, with apologies and instructions.

But Karen was younger than Mrs. Sjöblad had been, when Johnny disappeared. Karen would want to remarry in an unencumbered fashion, and Charlotte did not operate well with uncertainty. The trick was to do it without it seeming so. Roads were slippery at the moment; he would veer off the James MacDonald Bridge into the icy waters of the North Saskatchewan River.

He prepared the wizards' boxes. At its simplest, Kutisi was fire and steam. All he wanted was to enhance the relationship between them without breaking any laws of physics or killing anyone. There was a low-level buzz in his head, from trying and failing to fix the problem for so long. He was constantly on the edge of the solution, like trying to remember the name of a childhood friend, but today he would not even enter the painting bay.

The ghost would be in there.

New companies like Tesla and old companies like BASF had tried to hire Benedict, even to buy him out at an early stage of Kutisi, but no. Benedict had succumbed to the dangerous idea that if he were left alone in the most northerly big city in North America, lit by coal, he could change everything.

The Model X was not high enough off the ground to leap over the guardrails of the James MacDonald Bridge, and it would be a terrible waste of an efficient and beautiful car. He would have to buy one of those preposterous little pickups with huge tires and lift kits, a mini monster truck. An unusual percentage of them were yellow, with tinted windows. Why yellow? Benedict used his phone to search for used trucks. The blue-collar side of the economy, oil people and those who built things for oil people, had not been receiving six-figure salaries for a couple of years so there was a surplus of silly trucks for sale at decent prices. Distressed assets. Perhaps he could find one for under ten thousand dollars that did not smell like cigarette smoke inside.

The factory walls were painted soft purple, the colour of calm and creativity. Tables were metal, chairs were white. When Benedict was last in Stockholm, he did not find any uniformity in design, but he had wanted the factory to feel like his idea of Scandinavia: spare, sophisticated, tidy. Danielle, his director of design, had bought a

Colorado blue spruce over the weekend and arrived at seven in the morning to decorate it with ornaments she and her Strasbourgeois husband had made by hand. She strung garlands on the walls.

Each wizard's workstation had a chair, a table, a new set of tools, a lab coat, a box of gourmet granola bars, a small Nespresso machine, a computer that did not leave the factory, and printed specifications of Kutisi. With the specifications, Benedict had put together a startlingly honest appendix. In it, he outlined the problem he needed the wizards to solve at $25,000 American each for a week of work: *How do we bridge the gap between what Kutisi can do now and what we need it to do? That is, what we say it does?*

In the twenty minutes before the wizards were due to arrive, he locked himself in the bathroom with his computer and explored some of the used Toyota trucks for sale online. The cheapest one was $7,200 and it was orange, not yellow. Benedict had been feeling sick in his chest ever since Halloween night, and now it was beyond what he could accept. The bathroom was large, designed for the car dealership and its filthy employees, with a shower area that could hold eight or nine men at once. Was it normal, in the car business, for all those people to shower together?

If this gamble with the wizards did not work, he would have to be honest with Karen and Marie-Claude and Jessica Wolfe and declare two levels of bankruptcy, corporate and personal. He had allowed himself to think too much about this scenario. There was strategic value in plotting the end of things on the pre-Christmas calendar, knowing exactly when to drive off the James MacDonald Bridge to bring the greatest possible benefit to Karen and Poppy.

And Charlotte. What would happen to Charlotte without him? While she would never say such things to her mother or sister, she did confide in him from time to time about how she imagined her life would go, ever-increasing pain and a slow acceptance of opiates and their ugly derivatives. They would dull her senses. Her brain would fire differently, and her emotions would flare in unappetizing and unhappy ways for her and for her family. At some point, if they could not figure out what was wrong with her—it was a deeper problem than Crohn's—she would have to take drastic action.

It was logical. It had been logical for Johnny Sjöblad and it would be logical for him. The ghost was coming now, moving through the walls.

A knock on the bathroom door. "Chef?" It was the voice of Danielle, one of the only people who was allowed in the factory. She had no idea what went on inside the machines. Her job was to make them modular, transportable, and attractive.

"Yes, Danielle."

"Are you on the phone?"

He realized he had been speaking to himself. "No."

"Right. Okay." After a short pause, she said, "Marie-Claude just pulled up in the big truck."

"I'm coming."

"Oh good. Yeah. Are you okay, Chef?"

Chef. This is what Danielle, who had grown up in Lourdes, city of miracles, had started calling him.

"Absolutely. Perfect, Danielle, merci. Be right out."

Marie-Claude stood with the wizards, all but one of them men of her generation. Three of them wore suits, one wore chinos and a shirt, and the other—the bald, forty-nine-year-old physicist from Harvard—was in jeans and a soft pink hoodie that said "No Bad Days" next to a drawing of a couple of palm trees. He was chewing gum with his mouth open.

There was something that bound together scientists and researchers of this calibre, a fundamental disinterest in the social parts of their jobs. Though each of them had relied on it to succeed, Benedict knew they would rather get to work than talk about the weather or their flights. These were almost always his kind of people.

Almost always. The bald Harvard man who said everyone called him Dr. Darren spoke with a booming voice. He seemed a director of theatre, not the Innovative Nuclear Power Reactors and Fuel Cycles program at the International Atomic Energy Agency, and he brought an unwelcome flavour to the introductions by encouraging everyone to name their favourite food and favourite song.

"Unless we can attach two of our strong senses to each other's names—in this case, taste and sound—we'll forget. At least I will." He clapped his hands. "I'll go first. I'm Dr. Darren, like I said, and I love tuna tataki with a lime-soy-ginger jus drizzled over it, and my favourite song is 'More Than This' by Roxy Music. I hated that goddamn song as a teenager but now I love it. Old people, am I right?" He spit his gum into his hand and sang the first few lines of "More Than This," with his eyes closed for exaggerated effect. Then he looked around. "All right? Who's next? Not everybody has to sing."

Benedict was already exhausted, and he could tell by the ensuing festival of anus-clenching introversion that he was not alone. Once he learned nearly everyone's favourite food and song, Benedict led them on a mini tour and showed them where to put their bags and coats.

His partner was not "operational" and did not pretend to understand the science behind Kutisi. For a moment, Marie-Claude seemed to want to stay for whatever came next. The wizards did not mind. Sir Walter Jarrow, from Oxford, stood right next to her, without the faintest effort at pandemic distancing, and while it might have seemed normal a year ago, it had a curious intimacy about it.

"Perhaps I'll . . . let you all get to work?" Marie-Claude waited a moment for Benedict to invite her to stay. Something had changed in her face, the palsy had worsened. Even behind the mask Benedict could see it. She was tired. She was worried. When Benedict remained silent, she looked at Danielle, who had planned to do some Christmas shopping in the downtown mall. The legal capacity in stores was 15 per cent, and now that so many people had vacated the centre of the city there would be no lineups.

Danielle adjusted her Kutisi-branded mask. "You can join me, if you like. I want to buy my husband one of those old-fashioned, wool Hudson's Bay blankets; you know, the white one with the stripes? A real piece of Canada."

"I read we aren't supposed to have those anymore," said Marie-Claude. "Symbols of colonialism."

"Ah, *vraiment?*" Danielle turned and made her way toward the door. "*Partout c'est la honte.* Goodnight and good luck, men of science."

Marie-Claude followed her. The men of science thanked her for the ride from the airport and for the warm welcome. It was always less fun without Marie-Claude. The moment she and Danielle were gone, Sir Walter crossed his arms and exhaled mightily out his nose. It was quiet enough in the factory to hear the rustling of his tweed. His eyes were dark, from the shock of the eight-hour time difference. One of his Oxford colleagues had been the main voice in a takedown article in *Wired* online, expressing deep skepticism that Kutisi's claims were permitted by the laws of thermodynamics not to mention ready to scale, as the glowing article in the *New York Times* had promised.

Marie-Claude had not wanted to invite Sir Walter, given his close colleague's public denunciations, but Benedict had insisted. Now on the factory floor, the knight of the realm sighed with exasperation when Dr. Darren said he was the only one who wouldn't play the introduction game.

"You're killing the vibe, Walt." Dr. Darren leapt across the concrete floor and poked him in the belly. "Come on, your liege. Live a little!"

"Hamburgers, for Christ's sake, and the Brandenburg Concerto in B-flat major."

"There it is, your lordship, there it is right there." Dr. Darren winked. "Was that so hard?"

Benedict opened the folder he had prepared for their arrival. "Before we begin, before I present you with our challenge, I need you all to sign a non-disclosure agreement."

"I already signed the NDA." Sir Walter looked around, and the others nodded. "Before I left. The contract Marie-Claude sent us—"

"This one is different." Benedict handed them out, with pens. "Read it, if you like. In short, the penalties for sharing what you will see and do here, in these five days, are more strenuous."

"Strenuous?" Dr. Darren lifted his glasses to read.

Sir Walter looked up from the document. "Does Marie-Claude know about this?"

"No."

"Does anyone know? Any co-workers? Your *wife*?"

There were lots of things Benedict never told her. He never told her about his brother, Mark, and what his parents had done to him. He did not know what he was for, what he was here to do. At one time Benedict thought he knew but now he did not and there was no way to tell Karen. "My lawyer knows."

Sir Walter showed his teeth but he did not smile. "I'm happy to be here in your winter wonderland, Mr. Ross. But I suspect you haven't invited us to figure out a scaling strategy. It certainly isn't my expertise. Without having looked at the box in detail, it doesn't sound as if any part of your box needs *tweaking*, as you put it. It sounds impossible."

"I read your colleague's analysis in *Wired*. That's why you're here, Sir Walter."

"To do the impossible."

"Yes."

Sir Walter chuckled, and the others joined in. "You're fucked, aren't you?"

"Yes."

"Well." Sir Walter signed the final page of the NDA and removed his tweed jacket. "Onward then."

THIRTEEN

Forty-five of the city's most important philanthropists and leaders were invited to a special performance at the theatre. It was controversial on social media because the premier of the province had approved a one-night-only extension of the retail and religious rules—15 per cent capacity—for a pre-Christmas arts fundraiser.

Raising money wasn't the issue. A boozy gathering of 1 per cent of 1 per cent of the local one percenters was the issue. For Karen, it wasn't an issue at all. A few activists had stood at the entrance, taking photographs and shouting slogans. Was it the worst thing to be included in this crowd? Perhaps a photograph of her and Poppy would be included in the Twitter takedown, and Melissa would see it.

In the lobby, before and after the show, business leaders and city councillors and a few local celebrities introduced themselves and congratulated Karen for Kutisi. One or two of the men may have been flirting. It was difficult to tell, behind the masks. She carried the warm glow that came with being *spoken of*, and she adored it so much it inspired her to buy two juice boxes of overpriced, overwarm Merlot. Even the tall and gallant mayor congratulated her, and when that happened—during the intermission—Poppy squeezed her mother's hand and cried a little on their way back into the theatre.

"I can't believe this is happening," said Poppy.

It was the night of December seventeenth and the lobby was ornately decorated. A jazz quartet played holiday songs from the 1950s. The theatre's response to the activists was entirely sound: for artists this was going to be the hardest Christmas since the Great Depression. Tickets were five thousand dollars each.

Karen thought of Johnny Sjöblad during the first ghost scene in *A Christmas Carol*. When his crimes hit the newspapers, and spread through Western Canada, her feelings had a taste and a colour. Men came into their home in Edgemont and repossessed her jewellery, her bed frame, her Macintosh Classic II and her television, several pairs of her shoes and boots. They took her Cabriolet. They took her skis and her snowboard and her ice skates and her bicycle. She was seventeen years old, just about to graduate into the world, and suddenly the board of directors of the private school community that had been an enormous part of her life was having emergency meetings about whether or not to let her graduate with a Strathcona-Tweedsmuir diploma. The Glencoe Club removed them as members and banned them for life. There were columns about her father in the local, national, American, and British press. The phone rang at all hours, and when they picked up it was nearly always an investor who had been ruined by Johnny Sjöblad's lies. Once when Karen answered the phone, a man said he was going to break into the house in the night and rape her. The police were only half-interested when someone threatened them with violent assault or death. Her mother was removed from every one of her board appointments. Even though she had raised hundreds of thousands, if not millions, of dollars for local charities, she was on the front page of the *Calgary Sun* with a pun that barely made sense: "Jeanny gets rich-slapped." The *Globe and Mail* and the *Toronto Sun* dug up the Nazi sympathizer stories, and in the end it was so bad her mother struck a deal with Strathcona-Tweedsmuir to let Karen finish her classes by distance education. Did they refund the fifteen-thousand-dollar tuition or say a word about the money her mother had raised for the school from kindergarten to twelfth grade? Of course not. The chair of the board laughed when Jeanette Sjöblad suggested it.

When her father disappeared, the phone calls stopped. The newspaper stories shifted into mystery mode, with rumours and sightings and conspiracy theories about Johnny living it up in Bali with a new name, faking an Australian accent. Karen wanted to change her own name, to make up an entirely new history and family, but her mother convinced her to embrace the humiliation, to *own it* and make it the core of her being. Her mother wrote a book about her fall from the prairie upper class to a crummy apartment in the suburbs, but it was rambling and boring. None of the Canadian publishers was interested and she didn't have enough money to print and distribute it herself. Karen didn't finish reading her copy, which she received as a twentieth birthday present. Over time, people forgot. Hundreds of thousands of new people moved into Calgary, wiping out most memories of the social scene in the tough 1980s. By the time Karen graduated from the University of British Columbia with her strange but handsome genius boyfriend, Benedict Ross, hardly anyone remembered.

She remembered.

Karen was a slow and careful driver, especially in a snowstorm; men in shiny trucks honked and tailgated when she didn't drive fast enough. Poppy talked about the play all the way home. Reliving it was all that kept Karen from screaming out loud at some of the aggressive men in trucks. Her father had been one of them. She had

her Cabriolet, her mother had a Mercedes, and Johnny had his
Silverado. She breathed deeply and tried to imagine herself in a more
sophisticated part of the world, in a milder climate, with fern and fig
trees and no Silverados. She thought of the men, considered the
source of their frustration. In just a few years, they had gone from
rich to poor to really poor. The trucks probably cost eight or nine
hundred dollars a month and some of them would be going deeper
into debt every day, as she had done. Karen sympathized with them
as she pulled into the back lane. She silently forgave them.

In the garage, Karen found three more boxes of Christmas decorations. Poppy recited a few of the lines from the play along the
side of the house. *There's more of gravy than of grave about you.*
There was a bit in the middle of the show, when Ebenezer's fiancée
gives it to him for having changed, for caring only about money.
Benedict didn't seem to care about money, or the appearance of
having any, but . . .

The house felt different. A sour smell hung in the heat, as
though a sweaty work crew had just carried a couple of pianos up
the stairs. Poppy stopped talking. Neither of them turned on the
lights. Karen put a box of decorations on the tile floor of the foyer
and whispered, "Let's go back to the garage."

They ran, and when the garage door was closed and locked
behind them, she phoned Benedict. He and Charlotte had been at the
factory and they were walking home. They were a few blocks away.

"What do you mean it feels different?"

Karen was not sure how to explain. "It smells wrong. It feels
wrong."

"It feels like it's someone else's house now." Poppy held a
hockey stick. "Tell him that."

They stayed on the line together until he reached the house.
Then they joined Benedict and Charlotte in the foyer. He was
already on his way into the living room. "Hello?"

There was a bench in the foyer, where they kept hats and mittens. Charlotte sat on it, pale and a bit sweaty.

"Maybe stay here, girls." Karen followed her husband into the living room. He stood looking at the mantel above the fireplace, where her favourite piece of art had been removed—though not stolen. It was a painting of the summertime street she grew up on, in Edgemont, back when her dad was an executive and she was a tanning-bed-tanned high school girl on the volleyball team in short-shorts. Her father had gone out on his own, with an investment company. For his fifty-sixth birthday, her mother had commissioned this painting with the top artist in Calgary at the time, Tristan Gage. By the time Tristan finished it, her father was gone. The bastards had repossessed everything. Karen had taken the painting to Vancouver with her when she went to university. Now it lay on the floor, glistening with water. Up on the wall, in red paint, someone had written the word *emma* where the painting had hung.

There were long silences between Benedict's shouts. "Is anybody here?"

Karen pulled the phone from her back pocket and called 911. The man on the line dispatched a car immediately and wanted to keep her on the line because they did not know if the intruder was still in the house.

"Check the back door." The man on the phone had a calm voice and a Southeast Asian accent.

Karen ran across the main floor, checked it, and ran back to the foyer. "Locked."

"And the front door was locked too?"

"Yes. Should I go downstairs? The windows are—"

"Stay where you are, Ms. Sjöblad. Stay with your girls. Where is your husband?"

"Oh my God, I think he's downstairs."

"Stay with your girls. They're desperately scared, I imagine."

The operator had said a car was in the vicinity, and Karen could already hear it. Then see the lights around the corner, reflecting off the snow. Two in one month! What would her neighbours think? "They're almost here."

"I'll keep you on the line until the moment they arrive. Okay? Your husband, where is he now?"

"Still downstairs?"

"What did they write on the wall again?"

"Emma."

"Emma." The dispatcher paused, as though he were writing this down. "Do you know any Emmas?"

It began with her husband's scream, in and then out of a dream.

Karen had not wanted to get out of bed because the window nearest her was imperfect. Drafts came in. She closed her eyes and then Benedict was shouting. Still wrapped in the duvet, she lifted the blinds and looked out on the backyard. Light from the garage, triggered by a motion sensor, popped on and off. She remembered it was Halloween. It was not raining anymore and a light fog had come up. When she could see him, Benedict was on his knees in the yard, wearing blue pyjamas, next to a woman in black. Or was he on top of her? Karen's first thought was she had been a fool to think she knew this man. Beyond Benedict's silence had been a slow fire, growing every day, a twig here, a log there, every year until it was a hot roar beyond his control and on Halloween he could not help himself. He went out in the middle of the night, in his pyjamas, and jumped a woman. Then he dragged the woman here to—do what to her? What was he doing? He had not yet removed his clothes, or hers, at least not that she could see. Karen ran out of the bedroom, careful not to step on the dog who was not there, down to the back door.

"Leave that woman alone."

"Karen, no. I—"

"Benedict." She tried to whisper and shout at once. "Step away from her."

"But—"

"Step away from that woman. I'll be right out."

"Did you call the police?"

Karen picked up her phone on her way to the front door. Call the police on your husband for sexual assault? His name would be in the newspaper, his daughters' names. They would be ruined and she would be ruined—again. It was bad enough that Benedict and his company were widely mocked in the business community. Now he molested women in the yard at 3:24 in the morning. In the kitchen she paused at the magnetic wall of Japanese knives, to protect herself if it came to that, or just to punish him. Karen balled up a tea towel and screamed into it because she did not want to wake the girls, threw it on the floor, put on her jacket and boots and hat, and gathered up the same for her animal of a husband. She nearly slipped and fell on the rain-water that had frozen into a thin, invisible skating rink on the paving stones. By the time she reached him in the backyard, he was shivering, panicking, stuttering. Again, she urged Benedict to keep quiet as he put on the jacket and boots and hat.

"What the fuck are you doing out here?"

Benedict said nothing, stunned by the cold and by her presence and, she hoped, by the reality of a woman lying below him on the icy grass. His hat was crooked and his grey-black hair darted wildly out of it. Karen addressed herself to the woman on the frozen grass, who was only half-conscious and mumbling nonsense. Bad teeth. There was blood on and about her waist, but her jeans were buttoned to the top, a relief so profound Karen nearly clapped her hands. Close up, she could tell by the look of the woman and by her smell, booze breath and body odour and campfire, that she had come from the homeless camp by the old bus barns. Karen looked around: no lights were on in any of the neighbours' houses on either side of the alley.

The phone was heavy in Karen's pocket. All she had to do was dial 911 and it would be out of her control. Benedict would have to manage this himself, whatever it was. Perhaps the all-night journalists who monitored the police scanner would not bother rushing out to an injury of this sort. Karen worried one of the neighbours would look out, as the motion light continued to pop on and off, so she dragged the woman around the corner, away from the occasional glow of the garage light.

"I just ran and slid into her. I thought it was a man, breaking in." On the dark side of the garage now, with his bare feet in the boots and the parka around him, Benedict paced.

"Bullshit. I know what this is."

"The ice. And the pry bar, I have one like it. Sharp at both ends. She was using it to get into the garage and when I ran into her from behind, *I couldn't stop*, it went straight into her. She weighs nothing. She's a bird. I heard her trying to get into the house first. She was trying to get into the house when she was still a man and I thought of the girls. She's a bird though, as you can see. I'm not even wearing my glasses . . . "

Never in all their years together had Karen heard him say so many words in such a short period of time. He thought it was a man? Even from her bedroom window, half-asleep, Karen could tell the figure lying in the yard was a young woman. Benedict flopped on the grass again, his face in his hands. The woman reached for Karen and whispered something about bikes.

"You're going to be fine." Karen was no doctor but she felt the woman was not going to be remotely fine. "What's your name?"

The woman had closed her eyes at *fine*. Karen removed the thin wallet from the woman's front pocket and put it in her own jacket, even though it was wet with blood. Then, with her gloved hand, Karen picked up the weapon. The back lane was a riot of potholes, worse than Kandahar. The layer of ice on them was relatively thin so she cracked through the biggest pothole and washed the pry bar.

The thump-thump-thump of the heavy police boots on her violated floor returned Karen to her foyer, to the word *emma* painted in red above the mantel. The policewoman and her partner were dotted with new snow, and she reported this to the dispatcher, who had remained on the line with her.

"Karen? I'm going to let you go now, okay?"

You're going to be fine.

Poppy turned on the foyer light and welcomed the police with a big thank you and began crying on thank you number two. They reeked of hand sanitizer. The policewoman was the pretty redheaded one who had been here a week earlier to ask about Jak's Nazi. Constable McCaw. "Hello, Ms. Sjöblad."

"Hi again, Constable."

Before introducing themselves properly or taking off their boots, they walked directly into the living room. The short but beefy man asked if there was anyone else in the house, as he inspected the painting and the writing on the wall.

It took a moment to remember. Poppy crying into a jacket, Charlotte on the bench. "My husband. His name is Benedict. I think he's downstairs."

Neither pulled a gun. They muttered to one another and then split up, Constable McCaw going upstairs and the man down. It seemed pointless for Karen and the girls to remain in the cool foyer so she slipped into the living room and sat on the couch. Poppy joined her.

It was comforting to have police in the house. There was a part
of her that wanted to run upstairs and explain, to Constable McCaw,
that she had not mentioned the Nazi to anyone else in the family. If
she could kindly keep that bit to herself. But there was another part
of her who wanted everyone else in the family to know there was
something vile in the house—in her past, *in her blood*. Her missing
father and her Nazi grandfather and other ancestral misdeeds were
set to ruin Christmas for them.

What happened in an investigation like this? Would they look
on the top shelves of closets? Karen had placed the bloody wallet
with her dried-out weed and some foreign currency in a tin cookie
container with a painting of a fat baby on the top. Not that there
was anything incriminating in the wallet: a library card without a
name, $12.65, and a cracked photograph of an exhausted-looking
woman with tanned skin. Maybe the police knew what had happened here on Halloween night. That was their real reason for
showing up so quickly. Maybe they had written *emma* on the wall,
the police themselves, to draw the truth out of Karen and Benedict.
It was a set-up, a ruse, a sting. The police had seen Karen and
Benedict on CCTV, dragging the bloody woman through the alley.
Constable McCaw and her partner had been spying for weeks,
tapping their phones and collecting whatever proof and data they
needed to arrest and charge them with murder. They had assumed
Karen and Benedict knew the dead woman's name.

No. No, the name Emma had not been in the wallet. This was
a couple of young constables, not wizened detectives. If her name
was Emma, who had sneaked in to write it? Maybe, just maybe,
the young woman had lived through Halloween night. Either she
or one of her friends from the homeless camp had broken into
the house. It was both a relief and a different sort of threat: not of
a life in prison but torture and chaos, blackmail.

Emma wanted something.

Unless she had died and had written it on the wall. Unless
Johnny Sjöblad had done it. Wait. There was a smell in the living
room, and now that she had moved from panic to anger to fear,
she recognized it. "Do you smell that?"

Poppy crept to the painting, leaned over it, and slowly
straightened her back. "Oh geez. Yep. It's pee. They peed on
your painting."

Neither Karen nor Benedict had told Poppy about the urine
in the Tesla. Charlotte did know because they had asked if she
had ideas about removing the smell in the suv, given the chemical composition of piss.

"Uh, Mom? Why would someone pee on a painting? Why not
steal it, or steal something? Did they steal our stuff or just pee on
things? What else did they pee on?"

The policewoman walked down the stairs and looked in the
main floor bathroom and closets. "All the windows are locked
from the inside, at least up there. And you told dispatch the doors
were locked."

"From the inside, yes."

The ginger policewoman went to the back door, muttering to
herself. She was tall, with a dancer's grace that clashed with her
clunky boots. "Locked with the deadbolt like this?"

"Yes."

"The other . . . issue we had here. You said the door was
unlocked that day."

Karen motioned toward Poppy with her right eyebrow. *Shut
up about the Nazi in front of the kid.* All the doors were locked that
day too, but let's not go there. "Yes. So not relevant."

"Everything is relevant, Ms. Sjöblad." The policewoman went
downstairs to join her partner and Benedict. The smell of urine had
grown stronger now that Karen knew what it was. Poppy was crying on the couch again, her knees pulled up into her chest. "Imagine

being the sort of person who breaks into someone's house just to pee on something beautiful. Imagine all the things that must have happened to him, to do that."

"Or her."

"Imagine, Mom."

Karen had already imagined plenty. Her own father's final Christmas, when she was seventeen. Despite the death threats and his upcoming trial for securities fraud, wire fraud, mail fraud, money laundering, theft, and various crimes related to lying to government regulators and police, he was outrageously jolly on Christmas Eve. He drank too much eggnog and sang too loud. There were no presents because their bank accounts were frozen but her father wrote poems for her and for Jeanette, poems of regret and shame, poems asking for their forgiveness. He read them aloud Christmas morning, in his Ralph Lauren cardigan. They had a quarter share of a big house near Radium Hot Springs, and on Boxing Day Johnny said he was heading out there to meet with the repossession people. That morning, over Swedish pancakes with maple syrup, was the last time they saw him.

Her mother became a prescription drug addict. According to the popular theories, this trauma should have made Karen an absolute basket case. Instead here she was, a multimillionaire and an entrepreneur with her own design firm. *Malaise*, yes, she could accept that. She did allow a man with dreadlocks and feet warts to kiss her. But she didn't go around hurting people, stealing their bikes and power tools, pissing in their cars and on their art, and blaming it on something that had happened in the 1990s or the 1940s or the 1880s.

Poppy shifted and lay on the couch with her head on Karen's lap and Karen said, "Shhh," and petted her daughter's hair and tried to meditate it away: the blood of the thief in her backyard, the ghost of her father upstairs, Jak and his mouth and hair and Birkenstocks, and the Nazi.

The pandemic would break and they would leave this place and move to some progressive corner of America, with palm trees and organic markets, grapevines and hot sun and righteous rage. Her most glamorous design job had been as part of a team working on a luxury hotel brand, eight years ago. They stayed for two days at a spa in the Claremont district of Berkeley. Just off the grounds, beyond the pool and the tennis courts, there was a café that smelled of burnt coffee beans and fried bacon and onion and eggs, where prosperous but humble people read newspapers and ate and drank of a morning, and conversed, and hardly looked at their phones. It was dark but lamplit in there at eleven a.m. and the people who worked behind the counter had university degrees. Karen wanted so badly to be permanently among these Americans, cool and confident in a cool and confident climate, where it rained too much in certain seasons but never turned brown, never snowed. There were mountains alive with growth. They almost never had to wash their cars. Her meditation had fused with prosperity theory: thinking and believing and willing the universe into remoulding itself around her. Build the imperfect weather of the Pacific Northwest around her, and a reliable café with the lights out, surrounded by green shrubbery all year round and people who knew they deserved it.

When the police officers and Benedict reached the main floor, Karen opened her eyes. Back to the snowy flatlands of Belgravia, to the scent of urine. She eased Poppy off her lap and stood up to accept the verdict. The policewoman took off her hat and introduced herself to the whole room as Constable McCaw and her partner as Constable Park. Beautiful red hair! Why be a cop? She was about to say more, possibly about Nazis, but the smell emanating from the floor interrupted her. "Is that . . . urine on the painting?"

"And as you know, the people who broke into our garage a couple of weeks ago pissed in our car." Karen looked down at the pissed-on painting, along with everyone else. "I don't think you can fix that."

"New painting." Constable McCaw shook her head. "New carpet."

"Here's the thing." Constable Park reminded Karen of one of her high school boyfriends, Stan Yoon, who ended up being gay. "We can't find any sign of forced entry. The doors were locked and bolted; the windows, locked. It doesn't even look like someone *tried* to get in through the windows."

Benedict stood off to the side and stared at the pissed-on painting.

"So you're saying . . . " Karen reached down and mussed Poppy's hair, as she was on the verge of crying some more. "What are you saying?"

"All we can say, Ms. Sjöblad, is that no one broke in here tonight. We'll ask you to look carefully through the house to see if anything was taken or similarly ruined."

"What if the thief, or marauder, whatever you call a person who breaks into a house and pisses on things and writes messages on the wall, what if he's still in the house?"

"Or she." Poppy held back a sob. "Oh my God, what if he's in my closet?"

The police officers looked at each other, and a few minutes later they were playing high-stakes hide-and-seek, everyone looking in all the dark places a person could squeeze into: closets, under beds, storage areas. There was no point looking in the attic. After they had blown insulation into it, they had painted over the door and the integrity of the paint had not been disturbed.

It wasn't until they spoke of the paint on the attic door that Constable Park asked about the word *emma*. Did they know any Emmas?

Karen was alone on the second floor with Constable Park. Benedict was not a man who lied and they did not *know* they did not know an Emma.

"Nope." She prayed McCaw wouldn't ask Benedict the same question, wherever she was. "I told the dispatcher. And I know we don't have any red paint."

Constable Park led Karen back downstairs. He inspected the desecrated wall above the mantel where they kept a miniature porcelain New England Christmas village, complete with cotton snow. They had to sidestep the piss painting.

Constable Park pulled the ottoman over and stood up on it, to get a closer look at the wall. Karen briefly closed her eyes, returning to her meditation on the couch. *Please don't let it be blood. Please don't let it be blood.*

He didn't touch the paint but he smelled it and shrugged. "Paint, I guess. It wouldn't be this deep and clear if it were something else."

"Like blood?"

"I didn't want to be the one to say it." Constable Park climbed down. "Blood goes brown, anyway, when it oxidizes. It doesn't stay red like this. Can you give me the timeline again? Mr. Ross was out all day. Then your older daughter . . . "

"Charlotte. She went to see him downtown."

"And that was at what time?" The policeman pulled out his little notebook. "Late afternoon, you said?"

"Maybe four o'clock."

"You and Poppy stayed here until when?"

"We left at five thirty, so we could have dinner before the play. It was a thing in the lobby of the theatre."

"And you locked the door?"

"Locked and bolted, front and back, and as you saw the windows are all locked for the winter."

Constable Park looked up from his notebook. "It was locked when you returned."

"Yes."

"You and Poppy first. Charlotte and Benedict were . . . "

"A few blocks away."

"You're sure about that?"

Karen shrugged. "Yes."

"And you're sure there was no one else but you two in the house when you left?"

This was a nauseating thought. "I guess I . . . No, I can't be sure of that."

"And does anyone else have a key to your house?"

"Two of our neighbours have keys. We keep them in case someone gets locked out."

"Can you tell us about these neighbours?"

One set was with the Mushinskys, who were in their seventies. She had not seen them in almost a year, as Mr. Mushinsky had chronic bronchitis and they worried the virus would kill him. The other was a family from Morocco, Lena and Abbas, with three children, all under six. She did not want the constable knocking on her neighbours' doors unnecessarily at midnight so she explained how they could not have done this.

The constable made some notes. "Someone could have been in the house, earlier."

"I guess."

"Do you generally leave the doors open when you're home?"

So Constable McCaw hadn't spoken to her colleague about the Nazi thing. "Yeah."

"And no Emmas. Nothing strange lately? People hanging around?"

"The last community association newsletter mentioned a crime spree. Constable McCaw took the report, when we had our bikes and things stolen, and said there'd been a bit of a run in the neighbourhood. That homeless camp . . . I don't know."

While she could not judge his hidden mouth and nose, the rest of Constable Park's face was handsome. The top half of his body was cartoonishly thicker than the bottom. While she wasn't an expert in working out, she imagined him spending all his time in the gym doing bench presses and bicep curls, forgetting his legs. Stan Yoon had spent a lot of time on his upper thighs and ass, when she went to the gym with him back in grade eleven. Both their families had memberships at the Glencoe Club, where the oil executive kids gathered to lift weights, play video games, and make out. Stan's dad got a transfer to The Hague before Johnny Sjöblad's great undoing, so Stan Yoon never had a chance to turn on her like all the other Glencoe kids, like her classmates at Strathcona-Tweedsmuir.

"Do you collect a bit of the urine and do a DNA test?"

"Well . . . "

She heard, in the tone of his voice, that they could probably spend all day every day doing DNA tests. There likely wasn't enough lab space or technicians to do all the work, especially during a pandemic, and not enough people in the database for petty crimes like this to warrant it. The Ross-Sjöblads would change the locks, engage a security company, and call their insurer to add a painting and a rug to the list of stolen items from the garage. Constables Park and McCaw were not here to solve the crime. They were agents of a financial system, dressed up like protectors.

Karen yawned and tried to stifle it. Even if they had no way to protect her, she did not want the police to leave, as thinking of

Stan Yoon made her think of her dead liar of a father up in Charlotte's room again, standing over her as she slept. If the ghost of Johnny Sjöblad had been watching her these past months, he knew. He knew what Benedict had done to the woman in the yard. He had watched Jak kiss her and remove his trousers and underpants in her bedroom and maybe her father knew she was wondering what Constable Park would look like greased up with coconut oil in a pair of tight white briefs. Soon the house would be empty of police, with the scent of piss floating through it and the menace of knowing it could happen again, that some of the magic of the world was against her. The house watched and listened. It was against her.

Emma.

Again Karen yawned, though she was not tired. The living room stretched in front of her and the air chilled and carried an old smell beyond urine, an ancient smell, which she recognized from the day of Jak, the day her father returned. The yawn would not end and she felt lightheaded for a moment, woozy enough to bend over and put her hands on her knees. "I'm going to faint."

Constable Park said her name as a question as she toppled into darkness.

Johnny Sjöblad bent over Charlotte in the night, and with his cigarette-yellow lips he exhaled into her. Charlotte was sick and getting sicker, thin and getting thinner. The specialists could not figure it out. How could doctors know the girl's lost grandfather was breathing death into her in the night? Charlotte opened her eyes. When Karen opened her own eyes, those who had been playing hide-and-seek stood over her: Benedict and Poppy and Constable McCaw. Constable Park kneeled, his hand under Karen's head. She was close enough that she could smell garlic in the thick polyester blend of his slacks.

Karen sat up. "Where's Charlotte?"

FOURTEEN

In the factory, the best engineering minds in the world were two nights from the end. Benedict had felt their failure through the wall. He was failing too, in his painting bay workshop, failing in all the usual ways. He had done the environmental calculations and had decided he could not drive a jacked-up orange Toyota truck off the James MacDonald Bridge. It would mean leaking oil and gasoline and other noxious fluids into the river system that was the basis of the city's drinking water. Instead he would walk with the ghost across the High Level Bridge and jump off truckless. The insurance policy was a modern bit of work. Suicide was the result of a mental illness, not a financial strategy. Karen and the girls would be okay.

He was about to give up and write a note when the phone in his pocket vibrated with a text from Charlotte.

Mom and Poppy are going to the theatre tonight.

They had originally purchased season's tickets to the theatre because Karen had seen it in a book about marriage. It forced a couple to get dressed up, go to dinner, and spend an evening together once a month. In three years they had gone to the theatre twice. Every other time, Karen had either taken Poppy or her friend Melissa. She did not even ask him anymore. Tonight was a howlingly expensive fundraiser for the unfortunate artists, and even if Benedict could calm himself sufficiently to concentrate on *A Christmas Carol*, he could not imagine making small-talk with property developers in the lobby.

Okay.

There was a long pause, as Charlotte composed a response to this.

Mom says I should join you.

The good thing about Charlotte is she could come and work with him on Kutisi, and they could go three hours without speaking and it would be entirely acceptable for them both. Benedict had always found her to be an ideal companion. With Charlotte, there was never any pressure on him to be anyone other than who he was, and he was careful to ensure she felt similarly when they spent time together. It would be a different case with nearly everyone else in her life, as it was with him.

At first it had been terrifying to let the wizards in on his secret. Yet there was pleasure in it too, sharing his failure. The wizards' contracts protected him and it protected them. None of them would want to tie their reputations to a fraud and a charlatan.

Was he ready to share the truth with Charlotte? On his phone he typed several variations of *no* and erased every one of them. Benedict wanted to invite her into the secret.

That would be nice.

He sat on the couch and silently watched the ghost, which was now twice the size of Kutisi. When Charlotte arrived, he gave her a copy of the same package he had prepared for the wizards. She sat on the couch, reading through it with a pen, and when she was finished she said nothing. For hours they played with a small nuclear reactor without speaking, and despite the frustrations he found their time together in the painting bay of the factory to be perfect and at the end of it, Benedict told her so. He could jump off the bridge tomorrow, knowing they had shared something special. Neither of them had thought much of food so they ordered takeout hamburgers. Hers was wrapped in iceberg lettuce instead of a bun.

They sat on the patio furniture. He drank a beer and she had a glass of tap water.

Charlotte stared at him more intently than usual. With her therapist at the general hospital, they had been working on this— looking away from people, to avoid making them feel strangely, but not avoiding eye contact completely. One must aspire to Goldilocks eye contact. But Charlotte knew she could not make her father feel strange.

There was something she wanted to say, that she was working out how to say. Benedict decided to draw it from her. "I hope that was more interesting than staying at home working on . . . What are you working on?"

"Exponentially more interesting." Charlotte picked something from her teeth. "I'm playing with whether or not photons can be converted to chemical energy."

"Ah. Using water?"

She talked for a while about the experiment she was conducting in her bedroom but they both knew it was a way to avoid, however briefly, what she really wanted to say.

The beer was a wheat ale, brewed a block away from Kutisi. He thought of how it would feel, after jumping from the bridge, to hit the water. "Perhaps you'll come work for me someday."

She stared at him for a long time, as though there was something mysterious on his nose.

"The people working in the other room, what are they doing?"

"I gave them the same brief I gave you."

Then she found the part in her blonde hair and scratched it with her pinky finger. "I'm sorry."

"For what, darling?"

She pointed at Kutisi, its cover off, their tools in perfect order.

"Charlotte. The best engineering minds in the world, *in the world*, are working on it. They have a couple more days."

"It can't work, Daddy."

He looked away from her.

Two hours later, with the police, they found the note she had written on the back of an unopened envelope. The envelope had been sitting in the foyer for weeks, another form letter encouraging Karen to donate money to the New Democratic Party.

> *Dear Dad and Mom and Poppy: I did not want to disturb*
> *you but I was feeling poorly so I am walking to the hospital.*
> *I hope the police discover who is urinating on our possessions.*
> *Love, Charlotte.*

The police were eager to hit their own beds. Their report would show the culprit had most likely sneaked into the unlocked house while they were home and had waited until Karen and Poppy had left. The violator had entered with a small bucket of paint and a brush and had taken it with him upon leaving. Benedict wanted to tell the police about the woman in the backyard, but Karen dug her fingernails into the back of his hand when Constable McCaw asked if they had wronged anyone. Were they sure there was *no one* called Emma in their lives?

It all seemed simple and sinister enough, if pointless. The sleepy police gave them a list of things to do, to prevent it from happening again: change the locks immediately and keep them locked at all hours, home and away. Notice and jot down any oddities. Consider a home security system with video capability. When the constables were gone, Benedict ran to the hospital.

It can't work, Daddy.

This moved in his head like the choruses of the Christmas songs Karen played in the morning that stayed with him all day. Dolly Parton, George Michael, Bing Crosby, Mariah Carey. Benedict wished he had asked Charlotte to keep it a secret, what she had discovered about Kutisi, but she knew well enough to keep his failure, his fraud, to herself. The check-in app in the emergency room led him to a lengthy checklist. He expected the questions to slip from the virus into something deeper: what are you hiding?

The emergency room was as full as it could be, with the chairs spaced out appropriately. Those who were able to stand, stood. The room smelled thickly of hand sanitizer. *Elf* played on a number of flat screen televisions, affixed to the wall where art had once been. The volume was on low and there were subtitles. A man dressed as an elf was fighting with a man dressed as Santa.

Charlotte leaned against the wall in a corner of the emergency room reserved for patients who were not suffering from respiratory distress. She stood on a sticker in the shape of a Christmas tree. A nurse with circles under her eyes nearly as dark as Charlotte's stood a few feet from her. When Charlotte looked up, the nurse looked up.

"You're the dad?"

"I am."

"This place is . . . slammed. I can see, from her history and from the state of her, that she's in a terrible way. Do you have the pharmaceutical supports you need, when it really blows up like this?"

Charlotte grunted. "We do. I shouldn't have come. I panicked."

"Oh, you sweetie." The nurse was small and thin, in her late twenties. She had a nose ring. Perhaps she had been a gymnast when she was Poppy's age. "I'm so sorry about all this."

Though Benedict had been clear in his order, the chef must have accidentally done something glutenous with her dinner. Or perhaps, far worse, this wasn't about gluten at all. "So we shouldn't wait?"

The nurse shrugged. "I wouldn't."

Charlotte put a moist hand on his arm and he supported her weight when they crossed patches of ice and slush, as though she were eighty. Snow was lightly falling. It was late, and the pandemic had ruined the nightclub industry. A few cars passed on University Avenue but apart from that the city was quiet.

Where was the ghost?

"Daddy, what are you going to do?"

"About the break-in? There's a list of measures we can take."

"About Kutisi."

For the first block of homes in Belgravia, decorated for Christmas and Hanukkah, he considered his answer. Benedict wanted to be honest with her, yet he wanted the most optimistic and hopeful version of honesty. "These physicists, these engineers—"

"I see," she said.

Charlotte took two anti-inflammatory pills and said she was going to bed. Marie-Claude had been phoning so Benedict called her back. Then he went into Charlotte's room to tuck her in and it was so quiet he thought at first she had fallen asleep.

"There is something in our house, Daddy."

"No. No, there isn't. The police looked."

"You know what I mean."

Benedict knew what she meant.

"Daddy, I'm afraid."

"Please don't be afraid, Charlotte."

"I'm afraid that when you close the door and I turn out the light . . ."

"You'll feel better in the morning." He stood up from the corner of her single bed with its white duvet. White walls, white furniture, dark wood floor. There was no art on her walls, only a blown-up periodic table above her workstation. She wore pink flannel pajamas and the dark rings under her eyes had grown deeper. Something was eating away at his daughter, his baby, and every day she grew smaller. Benedict did not know how to stop it. He was afraid. He wanted to go away. "You'll get some sleep and you'll feel better."

She looked at him for a long time. "It's okay, Daddy. I know there is nothing you can do about it."

"Darling."

"You can't protect us."

There was one thing he could do. He returned to her bedside and turned out her light and remained silent, prepared if the ghost were to enter. He would try to protect her, even if it was with the prayers and songs he had memorized as a child—warrior God words that did not leave him even as he forgot other, more immediate things like the names of his employees. When Charlotte fell asleep, he kissed her on the forehead and crept out of her room.

Benedict rolled up the three-thousand-dollar rug, with the painting in it, and carried them both out onto a snowy patch of the backyard. Karen and Poppy were already in bed, so he spent some time on the hardwood, disinfecting the area where the urine had gone through. Then he swept the entire room, washed it with a mop, and treated it with an ecofriendly wood polish. He checked the internet for advice and discovered that recently applied latex paint will sometimes come off with soap and warm water. For an hour, Benedict scrubbed at *emma*. Much of it did come away. Then he gently sanded what remained and stood back against the opposite wall. The Christmas lights on the tree and on the mantel lent the room a soft blue glow. It was an attractive old plastic tree, perfectly proportioned, and there was a trail of LED lights on the New England village scene on the mantel. Other random Christmas trinkets dotted the room: a Santa on an end table, three wooden reindeer, dolls and weavings, tall white-and-red nutcrackers dressed as soldiers, a few Mexican lanterns hanging from the ceiling. Now he had to decide whether to go to bed or to repaint the wall, because even with the pot lights turned off, a faint shadow of *emma* remained. While there were no actual religious ornaments in the room, all of this Christmas decor, taken together, was holy for the Ross-Sjöblad family. There were Swedish elements that Karen had inherited from her own parents, and bits that were specific to them—like the jolly lanterns, from a sea-kayaking trip Karen and the girls had taken off Baja California. He would go into Kutisi in the morning, but it did not have to be at a specific hour. The wizards did not need supervision.

Again, the ghost was not with him. He thought, perhaps, it had something to do with the name. If the woman's name was Emma, and she had sneaked into the house to write this, the part of his brain that made ghosts was finally defeated by reason. The joy and relief this brought him was unexpected, and with a jolt of fresh energy he found three-quarters of a can of Navajo White in the basement, stirred it up, taped the accent boards, and put down three days' worth of newspapers along the wall. He had painted with College Pro one summer, during his undergraduate degree, and it came back to him. It took less than two hours. The adrenaline that had powered his heart since arriving home, first the frustration that came with powerlessness, the inability to protect Charlotte, and then the realization that he was not a murderer after all, faded as he finished. The woman was not the ghost. She was alive and she wanted vengeance.

Karen's soiled painting of her home in Calgary and the rug, from a Turkish import store, were outside. The wall was better than it had been before he started. By the time Benedict was ready to step down from the chair, it was three thirty in the morning and he could feel the deepness of the night, the silence of the city, heavy in the air.

It started low, almost imperceptible. Then it entered his chest, a small engine inside him. His shoulders were sore and he did not want to apply a third coat, his bed called out to him, but he wanted to be sure the wall would be perfectly white even in the sunrise hours. The sound grew, like crinkling thick paper—a lot of paper. He was standing on the chair in front of the mantel, and his balance was imperfect when he was tired, but for a moment he closed his eyes and asked it to go away. Now it was the sound of a roaring fire. He turned slowly and the ghost was there. Only it was much bigger now, so tall it had to crouch below the twelve-foot ceilings. Benedict wanted to scream a song of bloody Jesus at it to go away, to just scream, but he did not want to wake Karen or the girls. He did not want his family to know that what he had brought into their home was growing.

"What are you?"

In an instant he understood the ghost was not the woman he had murdered or not murdered in the yard on Halloween night. The ghost was Kutisi. His lie, his fraud, his failure, his betrayal of Karen and Charlotte and Poppy and Marie-Claude and his staff and everyone else who believed in him.

The fireplace was no longer a fireplace, but among the things the Assembly of God had not taken from his inheritance was an antique set of cast iron fireplace tools that had been his grand-parents'. They were so artful that Karen displayed them. Benedict would take the heavy poker from the set and stab the monster in its middle. It could swallow him up, make him a part of it, and kill his daughter before dawn, so he had to act swiftly. Without taking his eyes off the rotten thing, Benedict stepped down from the chair. His left foot slipped on the polished wood and he fell. The chair toppled with him. In the instant before he hit the ground, his panic turned to surrender. *Take me.* When he opened his eyes and remembered how he had come to lie on the floor of the paint-smelling living room, the ghost was gone, along with the sound of fire and the hum in his chest.

There was a lump on the back of his head, and he knew there were rules about concussions, but he was too dozy to muck around with that. Benedict brushed his teeth, and he was nearly asleep when the taste of poison replaced the mint and bloomed in his mouth. He checked his watch: a few minutes after four. Again, there were sounds on the back deck: footsteps. Then noises in the yard. Benedict crawled out of bed and lifted the blind and moved the curtain to see a figure breaking into the garage. There was no time to put on socks and he could not find his glasses. Where had he left them, before going to bed? The taste in his mouth was really foul. He clomped down the stairs and straight outside, where he was sure there had been more snow. The city was blurry.

Then he was outside, on top of the woman, and her mouth was opening and closing like a recently caught fish. He had another chance! The upstairs light popped on, their bedroom light. When they bought the blinds, the woman had said never to lift them by hand. They were too fragile, too dear, yet Karen did it all the time. She appeared under the blinds now.

Then as he prepared to press against the girl's chest, to bring her back to life, she was gone. The snow had returned. There was no blood on his hands.

Karen opened the window and did her loud whisper. "What the hell?"

It was far colder than on Halloween night, and there was a layer of hard-packed snow on the paving stones, not ice. Why had he not shovelled? The back of his head hurt, hurt so much it felt like one of the throbs could burst through his skull. Back in the house, where it was so deliciously warm he could have curled up right there on the hard tiles of the foyer, he made the habitual motion of taking off his shoes. Only he was not wearing shoes, so he wiped the melting snow from his bare feet.

When he walked into the living room it was back on the wall, exactly as it had been, only deeper against the fresh Navajo White: *emma*.

FIFTEEN

In the lobby before *A Christmas Carol*, every couple was assigned a separate white table with a few tapas: meat and vegetable skewers, a bit of kale salad, cheese, chips and dips. Poppy savoured each bite but only a few bites. When her mother went to the restroom, she filled her plate with food and flagged the waiter to take it away. He looked down at the untouched skewers and salad and cheese and back up at her.

"Is it not . . . good?"

"Very good. Thank you."

Now, lying in bed, it felt like her stomach was devouring itself. This was a feeling Poppy had come to adore, as pain meant progress, but it was never easy to sleep.

Her dad was downstairs painting. She had closed her door but she could smell the fumes when the furnace kicked in. You close your eyes and think only about your breath, in and out, and if any other thought comes into your mind you brush it away. Imagine yourself with a brush, sweeping thoughts of school or food or

singing or acting or Instagram or the word *Poppy* scraped into the
bottom of a desk by the pointy end of a compass one day.

Someone walked in the hall. Her mom, she hoped, on the
way to the toilet. Charlotte was a famously hard sleeper. She
peed her bed until she was nine. But it wasn't just one trip to the
toilet and back. These footsteps were constant, like someone was
pacing, and Poppy knew it was not her mom. Her room was cold
again and the hunger turned to dizziness. She could not concentrate on her breath, and it would never let her sleep. The house
would not let her sleep. Her dumb dance routine was part of the
Christmas concert and she needed sleep so she could remember
all the moves, so she could stay in time.

Poppy did not want to get up, or even to open her eyes, but she
had no choice. There was a woman in the hall with short white hair
and sunspots on her forehead, wearing a flannel nightie. She was
somehow young and old at once. There was a word for how skinny
she was, this woman, on the far side of anorexia, but Poppy could
not remember it. The woman's legs were bare from her knees
down, and they were impossibly thin. Bones, really, and covered
not in sun spots but sores.

"Who are you?"

The woman was almost as tall as Charlotte. She continued
pacing from one end of the hall to the other, hunched over, mumbling to herself.

"Are you Emma? Did you write your name on our wall?"

The woman stopped for a moment and looked up. There was
so much pain and worry and confusion in her tiny eyes—Poppy
had tiny eyes just like them—and in those awful legs that carried
it all. She could not tell what the woman had been mumbling.
They recognized one another. The woman opened her mouth to
scream.

Poppy opened the door to her parents' room. Only a tiny bit of light made it into their bedroom through the blind, from the street lamp in the alley, but still her mom could not handle it so she wore two sleeping masks.

"Mom."

Before she said what she wanted to say, had to say, Poppy paused. She knew the woman.

"Emma is here."

Her mother sat up and ripped the masks off, threw them. "What? Where?"

"In the hall."

She reached next to her. "Where is your father?"

"Downstairs. Painting."

Her mom looked around, in the light from the hallway. At first Poppy couldn't tell what she was doing and then she realized her mom was looking for a weapon. There was a pen on her side table. She held it like a hammer.

Together they crept through the bedroom and into the hall. It was not cold anymore. The thin woman wasn't in the hall and she wasn't in Poppy's bedroom or the office, where the fat woman had been. Her mom, still half-asleep, led Poppy back to bed and hugged her and kissed her.

"What did she look like?"

Poppy did not want to say. "Maybe she is the house."

"Shhh."

"But I don't see how she could write her name on the wall, Mom. She was too weak."

"That doesn't sound like Emma, honey."

"What?"

"Like how I imagine Emma." Her mom pulled up the duvet, tucked her in. "You just had a dream."

"She was . . ."

"Goodnight, my sweet."

Tears popped in her eyes. "Please don't leave. It might get cold again and the house will make me get up and see her. Sleep with me."

Her mom slipped under her covers and Poppy hugged her.

When her alarm went off in the morning, her mom was already up and Poppy did not feel she had slept at all. A Meghan Trainor Christmas song was playing downstairs. She was ashamed to have cried, to have needed her mom like that.

In the coming days, Poppy would swear she spoke to Charlotte that morning, about *emma* on the wall. Her mom and dad were in the kitchen, whispering about it. Both of them looked tired and miserable. None of this made sense: that her dad put a new coat of white paint *around* the red word. Why did he bother staying up so late, just to ignore the problem he was meant to solve? Her dad was a scientist: so precise and serious he only smiled if someone was taking a picture of him, and it never showed in his eyes. There was nothing jokey or forgetful about him, yet that is how her mom tried to sell it.

"Your dad was feeling silly last night. He was so tired. He thought he would start by painting around the word. The word itself: we'll do it today."

Poppy would never call her parents liars, not out loud, but it hurt her feelings that her mom would say something so obviously wrong, that she would think Poppy and Charlotte were dumb enough to believe one word of it. Charlotte was there, having porridge with her. *She must have been.* This is what she said later to the police: where else would Charlotte have been, at seven o'clock in the morning?

That is how Poppy remembered it: porridge together. But she was so tired her eyes actually hurt. Was she sure she had seen Charlotte at breakfast? No. Not sure of anything anymore.

After her shower, when it was time to walk to school, Charlotte was definitely gone. Her mom recalled Charlotte warning her about a morning she had to be at school early to prepare for a group presentation in English or maybe social studies. It was just like Charlotte to forget to tell her family she was leaving early.

It was cold for the first time in weeks, someone had pissed on their stuff, a fat woman and a thin woman had haunted her, her eyes were sore from crying, and she had hardly slept. Tonight was the Christmas dance recital so Poppy had to carry a bag with her shoes and costume, along with her lunch and dinner. She was on the verge of crying again so her mom drove her to school.

It was a sleepy afternoon. Exams were in a week and she would get an A in everything that mattered. While Poppy was no Charlotte, she understood how school worked. Even if she didn't get everything, she could memorize and repeat it back. She knew how to give her teachers exactly what they wanted in the long-answer bits. Something from the morning, as her mom and dad whispered at one another in the kitchen: Poppy was sure she heard her dad say he had painted over *emma*.

That it had come back.

If that was true, it meant she was right. The house was doing this. Poppy had not imagined the more-than-anorexic white-haired lady who shared her little eyes. The fat one could not have painted it. Unless they were the same person somehow, changing from one into the other. And if that was possible, maybe they—it—could become a paint brush. Or just *be paint*. There were no rules to any of it anymore, just as it didn't matter if you lied or stole. She did not have an account but when the pandemic was really bad, she looked on her mom's Twitter at what the American president had said and it gave her such a thrill, to know she could say or do *anything* as long as she had money.

Blaine was her friend again. So many kids who had ignored
her wanted to be her friend now, as though she could give them
something. It was stupid. Just because her dad's company had lots
of money didn't mean she had any. Obviously they didn't notice
but she was wearing the same clothes today that she wore back
in October, when they were apparently poor. At the theatre, all of
these people in suits and dresses made sparkle-eyes at her mom
and paid attention to her. The mayor even! She felt so good, in
the moment, but it was all starting to seem fake. On the way to the
car, her mom had explained that Kutisi had been invisible to them
all, even something shameful, but now it was different. Her dad
could build a factory here and he could give a whole bunch of
jobs to people who had worked in oil and gas and were now
unemployed. Her dad could solve a problem for the city, the whole
province, the whole country. Also, it was glamorous to be rich.
Everyone knew the mayor's name but he had not really built anything. He had not come up with anything new. Politicians do not
give. They take. All of those things that matter to a politician, not
one of them matters to your dad.

Your dad builds things.

There was a final dress rehearsal after school, to prepare for
the show at seven. Some days, when she was dancing, it felt like
everything was going too slow for Poppy. Every movement was
crisp and delicious, and there was enough air in her lungs for ten
performances in a row. She had not had one of those days in a long
time. Poppy had eaten three slices of red pepper and a carrot for
lunch, and with her ritual "Sorry, Mommy," she had thrown the
corn chowder into the silver garbage bin outside the old gymnasium. What annoyed her was that in two months she had only
lost seven pounds. If she looked at herself in the full-length mirror, in her bra and panties, she couldn't even tell.

Chubbin' it up.

Blaine was in the show, though she was not in Poppy's "Santa Baby" routine. "God Rest Ye Merry, Gentlemen" was a sombre dance to a spooky cello rendition of the song. "God Rest Ye" was only three people shuffling around barefoot on the junior high stage, to their own choreography; Aoife had won a competition in contemporary dance in Vancouver and convinced the teacher, Ms. Reyes, to let her choreograph. Since Blaine was her new best friend, she got to be in it along with a boy named Seth. They got to wear black tights and these red capes. Of course, Blaine also wore her Rolex. She always pretended to be cool about it, like it didn't matter. *Oh this?*

Poppy had no idea what Aoife's random and pretentious choreography had to do with the Jesus-y lyrics, but since it was goth and dark it was cool. If Billie Eilish had to choose a dance to be in, she would have chosen Blaine and Aoife's spooky rendition over stupid, embarrassing "Santa Baby." When the final dress rehearsal was done, and they were ninety minutes from curtain, they sat in front of their lockers and ate their dinners. Poppy was so hungry and so tired, but she had set a goal for herself to lose ten pounds by Christmas and to keep those pounds off even with all of the sweet temptations of holiday time. She had gained most of this weight in the late winter and spring, when they were isolated at home, when the only thing to do was eat tortilla chips and watch *Brooklyn Nine-Nine*.

Her mother had asked her not to tell anyone about the break-in, though she could not say why. Poppy suspected it was because they were supposed to have a fancy and perfect life, the life people advertise on Instagram, without anyone or anything pissing on paintings or writing *emma* on the wall. The truth frightened people. Maybe it was because Poppy had slept so shittily but she absolutely had to tell someone. Blaine was sitting across the white tile floor, next to Aoife, who was an absolute artist when it came to looking pretty and sad: green eyes, lots of makeup.

She started to tell the two of them what had happened, without going into detail. Someone had broken in, and they knew it instantly when they arrived at home. The smell, the feeling.

"Like feeling violated?" Blaine slipped a cookie into her mouth and offered Aoife one.

Poppy wanted a cookie. She wanted ten cookies. "Yeah but more than that. You know when you do something and you feel guilty about it, and no one knows, and then it seems like all at once *everybody knows?*"

Across the hall from her, with cookie in their mouths, Blaine and Aoife looked at one another and started laughing at the same time.

"Uh. No?" Aoife draped her left leg over Blaine's right leg, to broadcast her ownership. "That's so fucked up. What did you *do* anyway? You're the goodiest good girl in town."

Now that Blaine was allowed to be friends with Poppy again, Aoife wanted everyone to understand how things really worked. Blaine was *hers*. Normally this annoyed Poppy so much she chose to walk away and try not to cry, but today she was too tired and too hungry to care. When she had a cold, her mom gave her a drug called Actifed that helped her sleep. An hour after she took it, she would sit in front of the television in a wonderful haze. Everything was a bit funny and none of the usual things mattered. She felt a bit like that now, in the hallway. For a few minutes she closed her eyes and maybe she dozed, because when Ms. Reyes began clapping at the end of the hall it seemed to interrupt a dream.

Poppy walked behind Blaine and Aoife, who held hands. This had something to do with boys, with making them think you were mysterious and sexy. Blaine had asked Poppy to do it from time to time at the end of seventh grade.

Why?

We want them to talk about us, to think about us. We want to scare them a little.

Being mysterious was not a natural strength of Poppy's. She smiled too much and talked a lot when she was nervous. When someone was indifferent to her she tended to turn on the energy, which often transformed into "trying too hard," and in the middle of doing it she knew she was trying too hard but she could not stop. Both Blaine and Aoife were thinner than her, and Aoife already had quite a set of boobs. When she fell asleep at night, sometimes Poppy would imagine the perfect version of herself: maybe two inches shorter and forty pounds lighter, with perfect skin and eyes like Charlotte's, hair that always looked like she had spent a day at the beach. She was a fat-faced farm lady and her sister was an exotic Swedish princess, which was backward because Charlotte didn't even give a shit. *Chubbin' it up.* How many times a day did she hear those words, in Blaine's voice, reminding her? Walking behind them, on the way to the gym, she estimated: thirty. Thirty times a day while she was awake and conscious.

There were a bunch of Christmas trees on the way to the gymnasium. Each class had decorated one and put it out in the corridor. Someone had turned off the bright fluorescent lights so the trees, lit up for the evening, would twinkle cozily and remind us of what it felt like to be five with *The Grinch* on. Poppy wanted to curl up underneath one of the trees like she did when she was five. She would fall asleep and her dad would pick her up. Poppy was a light sleeper. She would wake immediately. "Be careful," her mom would say. "Gentle. Shhh." Her mom did not want her to wake up because it would be hard to get her back to sleep. Poppy would remain floppy and pretend to be asleep all the way up the stairs. As her dad lowered her onto her sheets, she would give him a kiss and whisper, "I love you." She wanted to be five again, when her dad still carried her, when she did gymnastics, when friends weren't a threatening mirror in front of her, when there were no thieves, and nightmares stayed nightmares.

When they arrived backstage Ms. Reyes gave them a pep talk about getting into the zone and feeling the movements in your bones rather than trying to remember them. "I know you remember. I just watched you do it. Now, in front of the audience, I want you to go *deep into yourselves* and let the music and the motion take you away: crisp when crisp, soft when soft, fast when fast, slow when slow."

It sounded like a speech for Blaine and Aoife, and for a couple of the other groups who had courageously decided to do Ms. Reyes's favourite: interpretive dance. How deep into yourself could you go with "Santa Baby"?

"Pardon me?" said Ms. Reyes.

It took a moment of her classmates looking at her for Poppy to realize she had accidentally asked this question that was not really a question out loud. There was silence, and Poppy hoped it would go away.

"Poppy?" There was hurt in her dance teacher's voice, or something like it. "Could you repeat that?"

"I meant for it to be my inside voice. I'm sorry, Ms. Reyes. I promise to go deep into myself."

Some of the kids laughed. Poppy had meant it sincerely but there had been an accidental slash of sarcasm in her voice. There were only two boys in the dance class and neither of them were like the other boys. Their friends were girls and they reacted more girlishly than girls in moments like this. "Oh my *God*," said Seth.

Poppy could tell Ms. Reyes was trying to figure out if she ought to ask for a one-on-one conversation. She was one of the youngest, coolest teachers at the school and everyone in dance loved her, even if she consigned them to the back of the chorus because they weren't thin and bendy like Blaine and Aoife. On a normal day this would seem a crisis. But tonight she was too tired and too hungry to care a terrible lot about Ms. Reyes's feelings. It was a stupid and embarrassing thing Ms. Reyes had said. She was in "Santa Baby" and the other regular girls were in "Wonderful Christmastime." They were more or less line dances, impossible to screw up, and lacking any real technical skill or imagination. The more she thought about it, the more Poppy realized it was Ms. Reyes who should be apologizing to her, to all of the regular girls.

It was so awful to be a regular girl. Would she always be a regular girl?

Everyone was looking at her. Blaine's already-huge eyes were open as wide as they could go and she mouthed, *What are you doing?* This was a gentle slap. Poppy did not want every girl in junior high dance to look at her, not for this, but she was too tired to remember what she had said.

Then she remembered.

"It's just that 'Santa Baby' is such a jolly song, that's all. You know how you play whale music, during savasana? On yoga Thursdays? 'Santa Baby' is not like that. How 'deep into yourself' can you go when you're asking Santa to hurry down the chimney? That's all I meant."

After a moment or two, Ms. Reyes nodded. "Poppy, are you okay?"

"Yep."

"You're not sick? Not on any . . . medication?"

"Medication? No, no, everything is cool. You can all just go back to looking at other stuff now, 'kay?"

And they did, eventually. Though she heard variations on *weird* for the next hour, as the special pandemic audience filled the squeaky hard plastic seats in the gym. All the windows were open and the chairs were spaced a metre and a half from one another. On the radio they talked about how the government allowed exceptions for Christmas things, that it had something to do with keeping the religious people and conspiracy ding dongs happy. Her mom had shouted at the radio, that it was a trap. Just lock us up! Or don't! She did not like having to decide between going to the Christmas concert or not. A lot of parents complained about the show, that the school was being irresponsible, that it was allowed. The school said what the government said. Parents didn't *have* to come. They didn't *have* to send their kids. Poppy peeked around the curtain to see where her parents and Charlotte were sitting but it was too dark, there were too many parkas, too much standing, and everyone wore masks. The actual concert would not matter to her dad and Charlotte. They would want to be somewhere else no matter what, even if she and her classmates performed a flawless version of *The Nutcracker*. It was a long program and more than half of it was interpretive dance, her mom's least favourite art form after pop country music. Why bother even memorizing it as a routine when you just run around barefoot pretending to be electrocuted, then pretending to be splashed with water, then swimming in the air, then rolling around, reaching for things that aren't there? "Santa Baby" was more of her mom's thing, an old-fashioned song-and-dance line without the singing, but Poppy was the third row from the back and Allison Michuki, one of the biggest girls in the school, was right in front of her.

This was another reason why Ms. Reyes shouldn't be offended. Tonight, Poppy was an entirely irrelevant figure in the show: third from the back, stuck behind Allison Michuki, in the least spectacular dance of the night. The dance specifically designed for the big, the mediocre, the forgotten. Why did she bother looking at or listening to Poppy at all? She was irrelevant, a ball of holiday lint.

It was a secret that Poppy felt these feelings or even noticed how it all worked. She was supposed to smile and accept it, and she had it good. Better than good! Anything she wanted, in the whole world, she got. What about actual poor kids, or desperately ugly ones, those anxious boys who couldn't finish an exam, the ones in rough schools who were already on drugs and in gangs and having sex in grade eight?

"Wonderful Christmastime" was first. Poppy's call time was not for another forty minutes so she paced back and forth, at the back of the stage, without getting in anyone's way. She thought of the obese woman in her dad's office, and the anorexic—*bulimic*, was that the word?—lady pacing the upstairs hallway. Poppy thought about them every thirty seconds or so, and something about these two women made other things seem less important. Like what Ms. Reyes and Aoife and even Blaine thought of her.

Two songs before "Santa Baby," she lined up with the rest of her troupe. Allison Michuki turned around, with her hands balled up under her chin. "Oh my God, I'm so freakin' nervous."

"Just go deep into yourself, Allison."

She winked. "You're gonna get in trouble again."

The song before "Santa Baby" was "God Rest Ye Merry, Gentlemen." The lights went out and Blaine and Aoife and Seth tiptoed into place. It was a dimly lit spectacle, with two of the red tracking lights moving haphazardly over the stage. No one would ever know it happened, if it happened, but Poppy went deep into herself and wished for Aoife to miss her big dive-and-somersault move. Aoife was supposed to take a couple of big steps and leap over Seth and land in a rolling ball, like a hedgehog, and bounce back on her feet, into Blaine's arms: Christmas grace and athleticism. Poppy imagined it going terribly wrong and when it came time Aoife took her two big, duck-footed steps and began to launch herself into the air. Just then, Seth sat up. The bottom of one of Aoife's legs crashed into his face and instead of somersaulting she belly-flopped in an ungainly fashion. It was not bad enough for anyone to be seriously hurt but Aoife was definitely winded.

For most of the audience, it would have seemed as good as anything else they had seen. If everything feels random, why not that? But then Aoife rolled on the floor, gasping for air. Seth held a hand over his face and said, "Fuck!" On the opposite side of the stage, Ms. Reyes waved her arms at Mr. Beifus, who ran the lights and sound from a computer board, and everything went dark. At "Christ our saviour" the song stopped, and after a few tense moments, when all they could hear was Aoife honking and thrashing on stage, someone in the audience began to clap. Seth and Blaine helped Aoife off the stage. There were tears in her eyes and Seth was holding his face and whispering, "Sorry" and "I don't know what happened to my brain."

While Poppy had conjured many terrible fantasies in her life, she saw herself the way Aoife saw her, as the goodiest good girl in town. She had never pinched or punched or kicked anyone, or lied to get anyone in trouble, or told on kids for the endless grotesqueries and assaults that marked late elementary and junior high school. But she had done something to Aoife with her mind. This was what people meant by the power of prayer. Ask for it, believe, and it is done.

Allison Michuki mock-jogged in front of her, and Poppy was shoved into her place on the stage. The air was different here, warm and stale, and it smelled a bit sour, like ten armpits leaking through baby powder. She felt cold-medicine woozy, like before, only now it wasn't pleasant at all. In movies and books there is always a villain, someone who wants the worst and tends not to get it. They fall off a cliff or disappear into a life of off-stage shame after the malice in their hearts is revealed. That was Poppy! Poppy in the movies! Aoife was the slim, perfect, and popular lawyer or rhythmic gymnast who overcomes cruelty and adversity to win the case or the gold medal. The song began playing, preposterously loud, and the lights popped green and red and bright yellow.

She made her moves, at first, and then at the opposite end of the gymnasium, above the heads of the parents and siblings who were too late to find a seat: *emma*.

It fit into other aspects of the last twenty-four hours she could not quite believe. The piss on the floor, the word at home, the woman in the hallway, and her new powers of mind control. At first, no way. Then why not? Why *wouldn't* the hauntedness follow her out of the house into the smelly gymnasium? Was the naked obese woman from her dad's office here too? The thin one? The house was not just the house. It was everything and it would follow her wherever she went.

Since Ms. Reyes had not placed her in a key role, it did not seem crucial to stay in line. Instead, Poppy danced out of the chorus line and into the forbidden open horseshoe at the front of the stage. It felt like she was lit from within by a thousand red bulbs. She could feel the other girls looking at her, though none of them did anything to help or stop her. Later that evening, when Poppy tried to go deep into herself, to understand, she confirmed the edge of the stage was irrelevant. It's not as though she thought, *I'm just going to dance off this*. She hadn't thought about it at all. All she wanted was to see if *emma* and the ghosts were really there, and to talk to her mom about it, what it meant not only for them but for the world.

If this can happen, anything can happen.

When she and Blaine had been proper friends, she would sleep over certain Saturday nights and go with her family to church on Sunday morning. She never felt her mom disapproved, exactly, but Poppy could tell something about church frightened her. It was a place of power and magic. This wasn't something she considered when she was six or seven years old, but the last time she went to church with Blaine she was already twelve. She knew a bit about the Bible and what the religion meant. The priest, or whatever he was called, was a womanish Mexican man named Juan Carlos and she found him sexy.

People could perform miracles. She had seen YouTube videos with cute street magicians in New York City making things disappear and levitating and animating objects. But dying on a cross and coming back to life a few days later was the big leagues. *If this can happen, anything can happen.*

She danced off the stage. It was two metres from the ground, the height of a tall man, not dangerously high but hardly a step. Members of the audience gasped and warned her, "No!" as she stepped off it, but she landed on her feet and continued dancing. Later, on social media, there were rumours she had floated. Gravity had a special relationship with her. That's why she wasn't hurt. Kids asked how she had done it, as though she were a street magician herself. Somehow, her mom and dad—they had both come—were so poorly situated in the back corner they did not see it, her alleged feat. *emma* was still there as she danced down the middle of the aisle and she could feel the eyes of the room on her instead of the kids on stage.

Poppy was more than halfway down the aisle, between the squeaky plastic chairs, when "Santa Baby" finished. In the brief silence she looked around to see if she could spot her parents. When she looked up again, *emma* was gone. The applause began, and the room went dark.

SIXTEEN

Poppy did not want to talk about what had happened in the gymnasium and Karen respected her for it. The eighties were a long time ago but Karen remembered moments from her early teens with filmic clarity: that time Martin Wozniak fondled her on a bus to Dinosaur Provincial Park; that time she opened a bathroom door at the ski cabin they rented outside Whistler and discovered her uncle masturbating his small, lean penis; that time she smoked hash in Kim Ryder's mom's Cutlass Ciera and spilled a nearly full Super Big Gulp of cream soda on the passenger seat; that time her friend Alanna, who was having trouble at home, broke into a car on the way to a grade ten dance and stole the stereo. Karen did not speak to her parents about these incidents. They just bubbled and roared away, their meaning expanding and changing in her personal encyclopedia of shame.

If Poppy ever did want to talk about it, the door was always open. That's what Karen said to her, when they got into the car, after the parents of other kids stared at her—at them—all the way out of the school and across the parking lot. *The door, sweetheart, is always open.*

Then Karen felt stupid for saying it. That's what bosses say in job interviews and in the movies. Did she have no original thoughts? Maybe she could stop talking entirely for a couple of weeks until she could rid herself completely of things she had heard on television. Back in university, one of her professors kept one of those laminated posters on her office wall with the line, "If the mind is shapely, the art will be shapely." Or something. Karen could not remember who had written that, but she thought about it all the time—the dangers of unshapeliness.

When Poppy revealed herself in a polyester elf costume on stage, under the hot lights, Karen did not recognize her. Her baby had become a full-figured woman. Only on stage, she wasn't nearly as full-figured as Karen had expected. Was it the lights? Had something changed, in the past few weeks or months, and had she been so preoccupied with bankruptcy and non-bankruptcy and a woman bleeding in the backyard that she had failed to notice?

Karen was so busy thinking these thoughts that she looked at her own hands for much of "Santa Baby." It had been so hard to see Poppy anyway, three or four rows back. She looked at other things, like the way some masks yanked comically at parents' ears. It was not until everyone around her gasped that Karen looked up and saw Poppy wasn't on stage anymore. She was on the gym floor, and then she spun and vamped in the aisle between the chairs. Even the girls on stage were watching her.

Poppy *had* been doing the hard work of self-fulfillment and personal transformation.

They were a few blocks from Belgravia now, waiting for the train to pass, when Karen realized she did not really want to go home. Where else could they go, could she go, instead? Something was wrong, and it was growing every day. The

Christian radio station that redeemed itself every November and December by devoting its playlist to holiday jams, 96.9 True FM, was playing a choral version of "In the Bleak Midwinter." Every other year this would have filled her with warmth and hope, especially as they waited in traffic across the street from an exceedingly jolly Christmas tree farm. She might have reached for Benedict's hand, the one he kept on the middle console, and squeezed it.

The silence was too much. "Did Charlotte tell you she wasn't coming?"

Benedict shook his head. It was not surprising that Charlotte did not *want* to go to a sweaty, crowded dance recital in a gymnasium during a pandemic. But normally she did go to such things, to support her sister. She would do anything to support Poppy.

"She didn't tell me either." Poppy had turned toward the Christmas tree farm.

"That was pretty cool, your solo bit." Karen genuinely wished she had seen the rest of it and planned to ask Benedict to describe the routine. "You said 'Santa Baby' was a regular old number but—"

"Yeah," said Poppy.

"People liked it!" Karen's job, normally a job she shared with Poppy, was to inject energy and enthusiasm into family discussions. "It was, I mean . . . there you were."

Poppy murmured. "It's not what they were expecting."

"The rhythm took you."

"I guess it did."

"But . . . it was choreographed that way."

For a while Poppy didn't respond. Then, quietly, "No."

"So you . . . " The train passed and the barrier lifted, traffic began to flow along University Avenue. Karen would have been just as content to sit in traffic for another hour or more. Despite reaching a destination she had imagined her whole life—wealth and social relevance—Karen wanted to cry.

The garage door opened. No bikes. No skis or snowboards.

"How is everything going at the factory? The engineers are here another day or two?"

"Tonight and tomorrow." Benedict drove in. "They leave Sunday morning."

Inside the house, which smelled faintly of fresh latex paint, Karen called for Charlotte. It was at first silent, as she had expected. Charlotte was far too logical to do what Karen and Poppy tended to do, communicate across floors by shouting. The space above the fireplace was white again. She had hired a couple of university student painters to do the entire wall. It had cost an extra ninety dollars to use low-VOC paint. She asked one of them, whose name was Jet—Jet!—why there would be anything *but* low-VOC paint given what we know about the dangers of volatile organic compounds.

"Same reason we use dangerous herbicides and pesticides when we grow food." Jet spoke flatly, as though he expected the worst. He and his partner, Chris, wore white coveralls and white hats as they worked and listened to Drake on a little paint-spattered Bluetooth speaker. "Same reason we didn't prepare for a pandemic even though we were warned for years. Same reason we pump animals full of growth hormones and antibiotics, and keep them in massive pens so they can't move. Same reason we burn diesel and coal and—"

"'Cause we're humans," said Chris, the cute one, tall and sandy-haired and flat-tummied.

Karen admired their work. No more *emma*. Seven hundred dollars well spent. "Charlotte! Please come down."

Of course she would be upstairs in her room, working on whatever she was working on these days. Charlotte and Benedict could sit up there for hours, hardly speaking, trying to solve an unsolvable riddle from the annals of physics and chemistry. Charlotte kept putting a huge, warped periodic table on her wall, stained yellow by nicotine and the sun, that she had bought for a dollar fifty at the estate sale of a deceased professor. Karen would take it down and three days later it would be up again, on the same part of the wall. She did not like to think of Charlotte up there alone, now that the house was possessed by her father.

Karen turned on the Christmas tree lights. Normally in December, even when she had been poor, a Christmas tree lit up in the living room was a talisman against all forces of anguish and desperation and doubt. Now that the living room had been pissed on and violated, all of the good sorcery was gone. Her dead father inhabited it. And somehow a marauder had entered their home, did her strange business, and exited *with the doors locked.*

There was a beanbag chair in the corner that had been around since the girls were little. They tended to forget it. Poppy dragged the beanbag chair out, shoved it under the plastic boughs of the tree, mushed it the way she liked it, and lay there like a wrapped present. She pulled out her phone.

"I'll make us some eggs if you go see what your sister is up to." The kitchen was just as Karen had left it; obviously Charlotte had not fixed herself anything to eat. "See if she is feeling well enough for dinner."

Benedict slowly climbed the stairs. "I'll ask her."

"Fuck," said Poppy.

"Ouch. You say that now?" They had lost certain aspects of historic designation for the old house when they had knocked down the wall separating the kitchen from the living room, replacing it with a couple of beams lined with old bricks. "Please, sweetheart. Just be thirteen."

"All the kids are talking about me."

"How?"

"On Instagram. They say I floated."

"Floated?"

"Mom, when I was on the stage I saw Emma."

Karen dropped an egg. It broke on the floor with an awful sound, and some of the yoke seeped into her wool slipper. She took a few steps into the living room. "What do you mean you saw Emma? Last night you—"

"I came out to dance the stupid dance, in the back, where the rest of the nobodies dance, and it was painted on the opposite wall of the gym. In red. Just like it was painted here."

Karen sat at a dining room chair. "You're not a nobody."

"Mom. Who is Emma?"

"I don't know."

"Yeah, I'm sorry but I think you do."

Benedict came down the stairs and looked at Poppy, lying on the beanbag chair with her iPhone. He scratched the back of his head. "She isn't up there."

"Charlotte!" Karen walked to the top of the basement stairs. The lights were off down there. "Char?"

Without her asking, Benedict went down. When he came up a few minutes later he put his jacket back on. "Yesterday she went to the emergency room without us."

Rather than return to the conversation about Emma, when Benedict stepped back out into the cold, Karen commanded Siri to play a Nat King Cole Christmas playlist. She did not want to think about Charlotte in the hospital or the word *emma* on the wall of the gymnasium. A few minutes later Poppy was asleep. When the eggs were scrambled and the broccolini was steamed, Benedict re-entered and without removing his jacket he walked across the living room and into the kitchen. "She isn't there."

"Maybe they admitted her? Was she that bad last night?"

"No."

"No to what? The hospital is out? What if they're just too concerned about the virus to keep proper records?"

Benedict sat at the little table in the kitchen.

Karen went to give him a plate of eggs and greens but her hands were too shaky and the food slipped off the plate and on to his lap. Then she didn't know what to do about it.

"What did she say this morning?" Benedict scooped some of the food off his pants and on to the table.

Karen thought back. The mornings blended together. "She . . . I guess she left early."

"Don't guess. Did you speak to her?"

"I don't know. No. I think no."

They determined the last time either of them had seen Charlotte was after she and Benedict had returned from the emergency room. She had been afraid. Benedict had stayed with her until she fell asleep. They texted her. They called her and when she heard the phone ring Karen ran to it, said her name. But the phone was on the bench in the foyer. They split up and searched the house, like they had done last night when they wanted to find a marauder. Last night Charlotte had written a note on an envelope. Perhaps there was something like that up in her room, in the office? As Karen searched, she muttered affirmations to herself. *Charlotte is here. Everything is okay. She's feeling better.*

Charlotte was not there.

For twenty minutes, as Benedict wrote words in oblong bubbles on an actual piece of paper, Karen locked herself in the bathroom and stared at herself in the mirror. Her pubic hair was growing in properly and it itched her so she scratched it. She had not eaten since her smoothie at lunch and something about Benedict's instinct to draw up a *strategic plan* to find their missing daughter ruined her. She washed her hands for a long time, dried them, and washed them again. Where does Charlotte go when the banal anarchy of modern family life is too much for her? Karen opened the bathroom door and sprinted across the living room, into the foyer, and out into the snow in her socks. She ran around the house to the backyard.

"Charlotte?"

A rope ladder was the only way up to the treehouse. It was half-frozen, slippery and shaky, and Karen imagined a stranger watching her—a stranger watching her on video. *What is that Karen doing?* Inside there were a couple of folding chairs, from the folk music festival, and a coffee table from their last iteration of downstairs furniture. Charlotte had not been in here since summer. For the first time since running out the front door, Karen felt the cold. Her wool socks were caked with snow, which made it extra difficult to climb down. On her way back into the house she laughed and cried at once.

Karen washed the mess her makeup had made, took several deep breaths to seem a normal mother, calm, in control, and woke up Poppy. They needed to know when she had last seen her sister. Also, she should eat. Fried eggs? Scrambled? Poppy did not want to eat, she said, because she'd brought dinner to school. And Charlotte? This morning. Yes, definitely this morning. No. Wait. Hold on. Was that yesterday? This morning, over porridge maybe? Maybe not. Why?

There was nowhere else to look. They could not enter her mind or her heart because she was not that sort of girl. Charlotte did not feel sorry for herself or do impulsive things or seek attention or make emotional decisions that could get her in trouble.

The next oblong bubble on Benedict's plan was: call the authorities.

Karen phoned Constable McCaw's mobile number. It turned out she and Constable Park were on shift again and would come by the house within the hour. Benedict stood in the middle of the living room as they waited. The house smelled of eggs and steamed broccolini. None of them had eaten or would eat, not now. Benedict looked down, frozen and unresponsive. Karen lied to Poppy about how it was no big deal and tucked her into bed.

The Halloween woman, Emma, had done this. Sex with her yoga teacher could not make it go away and money could not make it go away, Christmas music and the tree and the movies and the play could not make it go away. Giving ten thousand dollars to charity in one night could not make it go away. A new house on Saskatchewan Drive would be just as haunted. Emma's revenge was perfect.

She wanted Benedict to straighten his neck, to walk across the room with a normal worried-dad look on his face and speak to the officers when they arrived, but he remained standing and staring in the middle of the living room.

Before she met Benedict, Karen knew only one person like him: a boy named Warner in grade six. He was astonishingly smart but not a social wonder. One day the other boys made fun of him so cruelly, he snapped. He stiffened in his desk and began throwing everything out of it, his pencil case and his erasers, his books, his compass and protractor, and a few cut-out valentines that had been in there for months, including one from Karen because her mom made her give a valentine to everyone. While this response only made the cruel boys in the class crueller, like wolves who want to remove the limping one from their pack, it was one of the few instances in her own childhood that grew her heart. She thought of

Warner all the time and tried to find a trace of him on the internet, of his success. Karen wished she had walked across the room and held him, instead of remaining on the outer perimeter with the others who pretended to be afraid of him. The boys who had been cruel to Warner would have been the perfect age to profit from the long oil boom that ended in 2014. They would have big trucks in the garage, and snow machines and quads for hunting, maybe a boat each, but now they would be laid off and they would be blaming George Soros and Greenpeace and the cute prime minister for making it all go away. She wanted Warner to have owned one of the companies that had employed his tormentors, and she wanted him to have sold it for many millions of dollars before the crash.

She wanted Benedict to stand up straight, to welcome the police into their house and to berate them for their incompetence. She wanted to berate Benedict for his incompetence. Sure, he could invent a clean way to heat the homes of Finland but he couldn't do the simplest thing in the world: keep his family safe.

When Constables McCaw and Park arrived, Karen kept them in the foyer. Last night they had tromped through every room in the house with their boots on, and of course it was her job to clean it. Not this time, constables. And what was the point of them? Why were they even police when all they did was take notes?

They took notes. When Karen reached a point of exasperation in herself, in them, certainly in her ghoul of a husband slouching in the living room, both constables handed her a tissue.

"I guess this answers our questions, about who came in and wrote on your wall." Constable Park looked at the bare white wall above the mantel. "Who took the painting down and . . . "

"You mean Charlotte?"

Constable McCaw looked at Constable Park and he did not respond.

"Jesus Christ, man, Charlotte wouldn't have done that," said Karen. "If you knew her you'd understand. If it answers anything, it's that someone means us harm. Someone might have hurt her. If you're coming in the house, you're taking your boots off this time."

Constable McCaw bent over and removed her boots. With a sigh, Constable Park did too.

"We're gonna make a list of all her friends, all the places she likes to go. This almost always turns out just fine, Ms. Sjöblad." Constable McCaw looked at Benedict standing there, just standing there in the middle of the room. "How are you faring, Mr. Ross?"

Benedict did not answer, and when Constable McCaw looked to her for a translation, all Karen could do was shrug.

SEVENTEEN

After her mom tucked her in, Poppy sneaked out of her bedroom and sat at the top of the stairs. She was exhausted but she had only pretended to be sleepy. Exhausted and sleepy were two different things and there was no way she could sleep knowing Charlotte was missing. There was a long list of things she had done to her sister over the years and it seemed to Poppy every last one of them contributed to this moment. She stole all the best Halloween candy from Charlotte and mocked her at school to impress idiots. She wanted Charlotte to get fat and to get pimples and to be stricken dumb, so for once Poppy would be the mysterious and special one. Without even trying, *without even wanting it*, Charlotte was the centre: sick and pretty and brilliant and strange. And gentle and kind. So deeply, frustratingly kind to Poppy—always.

Downstairs her mom listed all the places she figured Charlotte could be. It was a short list and Poppy would have made it even shorter. When the policewoman and policeman asked for the names of Charlotte's friends, Poppy nearly laughed—though this was the opposite of a funny time. Come on. What would Charlotte do with a friend?

"I could reach out to her friends' parents," said her mom.

Poppy could feel it from the top of the stairs: her mom did not want to tell the truth because she was ashamed.

The policewoman talked about how Charlotte did not fit the profile for a classic runaway. She didn't fit the profile of any teenager. She wasn't on social media and she had left her phone. The last texts were from the night before, when she told her dad she was going to meet him at the factory. Her dad stood slouching in the middle of the room. Even from the top of the stairs, it was obvious to Poppy the police figured her dad for a kook. And if you're investigating a disappearance, it's probably going to cross your mind that the kook did something kooky. Poppy wanted him to stand up straight and to defend himself, to say normal things so the police would know he was normal in all the ways he needed to be. He loved Charlotte. He loved Poppy. They loved him. It was not the sort of love you see in the movies but why did it have to be? He was a strange and good dad who was building something that would actually change the world. The police's job was to make him seem like a strange and bad dad, to humiliate him right in front of her mom, to give her mom more reasons to divorce him. An awful job, to do that to people all day and all night. If you were his daughter it all made sense, but looking from the outside Poppy could see there was something wrong with her dad. She did not want to see it but there he was. He was not a strong man, a fighter. He could not protect them from the people who were breaking into their garage and their house and maybe stealing Charlotte into sex slavery. They read his text conversations with Charlotte aloud and it was true: he sounded like a robot kook. But the number one theory for her sister's disappearance was stomach-related. Something had gone hay-wire with her body, her fever spiked, and she . . .

Poppy imagined the view from the High Level Bridge: snow falling, the ice and snow and the black water flowing.

"I hate to say this out loud but I don't have a choice," said the red-headed policewoman. "Did Charlotte suffer from depression, anxiety, suicidal ideation?"

Her mom answered quickly, though not with a lot of confidence.

The policeman went out with her dad, in the squad car, to look. Her mom and the policewoman stayed to phone all the hospitals in the city. Poppy went on Instagram, where kids posted pictures from the dance recital and argued about whether or not she had floated. It felt good to be talked about but it felt wrong in the house, wrong to be without Charlotte, wrong that she couldn't help, wrong that it was her fault, wrong the house did not want them anymore.

Emma. Who *was* Emma? It wasn't just a random name. Could Emma have taken Charlotte into sex slavery?

The best picture of them together, looking sisterly, was in Huatulco last January before the pandemic kicked in. They had gone at the last minute with their mom to a five-star resort that was a sweet deal because the beach was rocky and dangerous. Every night there was a pretty sunset, and once after they had gone swimming in the pool, her mom took a picture of them holding virgin margaritas. Poppy had a tan and didn't look chubby at all.

At just after ten there was a knock on the door and someone else came in, a child psychologist and expert in missing kids named Carl. He cleared his throat a lot. Someone outside was playing "Do They Know It's Christmas?"—maybe one of those douchebags who walked around playing music loud from their phones. In social studies, Mr. Bischoff had asked them to write essays about how "Do They Know It's Christmas?" is a racist and colonialist song. A lot of the kids got pretty worked up about it, as though they were starving in Ethiopia in the 1980s themselves and feeling insulted by the whole thing. The white kids were the angriest. It was a simple essay to write because she knew exactly what Mr. Bischoff wanted them to say, and she said it, but in her secret self-hating heart she loved the song, especially the part where George Michael comes in. She knew he was gay and dead, but it was pretty much the hottest thing in human history.

When her mom asked Crisis Team Carl what happened next, he didn't say much. They would search all available avenues, seek all available avenues, scour all available avenues. All the things you can do with an avenue! Crisis Team Carl talked about the holiday season, the stress and the misery of it, cloaked in joy and peace and love and how all of it feels like ashes come Boxing Day.

Poppy did not know how to pray, had learned very little at Blaine's church, but she sneaked back to her bedroom and opened her little Bible randomly and read from it and she had no idea what the lines meant. Even so, she said the words out loud and hoped the holiness of them alone would help keep her sister safe. She made a cross over her chest, like in movies. Then she closed her eyes and made up her own version of a prayer: *God protect me from the evil spirits I promise never to hurt people or animals or lie please God bring Charlotte home so I can love her better and never make fun of her to impress idiots or want her to get fat or sick or stupid again.* She posted that picture of her and Charlotte from Huatulco on Instagram and wrote, "My sweet sister is out there somewhere. Please keep an eye out for her and if you see Charlotte tell her to come home and that her sister loves her." She tagged it #IMissYou and #FindCharlotte.

For the next half hour she lay in bed, exhausted but not sleepy, and said the words of her prayer over and over again. Then she checked her phone. It was Friday night and school was out now for the holiday break, so kids were still up. Her post already had over one hundred likes, more than double her previous record. In half an hour! She tried not to think about Charlotte jumping off the bridge because her tummy hurt too much, because her fever was too high and making her delirious, the wind as she fell, her bones and guts on impact, the water. Sleep would never come so Poppy went downstairs in her pyjamas.

Her mom stood up from the couch. "Poppy. You should be asleep, sweetie."

"Can't we go and look for her? Maybe she's out walking."

The red-headed policewoman waved. "Hey Poppy. Sorry about all this. We're going to work real hard to find your sister."

Crisis Team Carl stood up from the wing chair where Daphne used to sleep. Carl was a portly man in a cream fisherman's sweater and his grey socks were half pulled off. He had a goatee. The chair had little red-brown hairs on it you could never vacuum off and still smelled like Daphne when you got really close. It annoyed her that Carl had been sitting on it. "Poppy, you say? Your name is Poppy? I like your jammies."

Oh good. Carl thought she was seven. Behind her, upstairs, Poppy could hear the big woman shouting from her dad's office, "Aliya! Get in here with my cream!" It made her heart beat so fast, poison fast, and her hands were cold and moist. Poppy wished the screaming woman away but it only made things worse. There were cuss words up there, and banging. The woman was frustrated and alone and she regretted all the cruel things she had said in hot moments, things she could not take back, slammed doors and ter- rible insults, and now the only person who saw her and touched her was someone who was paid to do it. All the woman could do now was scream and smash things until it exhausted her and then it was just quiet. No one was listening. No one was coming. All of that was over because of her selfishness and there was nothing she could do to bring it back.

Poppy had waved at the policewoman but did not speak to Carl because she was sure her voice would not work. So they could not see her face, she walked into the foyer, where she stepped in a puddle of melted snow from the police boots. Now her socks were wet. She picked up the nearest shoe—one of her dad's—and prepared to break the window with it.

Poppy deserved all of this. It was her fault. She could not tell her mom or Crisis Team Carl the biggest and darkest truth: that she resented brilliant and beautiful Charlotte for her effortless brilliance and beauty.

"Sweetie, it's after eleven. And your sister's going to be fine." Her mom leaned on the doorjamb. By the tone in her voice, Poppy could tell two things. Her mom did not really think Charlotte was going to be fine and she did not really think Poppy was going out to look for her. Where would Charlotte go, anyway? Charlotte had no friends, no location-based hobbies, no remaining grandparents, no enemies.

Poppy dropped her dad's shoe and slipped her wet-socked foot into her own boot. Her boots were warm and pretty, with flowers on them, $150 boots. It was a lot but it never felt like a lot. Nothing ever did. She got whatever she wanted and the storage room in the basement and the loft in the garage were full of the wants she didn't want anymore.

"You're not going out, Pop. Not now. You can help us look tomorrow."

Poppy put on her second boot and pulled her thousand-dollar Canada Goose jacket from the hook. It was in the news: the stock market was the highest ever but there were so many homeless and poor at the camp by the old library; so many people didn't have jobs.

Crisis Team Carl, searching every available avenue from the middle of their living room, blew into his cup of tea.

"Poppy." Her mom whispered through closed lips, like an angry ventriloquist. "Listen to me."

"You want me to stay?"

"Yes."

"Who's Emma?"

Karen turned around, briefly, and when she looked back at Poppy there was something new in her eyes. A real warning of danger, of punishment. "Not. Now."

"When? Charlotte's missing for real now, Mom. Have you ever heard of sex slavery?"

The policewoman took a step closer to the foyer. "Pardon me?"

"These people are always trying to break into our house!" Poppy spoke past her mom to the policewoman. "First they steal stuff from our garage. Then they get in here and pee on things. One of them is named Emma, she must be, and my mom knows it."

"Poppy," said Karen.

"Either that or Charlotte jumped off the bridge." Poppy pointed at Carl. "That's what you think, isn't it?"

There was silence for a while, interrupted only by Carl slurping his tea. Poppy waited for her mother to explain about Emma, as it was now so obvious she knew something and did not want to talk about it. But her mother didn't explain. She just stood there in the dark.

"These are natural feelings to express, Poppy, completely natural and normal," said Carl.

"All right. Cool. Thanks, Carl!" Poppy opened the door and walked out into the cold.

It was the sort of cold that hurt her eyes. Snow was falling. She walked to the end of the block and turned left toward the bank of the river. This was the route she had always taken with Daphne. No one else was walking at this hour. Poppy herself had never been out this late and had never imagined being out this late alone.

Where was she going, anyway?

Charlotte hid nothing and had no hiding places. For Christmas last year, Poppy had bought Charlotte a diary. It was a Moleskine one from that eucalyptus-smelling stationary shop on 124th Street. For most of January she had hassled Charlotte about it, about writing in her diary every night. Then Charlotte began to use it, but only for notes on her experiments.

"What about your thoughts and feelings?" Poppy had said, when she spotted the open diary on Charlotte's lab table.

Charlotte handed her secret diary to Poppy. "These are my thoughts and feelings."

They were formulas and points on what had worked and not worked in her latest experiment. Who keeps her diary open on her table? Charlotte could be floating dead in the river, escorted by the ugly sturgeon, on her way to Hudson's Bay. Or she could be passed out in the back of a big brown SUV with tinted windows while people with bad teeth smoked inside. Russians, probably. They were driving her to Vancouver. They would keep her drugged and lock her in some hotel room. It would be called the Belvedere and it would have a neon sign, and the owner and everyone who worked at the Belvedere would be in on the scam.

Emma was someone who broke into the houses and garages of families with pretty teenage daughters. She was a scout for bald Russians in leather jackets with cigarettes and neck tattoos who sneaked into houses at night and took girls.

But why did they write *emma* on the wall, and why had she seen it in the gymnasium? Wouldn't they prefer to be sneaky, to get away with their crimes? Why had Poppy floated? The fat woman and the thin woman—her ghosts—what did they want? Did all of this mean she was going crazy? Is that what had happened to Charlotte?

Poppy stood at a little wooden fence, one of the barriers to keep people from falling down the bank. Until a couple of years ago, naughty kids from all over the city came here to drink and smoke weed and probably have sex. It was part of an old road that everyone called the End of the World. You stood there and overlooked the whole valley: the river, the old fort, the fancy new houses like the fancy new houses behind her.

When Poppy heard her mom calling, she had two choices. She could either run away or go back to her. Running away in the snow and walking through the valley trails for an hour might cause her mom a bit more pain, and it would feel pretty good to ease into the centre of attention, but it was bad-good, and Poppy already knew she would end up regretting it. "She's not herself" was probably what her mom had been saying to the policewoman and Crisis Team Carl, and she was right about that. But Poppy wasn't *that* not herself. She knew there was plenty more bad than good in bad-good feelings.

A bunch of the evergreen trees outside were decorated for Christmas. It was a bit wonderful and a bit littering because the decorations sometimes blew off. The boughs waved in the wind, setting off bells and chimes. Poppy walked back across the field to her mom as the snow blew in chaotic circles up and into her face. Wherever her dad and the policeman were looking for Charlotte, there would not be much to see. She liked this sort of blowing everywhere snow when she could look out at it from inside the warm house, ideally with a cup of hot chocolate. Only now, even when the house was warm it wasn't warm. Something had come and it had contaminated all that had made her safe and happy: the tree lit up, the holiday special, the smell of freshly baked every-thing, her mom's mulled wine, her dad in his pyjamas—her dad not working for a whole day or two. It was gone forever. Charlotte was gone forever, with the sturgeon, because Poppy had not loved her enough. Poppy had lied and pretended. People thought she was good but she was bad, and she liked being bad. She had sum-moned evil into their lives with her meanness, her jealousy, and her vanity. By the time she reached her mother on the corner, she was exhausted *and* sleepy. Her mom embraced her.

"Poppy—"

"Mom, I made this happen. I was embarrassed about Charlotte, that kids wouldn't think I was cool if they saw me with her." The sobbing started and there would be no way to stop it now. "I took her candies. I wanted her to be gross like me. She's only smart and good. She doesn't hurt anyone. She's a dolphin, basically, and I was embarrassed by her and *she knew it*. And I'm mad at her for being so pretty and not even giving a crap. Then I wanted that bitch Aoife to get hurt and she did get hurt. There's a fat lady and a skinny lady, ghost ladies, who live in the house now. *And they're me, only old*. Emma came with the bald Russians and their ciga-rettes to take Charlotte away because I invited them with my wicked thoughts. When we were in the car in the summertime, Charlotte ducked from the skateboarder boys because *she knew I was ashamed of her*. And I want to change bodies with her. That's why it's all happening to us. Emma came because I asked her to come. I'm going crazy, I think. And maybe Charlotte jumped in the river."

Her nose was running so much, from her crying, that she had to pull away from her mom's parka or risk transferring a quarter cup of snot onto it. The policewoman reached with a tissue. Poppy had not seen the policewoman and would not have unburdened herself so completely if she had seen her.

"Come back home." Her mom led her away from the valley. "We'll knock on every one of these doors in the morning if your dad doesn't come home with her."

EIGHTEEN

By the pink sunrise just before nine on Saturday morning, there was a team of well-caffeinated professionals in the house. Four police, the psychologist named Carl, two abduction experts, two social workers, and an autism specialist who squinted at Benedict from across the room.

They talked and talked and talked, and Karen filled their cups of coffee. She watched her husband, who stood next to the dining table watching . . . what? He had not slept. He did not engage in the conversation; when one of the team asked him a question, Karen apologized and answered for him.

From across the room, she could feel something burning up inside Benedict. Karen had never seen him lose his temper, but she imagined him now picking up a nearby poinsettia in a terra-cotta pot and smashing it at the feet of the experts. Carl and the social workers spoke authoritatively, though without evidence. These were fingernails scratching at the insides of her husband: no matter how special she seems, Charlotte is just a teenager, after all, with deep needs and desires. These needs and desires, coupled with her medical challenges and the recent chaos in the house, the public attention, created a *perfect storm*.

The cliché seemed to be too much for him. Benedict went into the kitchen and just stood there.

It was deeply cold but cloudless now. The sun was low in the sky and the new snow covered the sand and the dust and the everywhere brown filth of winter. Another blizzard was due that evening—a proper one—and there was something quick and flinty in the air that foretold it. Karen had not spoken to Benedict, not for hours, but all through their sleepless night he had been quickening with the air. She expected him at any moment now to do what he did not do, to order everyone out of the house, some adult version of what that boy Warner had done in grade six. Throw everything. Throw them out. Embarrass her. Reveal the truth.

The detective in charge—a tall, well-muscled, Indo-Canadian man who first introduced himself by bellowing, "Call me Sammy!"— spoke with absolute confidence about Charlotte suffering a breakdown. Call Me Sammy was handsome and not yet forty. Despite his size, his hands were delicate and pretty. His turban was baby blue. There had been a controversy, back in the nineties, about whether or not Sikhs could wear their turbans and ceremonial knives in the Royal Canadian Mounted Police. Like most of these controversies, they seemed ridiculous twenty years later. The others agreed with Call Me Sammy: the girl had suffered an anxiety attack, possibly an extreme one. The professionals spoke about her as though they knew her and looked pityingly at Karen when she argued that Charlotte wasn't like that.

Charlotte wasn't like that. She wore black because it was simple, efficient, and hid stains. The darkness on and about her eyes wasn't goth makeup. It was her skin. There were no boyfriends or online *bad actors* and if she had any trouble with emotion it was a lack. A girl doesn't jump off a bridge because she doesn't feel something. A girl jumps off a bridge because she is in pain.

Benedict walked back into the living room and said his first words all morning. "I have a confession."

Karen leapt up.

Call Me Sammy pointed at Constable McCaw. "Here we go. Notepad!"

"Ben?"

He pointed above the fireplace. "Charlotte did not paint *emma*. We know an Emma, or we think we do. She tried to break into our house, our garage, on Halloween night, and I accidentally killed her. Only I didn't kill her, because she wrote her name on our wall."

It was quiet now. Constable McCaw, who had been taking notes, looked up at Benedict, then at Karen. Then she exhaled, closed her eyes, and shook her head. "Jesus Christ," she said.

Poppy had been sitting on the stairs, watching and listening. "I knew it, *Karen*." She stomped up to her room. "Liars!"

Call Me Sammy transformed. He dismissed the experts, who slowly exited the house without looking back at Benedict and Karen. He interviewed Benedict in the kitchen and Constable McCaw interviewed Karen in the living room and then they sat on the couch together like naughty children while Call Me Sammy spoke on his cellular phone with headquarters. His voice was different now, more doubtful, and he spoke in code.

At one point, a moment of resolution, Call Me Sammy sat at the dining room table and made notes. "Uh huh," he said, several times.

Constable McCaw sat in the dog's chair. It was clearly not a thing a police officer is supposed to say, because she whispered it, but while Call Me Sammy was at the dining room table she pulled down her mask and looked directly at Karen and said, "I'm really disappointed in you."

In me? Karen wanted to say. She wanted to say something to defend herself, not only from this but from every choice she had made in her adult life. Did any of these middle-aged experts of the teen heart understand what it was like to grow up with Johnny and Jeanette Sjöblad and the secret Swedish Nazi grandparents? To begin dating a man like Benedict in university, for good reasons and bad reasons, and then realize you were forty? That you couldn't go back and start again?

In her official interview, Karen said nothing of her deepest fears, that Benedict was not telling the truth, that he had snatched up the woman and had stabbed her with a pry bar and had dragged her into the yard to force his way into her. And if he could do that to a stranger, *what might he do to their daughter?*

When she regained consciousness, they coaxed Emma to stand, to put one arm over each of their shoulders. They walked north to the emergency room of the university hospital. There were no cars on the roads of Belgravia, the lights of the houses were off. They ducked CCTV cameras near the LRT stop while Emma mumbled about her own mother. Her breath was sweet with alcohol. The bunnies on the Corbett Hall field had early patches of white in their fur. There were people outside the emergency room doors in and out of wheelchairs, smoking, so they lowered Emma to a wooden bench around the corner, in the quiet and the dark, and Karen ran to the ambulance bay. She told the nurse, who wore dog ears for Halloween, about the wounded woman on the bench and from the parking lot they watched paramedics address themselves to Emma.

Karen did not ask Benedict what she should have asked, on the walk home, or in the bathroom as they washed the woman's blood from their hands. She did not really want to know.

/ Call Me Sammy shoved the chair back from the dining room table, with a sound that Karen despised: the shriek of a wooden leg digging into their oak floors.

"Well." Call Me Sammy looked down at Benedict, then Karen, then Benedict again. "The forensics team was on their way but we called it off. Do you know why?"

"She's dead?" said Karen.

"You're a couple of very, very lucky sons of bitches. Emma, Emma Scofield, nineteen, was released from the University of Alberta Hospital on the afternoon of one November after treatment for minor injuries and a medical way to describe *sobering up a bit*. I won't bore you with the details. She had stitches. No ID. No fixed address. The kid was blitzed out of her mind, it turns out. She probably doesn't even remember you fuckheads because there are no notes, none, about how she came to be superficially stabbed in the abdomen."

Constable McCaw stood up and joined Call Me Sammy looking down on them. Was he allowed to call them fuckheads?

Karen reached for a tissue and dabbed her eyes again. "Are you sure?"

"Positive." Call Me Sammy whispered something to the constable and crossed his arms. "New theory. Your Charlotte knew what went down Halloween night. She wanted you two to come clean, to do the right thing. Guess what? You didn't."

"You failed Charlotte," said Constable McCaw.

"*That's* why she painted *emma* on the wall. Makes sense, doesn't it? When you're totally ashamed of your mom and dad. There's a friendship you two don't know about, maybe a boyfriend. She's in some basement in the suburbs, bingeing *The Queen's Gambit* and hoping you two are sweating. How about that?"

Ninety minutes later, the experts were back and despite Call Me Sammy's theory they returned to the original plan: to split up and go door to door in Belgravia with a colour photocopy of Charlotte's face and a rehearsed set of questions. Poppy agreed to go with Karen because even though she was furious she did not want to go with a social worker or stay home alone. On the toilet, before they left, Karen scanned Poppy's Instagram. There was a picture of the girls together in Mexico. Her followers and others commented on the picture. Someone had spotted Charlotte at the big mall last night. She was playing shinny. She was carolling without a mask in the Hamptons; one of the west end suburbs, with identical vinyl-sided homes, front garages, and no trees was called the Hamptons. So many emojis.

Karen could feel the secrets rising in sweet Poppy, the guile, and the beige desire to be liked. When she was home-schooling in the early weeks of the pandemic, Poppy would watch television series about young lovers, about people baking cakes, about drag queens. She would take pictures of herself and put them on Instagram with ungrammatical captions. This Instagram post was about her sister's disappearance but it was also about her. There was nothing Karen could do about any of this.

When they finished with the houses, they walked the trails along the mostly frozen river, even though Charlotte never went for walks—not now that Daphne was dead. Dog people smiled and said hello as they passed. There were a few trees with Christmas decorations and laminated pictures and messages from neighbourhood pets. *Merry Xmas from Barry the Basset Hound.*

Poppy did not speak to Karen, even when Karen tried to explain herself. The only reason they were looking for Charlotte along the trails was because the police and experts told them to look for her here. During the lockdown Charlotte did what she always did when there were no other demands on her time: she built, tried, and tested things in her little laboratory. She gave Benedict obscure lists of chemicals and material to get at the hardware store and at the mass spectrometry facility, the molecular biology service unit, the machine intelligence institute, the geochronology lab, and the nuclear magnetic resonance project on campus. She suffered an illness no one understood.

They passed the muddy little pond Daphne had loved. In the summertime it was rank standing water, so they would have to take her to the river for a swim afterward. When Daphne found dead squirrels and fish, on the paths or along the river, she would roll in them. No, Daphne, no! It meant they would have to endure the smell of her all the way home and give her a bath. When they were poor, in the summertime, bound for the modern equivalent of debtors' prison, they were happy to bathe Daphne after a walk.

Karen was regretful and nostalgic at once. She wanted to tell Poppy all of this, not to make excuses but simply to share. No one knows how to do anything, really.

They went up the steep part, and the melting-freezing cycle had made the path precarious so they went into the bush a bit and used birch trees and evergreens to brace themselves. Poppy started crying. "It's my fault Charlotte jumped off the bridge."

"Darling, she didn't jump off the bridge. And none of this is your fault."

Poppy shook her head. She was crying again, different crying now. "It is my fault. I was the worst sister, so selfish and so jealous. If I can have her back . . . "

"She'll come back."

They were nearly at the house now. Karen put her arm around Poppy and she didn't swat it away, which was a gift. Karen apologized. It smelled different inside, as men's cologne spray mixed with coffee. Benedict endured his fourth interview with the police, this time with Call Me Sammy and a new man in a suit. A policewoman in uniform took notes. Karen could hear the whole thing from the foyer. She did not want Poppy to hear but there was no way to avoid it.

"Did you hurt Charlotte?" said Call Me Sammy.

"No."

"The way you hurt Emma?"

"I told you I didn't know Emma was Emma, and even when I thought it was a man I didn't want to hurt him. I slid into him."

"Do you think Charlotte could have jumped off the bridge?"

They did not hear his answer.

"What would she be trying to escape, Benedict? What *shame*?"

NINETEEN

B enedict guessed the High Level Bridge was somewhat more than 150 feet high. He remembered the moment, in high school physics, when he first learned the formula for gravity. Benedict translated feet and pounds to metric, which a scientist of his generation tends to do. The bridge was about fifty metres tall and he weighed about eighty kilograms. If Charlotte, or if Benedict, crashed into the miserable water, they would be falling faster than 100 kilometres per hour—faster than a car on a secondary highway.

Charlotte would have calculated this just as easily, only faster, with more precision. When the police departed the house was quiet. Dusk had arrived and the Christmas lights were on. The white ghost hovered silently in the backyard, enormous now, taller than the treehouse and camouflaged in the snow. Benedict knew what had happened, though he could not have explained to the police. The ghost had sucked Charlotte into itself because he had shared his lie with her.

In the living room, Karen and Poppy cleaned the floor and the tables. Not all of the police and social workers and psychologists had removed their shoes at the door. It was contrary to pandemic regulations to be inside a house like this, and perhaps wearing shoes made it feel legitimate. Christmas music played again: more Dolly Parton.

Benedict knew how Karen had been feeling this past long while, at least until he had secured the Sinotechnika investment. There was a reason people stayed married, and that reason had withered. His wife was not sneaky. When he would grab the nearest laptop, from time to time, the browser would refresh on a real estate ad for a two- or three-bedroom condominium in Vancouver or on the island. Benedict was often on the verge of bringing it up with her in bed at night, and then he would vow to do it another night and lie awake. If the experts were right and Charlotte had jumped off the bridge, it would make it easier for Benedict to jump. The legal fees, compared to a divorce, would be minimal. Mortgage and life insurance would take care of their real estate conundrum. Karen was insulated from any claims against him for mismanaging Kutisi.

There was one remaining issue.

He sneaked off to the factory to use the big printer. It was Saturday the nineteenth of December, the last day of the wizards, and quiet on the floor apart from the whispers and murmurs of the three Germans, who had formed a team. Benedict could not speak their language but he knew what a breakthrough sounded like and he did not hear it. Though it was unclear what had happened exactly, Dr. Darren had been drinking in the factory until late Friday night and had knocked over the Christmas tree. Several of Danielle's handmade ornaments were ruined. The garland was ripped and lay on the floor.

Sir Walter Jarrow had already given up, but to earn his $25,000 without breaking his contractual obligations he took his Kutisi box apart and put it back together again. Dr. Darren started and stopped the digital clock app on his phone as a performance measure of some sort, but Benedict had no idea what he was doing.

There were two hours left. Then the men would retire to their hotel rooms to freshen up and meet for a goodbye dinner. Marie-Claude did not yet know they were spending 200,000 American dollars of Sinotechnika's money on a confirmation of their failure. She did not know Charlotte was missing. Benedict had not responded to any of her texts.

If Benedict jumped off the bridge, Marie-Claude would dismantle the company—in her seventies!—and work through the legal aspects of bankruptcy protection. While the Ross-Sjöblad family had nothing to lose, since the government didn't even take your house anymore, Marie-Claude had plenty of assets. Some of them were in the U.S., where Sinotechnika's clever lawyers would immediately seize them. Marie-Claude thought she was ending her career with a climate change breakthrough, not a scandal. In the early days she had worried most about an accident, about something she did not understand in the core of the little nuclear reactor going sour and becoming a tiny Chernobyl. That would be a legacy: a million and a half angry refugees crossing the Rockies into British Columbia, demanding suburban houses and suvs and fast internet.

On Monday morning, Jessica's Gandalf would arrive to see if Kutisi was everything Benedict had claimed. How much had they spent of Sinotechnika's money? Three million, tops, paying off their liabilities and pumping some resources into future action. Gosh, when Marie-Claude's company, Aarhus Energy, was at its most prosperous they would write off three-million-dollar mistakes all the time. Back in July, the French oil giant Total had written off $9.3 billion in stranded oil sands assets. Three million was nothing! In April, when a barrel of oil was trading at negative thirty dollars, the government stepped in to help keep what remained of Aarhus alive—along with hundreds of other oil companies that had bet everything on the forever rise of fossil fuels.

Emma was alive. He was the dead one, he and his machine. Benedict had slowly become Kutisi. He had dreamed his way into its lifelessness and had dragged his family and his partner along.

Benedict finished making photocopies of Charlotte's face and stuffed them in his backpack with his heavy handyman stapler. He did not bother going into the painting bay to evaluate his failure. Instead he set the fallen Christmas tree upright and walked out of the factory without saying goodbye to the unsuccessful wizards.

"See you at tea," said Sir Walter.

A new storm had moved in from the mountains. It was snowing again. He stapled posters to poles and boards on 104th Street, with his name and phone number. He was at 109th Street when he received the first call about Charlotte, but it was from a crazy person with sexual thoughts about her. The second was from someone who recognized his name and wanted a job. The third was from a "citizen journalist."

His phone vibrated again. It was Karen and he did not have the courage to speak to her just then.

A blizzard warning, earlier in the afternoon, had come with advice not to drive unless it was absolutely necessary. Yet everyone was in their cars and SUVs and vanity pickup trucks, creeping up and down Jasper Avenue on a thickening layer of slippery slush. Karen called again. He put up another seven posters.

Christmas gaiety hung from the heights of 124th Street. He ducked between shoppers, giving them plenty of space, all of them better prepared for the weather than he was, in the down parkas of the upper middle class that Karen and the girls wore all winter.

His feet were soaking wet, and snow was caked in his hair. Karen liked this neighbourhood. The commercial art galleries were here, and if they lived in Glenora among the established wealth of the new city, they would stroll here on warm summertime evenings for ice cream and single malt whisky.

From Karen:

Where are you?

Then, seven minutes later, she wrote:

Come to Candy Cane Lane right now

There was a bridge over Groat Road, which snaked from the north side into the valley. Before he stopped on the bridge deck and looked over, toward the river, Benedict knew what he would see. His ghost hovered over the road. He could dive off the bridge and find Charlotte inside, swirling there. *It can't work, Daddy.* There was no suicide barrier. It took only a moment to swing one leg over, though his other leather dress shoe slipped in the snow and he fell back. He lay on the wet snow a moment in his navy blue suit. Behind him, drivers honked. Someone shouted, "Don't do it, buddy!"

His phone was still in his hand. Another text from Karen:

Please

Candy Cane Lane was in the near western suburbs. For as long as Benedict had been alive, it had been a ritual to walk or drive slowly past the over-decorated houses in December. Before his parents were born again, they would take him to look at the garish blinking lights and animatronic Santas. Then his parents entered a new phase of Christmas austerity, where celebrating the birth of Jesus was darkened by the strange rejoicing at the ancient boy's sacrificial death. It was too grim to be a carol but Benedict remembered a man with a beard and an acoustic guitar playing a song called "He Was Born to Die for Us" in the fluorescent-lit, beige-carpeted megachurch of the Assembly of God, where they spent every Christmas Eve. The chorus was about being covered in the blood of Jesus. After the removal of his brother and his miracle in the hospital, when his parents joined the church, Candy Cane Lane became a devilish distraction from the solemn and gory truth. The Assembly of God didn't even have a tree.

His phone vibrated in his pocket several more times. All he could do was walk, so he walked westward on what his city did best: a corridor for cars. Everything was so wet, as the heavy flakes fell, that by the time he made it past the mansions of Glenora there was nowhere to put up the posters with his darling Charlotte's face on them. He pulled another one out and looked at it every few steps.

It did not take as long as Benedict had imagined. The ghost hovered above him in the parking lot of the Reformed Christian Church like a slow-motion fighter in a ring. He was tiny before it. The RCC was a white dome at the entrance to the world's hap-hap-happiest neighbourhood. Snow passed and whirled through the monster. There were signs blocking the flow of cars into the church parking lot, threatening fines and towing charges. On the other side of the ghost, a few couples and families in masks walked on the sidewalks that led to the lights of Candy Cane Lane. There was a long line of cars and trucks, preparing to turn in.

The new snow had not yet been ruined by a slurry of salt and sand. It was wet enough to stick to the evergreen boughs. As children walked past the monster, Benedict worried it might snatch up one of them and begin eating—or just absorb the child into itself, as it had done with Charlotte. The ghost was his responsibility. He had called it into being with his machine, his lies, his insincerity, his betrayals of science. A business plan! Benedict knew how to write a business plan. Yes, he could outline, step by step, how to destroy the monster, the financial and human resources he would need, the short- and long-term strategies, and the output—the sweet reward. He would help build a world without expanding ghosts of shame that eat the small and the fragile, that do not feel.

Benedict looked at the soaking wet photocopy of his daughter's impossibly beautiful face. The ghost had taken her from him, through his own vile invitation. He decided not to walk around the creature or to go in the opposite direction.

"Give her back to me!"

It did not respond. The ghost expanded and shrunk somewhat like a bag of air, and for the first time Benedict could see that it was fragile. That it could be beaten. There was another hand-painted sign in the snow, reminding visitors to give generously to the food bank. Benedict pulled the sign out of the ground and ripped the words on white plastic from the top. Industrial staples flew out. Now he had a weapon. And what was he afraid of? He knew what Charlotte would want of him, not vengeance but honesty and rigour. He knew how it worked with monsters. You could send your employees, your minions, your heroes out to slaughter it but the ghost would defeat them one by one. *It has to be you*. And if you do not defeat the monster, it will devour your villagers. First Charlotte and then Poppy and Karen and Marie-Claude, all that remained of him.

The blizzard arrived with a howl from the west and blew him from behind. The snow swirled in the parking lot and rose up and about the ghost. Benedict was so afraid. He raised the stake. This is what he should have done when it first arrived in the basement, on the night of the break-in. If he had summoned the courage to attack the monster on November thirtieth, Charlotte would still be with them.

He shouted mightily and began to run. The thing was so big he would have to jump at the right moment, and the wind would carry him. As he prepared to leap and fly, he felt something on his right. It was in silhouette, as the lights of busy 149th Street were behind it. A small car? Why was it not stopping?

A tall and rather obese growling man tackled him and together they landed in the snow on a patch of frozen grass. Benedict could not breathe, as he tried to stand up, and he gasped for air. The great ghost had disappeared. In its place stood Karen. By the time his breath was easing into its normal function, the bison of a man who had tackled him was standing over him with the wooden stake and shouting. "Huh? You figure I should put this up your ass, fucko?"

"No."

A big blonde woman in a black fur coat came around to speak to the bison, who dropped the stake. Then Karen approached Benedict with a big smile and tears in her eyes and bent down to hug his head. She addressed the small crowd, "It's his sense of humour! An inside joke we have between us. Husband and wife? Vampires? Vampires! Thank you, everyone. Happy Christmas."

Once they were gone, Karen sat next to him in the parking lot and sobbed. Then she lay in the snow and he lay next to her. And for a while that was it: her sobs faded and she wiped her eyes with her mittens and they lay next to one another in silence, on the outskirts of the pretty lights of Candy Cane Lane. They lay long enough for snow to first melt and then collect on their faces.

Benedict moved closer to Karen, for her warmth and to somehow share that he could not make it through the weekend without his daughter. Kutisi did not matter. The ghost did not matter. The snow and the wind and their debts and prison did not matter. All that mattered was Charlotte and if they could not find her, if Charlotte could not find them, there was no way he could see himself through to Monday. He wanted Karen to understand, to feel his feelings, but he did not know how to begin, the words to say and how to say them.

"What, uh . . . " Karen slowly turned to him. "What just happened there? I think you were trying to kill me with a stick."

"I thought you were a ghost."

"When I was screaming at you?"

"Didn't hear that. You were a ghost. A big one."

"Am I *always* a big ghost or just then?"

He was so cold his mouth wasn't working terribly well. "Remember the night they broke into the garage and took the bikes and urinated in the Tesla?"

Karen turned on her side and they looked at one another.

"Remember I saw a ghost when I was sick? That was it. I thought I saw it because of the fever but it wasn't the fever, Karen. The ghost never went away. Then I decided the ghost was the woman."

"Emma Scofield."

"But it wasn't her either. The ghost is my lie. It just grew, and it took Charlotte from us. My lies took her."

She nodded as though this were an entirely normal sort of thing. "What lies?"

"The wizards are leaving tomorrow." Now that Benedict had started talking, he thought he might as well continue. "I know it doesn't matter, next to Charlotte, one thousand failed Kutisis do not matter. But it doesn't work."

"What doesn't work?" Karen sat up. The snow slid on her face. "Your machine?"

"It never did."

"Your wizards couldn't make it go?"

"The best engineering minds in the world."

"But your investors."

"I lied to them. I lied to Marie-Claude. I lied to you."

Karen turned away from him.

"A man from Sinotechnika is coming on Monday, the wizard of wizards, to inspect the box. We were never moving to a fancy house on Saskatchewan Drive. We're not richer than we were last month. We're a lot poorer. I am a fraud and I will be punished for it. We all will, I guess. That's why Charlotte is gone, why the ghost took her. She came with me to the factory and we worked together. She knew I was lying, that I am a charlatan, and—"

"Ben. This is so fucked up. I hate you right now. But it's not why Charlotte is gone."

"She knew it didn't work, that it can't work, that I have ruined us."

Karen turned back to him. Benedict knew, by the look on her face, that she was about to scream, scream anger and betrayal and impossible frustration. Then she took a big breath and calmed herself. She sobbed, just once, and then: "I've been seeing a ghost in the house too, the ghost of my dad. He was also a liar, and the son of a Nazi. And I'm a liar."

Folks walking away from Candy Cane Lane, as the wind came up ugly, watched them like they were passing a bloody car accident. Benedict did not want to know what Karen had been lying about so he did not ask.

"I kissed my yoga teacher. Well, he kissed me. I was really going through something. I guess I still am."

"Do you love him?"

"Oh God, no. I'm sorry."

"The girls should take your name, take Sjöblad, when I'm gone, to protect them from this—from what's coming."

Karen looked at him like *he* was the ghost. "When you're gone?"

Now that he was no longer moving, Benedict was profoundly cold. If he did not put a jacket on, soon, his scientific advice to himself was that he would die right here in the parking lot of the

Reformed Christian Church. He was on the verge of hypothermia. What was he supposed to say about Karen kissing her yoga teacher? It was not a surprise to him that she was unhappy; she had been unhappy for a long time. He worried about finances. Karen *felt* their net worth in her viscera, the lack in her life, and she wanted things Benedict did not know how to give. Things of the heart. He did not ask for her help in this. It all haunted her like the fifty-foot ghost haunted him.

"Ben, she's here."

In an instant, everything changed in him. "Charlotte's here?"

"Emma. Emma is here." Karen stood up, wiped the wet snow off herself, and reached for his hand. The wind was so strong she had to half shout. "Charlotte's not gone because you're a lying charlatan. She's gone because of what we did to Emma. Let's go."

It was unusual to be among the few people who dared to be out in a virus-drenched blizzard. There were dogs. None of the dogs were as good as Daphne. A few minutes later they were in the bright corridor of Candy Cane Lane. When Benedict imagined Candy Cane Lane, from a long and distant night in June, it glowed softly with incandescent bulbs. The modern reality was different. Karen led him south down 148th Street past laser showers and explosions of rainbow LED. The painted plywood Santas of his youth were now giant inflated plastic airship Grinches and Frostys and Rudolphs, all based on cartoons that were old when he was young. People needed this place. Benedict decided it would be a good idea to go to the hospital and tell them he was suffering a psychotic episode. That he had tried to kill his wife a few minutes ago. The tips of his ears felt hot now. His hands had entered that place where they are beyond cold: numb and throbbing.

"I wanted it to be true and I wanted you to be proud, you and the girls. My parents, you know, they were believers. *Actual believers.* The ghost came that night, at the end of November, the night they pissed in the car, and I thought if there is a ghost in our basement anything is possible. Marie-Claude said believe. *Believe!* And it felt so good. I know why my mom and dad fell so deeply into believing. It made them whole. I told the investors what I wanted Kutisi to be, and when they asked if we were there yet, with the tech, *I believed* and we were there. I saw our silver boxes in every city and town in the world, the coal-fired power plants of America and China and Europe and Australia empty and shuttered, turned into conference centres and modern art museums, the global transportation system electrified. I saw it all, and I helped them see it. It's prison for me or . . . or what? I'll jump off the bridge for you, or make it an accident. And if I go away, it all goes away: the ghost and Gandalf and Jessica Wolfe. My darlings will be safe. Charlotte will come home from wherever she is. It will be undone, all of it. Charlotte will come home to you."

Karen squeezed his hand. "Shhh."

The food bank had set up a manger and some actual farm animals. There were two sheep, a donkey, and a goat wearing a sweater. There were also two pigs in a little pen, which stretched Benedict's understanding of farm life in ancient Israel. There were some people with togas over their parkas, and snow boots, and there was a baby Jesus doll that looked—from a distance— like a Cabbage Patch Kid. Benedict had received one of those for Christmas one year from his grandmother. His parents allowed him to keep the doll but only because he agreed to name it Paul, after their favourite apostle. He desperately wanted that goat's sweater. The food bank scene was split in half, with this quasi-sacred bit on one side and the pantheon of corporate jingle-jingling on the other. Santa was a tall man Benedict recognized from fundraisers, the CEO of the food bank, and according to a sign on the side of a huge wrapped present the elves were from the local coalition of women's shelters.

Emma Scofield, the girl he thought he had murdered, stood with two other elves behind bins of donated food. Families emptied bags into the bins and the young women were meant to thank them. One of the women took care of it for the other two. She was bright-eyed and energetic, like she had just finished a large cup of powerful coffee. "Oh my God, *thank* you," she said, to everyone who arrived with a bag of food, like each of them had shocked her with generosity. "Merry *Christmas*!"

The other two women didn't have to say anything. Emma was the one in the middle. On the other side of her, an obese elf shook two lines of bells in a lazy and indifferent fashion. Emma was alert, as though she expected an angry boyfriend to arrive.

Benedict's phone was vibrating in his pocket. He pulled it out and peeked at it. There were several voice mails from Marie-Claude, and a few unread texts on his home screen asking him to call her. Their employees would be jobless on the twenty-third of December but he had been careful about Marie-Claude, what she knew and when she knew it. She would lose the entirety of her investment but she would not go to minimum-security prison.

A man put a small bag in one of the bins and the three elves jingled their bells. A group of five carollers passed on the sidewalk singing the final bit of "Silent Night" into the wind.

"How did you find her?"

"Constable McCaw found her." Karen crossed her arms. "I overheard her whispering about it in the kitchen."

Emma Scofield looked like he felt, like she had not slept in sixty hours. She was divorced from the snow blowing into her face, from her elf costume, from the job she was meant to do, and from Christmas: the lights, the carolling, the vats before her literally full of the spirit of giving. Benedict eyed the goat. He was a few minutes away from needing hospitalization. Karen was in the middle of telling Benedict why they were here, to ask Emma if she had stolen the bicycles and pissed in the car, if she had broken into the house and wrecked her painting of old Calgary, if she had done something to Charlotte.

"She knows where Charlotte is." Karen had to shout at him to be heard over the carollers, who had moved on to "White Christmas," and the wind and the bells. "The cops won't even ask her."

Benedict was relieved to see the bird woman standing there, over a bin of food for the needy. A man pushing a cart kitted out with huge thermoses full of coffee and hot chocolate rang his bell next to them.

"I'm going to ask her right now." The snow had melted on Karen's face and her eye makeup had dripped and smeared. "She knows."

The cheerful elf greeted them. Karen ignored her and shouted over the music and the jingling and the wind. Karen shouted at Emma about Charlotte and urine, and the bird woman did not seem to understand. Then all was quiet. Benedict made eye contact with Emma. He expected this to be a moment of insight and understanding. They had been through so much together since Halloween night. But the woman did not recognize him.

Emma swallowed and looked away from Benedict, to the CEO of the food bank dressed as Santa Claus—her protector. Santa was ministering to a small girl who had come to see him with her Christmas wishes.

The ghost hovered beyond Santa, so tall now the blizzard obscured its face.

With a jingle of her bells, Emma waved Santa over. "Please."

TWENTY

The basement was set up like a tiny movie theatre, with reclining leather chairs the perfect distance from the big screen. Speakers were embedded in the ceiling and the walls. Charlotte designed it when she was ten.

Ten!

When she was seven, a specialist named Dr. Linnaeus told her parents that Charlotte would never be a salesperson or give a TED Talk or run for prime minister. The doctor had become a legend in the Ross-Sjöblad household. If Charlotte wanted to be a salesperson she would take salesperson-ing apart, study its components, improve them, put it all back together, and become the best salesperson in history—or TED Talker or prime ministerial candidate.

Charlotte was bad at everything that did not matter. She didn't care about music or apps or clothes or YouTubers or boys or whatever everyone was watching on Netflix. She didn't know how to talk about teenager shit like popularity and breakups, and if she wasn't invited to someone's stupid "spa day" birthday party, she wouldn't even know it. Charlotte wasn't just good at everything that did matter, like home theatres and chemical reactions, she was the best. Better than anyone! Actual goddamn freaking Apple came to their house to talk to her and give her free stuff after she fixed the crappy HomePod.

There was a bottle of kombucha in the fridge and artisanal salted caramel ice cream in the freezer. Poppy put it on a tray and carried it downstairs. All she had eaten, all day, was two spoonfuls of cereal and three bites of a grilled cheese sandwich. In the basement, on the most acoustically perfect home theatre system in the world, she turned on *Love Actually*. It was rated 14A, which is why her mom wouldn't watch it with her, but she would be fourteen in seven months. Her friends talked about it all the time and she pretended to have seen it. She had heard about a few of the scenes so often—stand-ins for the sex scenes in a movie having really cute conversations, and the Mr. Darcy guy proposing to a Portuguese lady in a restaurant after learning Portuguese for her—that she could recount them without anyone knowing she hadn't seen it.

Could Charlotte do that? No. But Charlotte would recognize that pretending to have seen a movie to fit in was ridiculous and pointless and dishonest and weak.

It was blizzarding. The lights were dim outside the house but she could watch it swirl as the snow slowly piled up during the boring bits in the first ten minutes of the movie. There was no Christmas tree in the basement, which was a problem. For the home theatre to work properly the lights had to be out, but Poppy didn't like the dark so much anymore. The soft glow of a Christmas tree would be just the thing. Twenty minutes into the movie, she brought the kombucha and the ice cream back upstairs without having any of it. Keira Knightley was in the movie, thin as a whippet, and after all her hard work the last thing Poppy needed was to feel like an undisciplined walrus watching teenage Keira Knightley.

If Charlotte had jumped off the bridge and Poppy was all her parents had left, their only kid forever, she would end up disappointing them so much. She wasn't as pretty or as skinny and would never be, and she wasn't even in the same universe of smart.

Charlotte! How could she watch a movie when her sister was bobbing underneath a layer of ice in the North Saskatchewan River on her way to the Atlantic Ocean? And nothing in *Love Actually* felt real anyway. At first, when Blaine said she wanted to be her friend again, when she apologized for the nonsense and said it was her mom's doing, Poppy felt like a million sparklers were going off in the school washroom. She didn't *love* Blaine but she loved her. Maybe she did love her. It's not that she didn't find boys sexy, some of them. Sexy wasn't the word for how she felt about Blaine, and a couple of other girls if she was honest. She did think about lying naked with them in the dark, in the summertime, with a bit of a sunburn, maybe after a swim in some lake, smelling like a lake. She thought about touching them softly and singing along to slow songs with them.

The door to the rec room, a room she really hated because it was smelly and cold, with a light that barely worked, had been closed. She was sure of it. Now, halfway into the movie, with her stomach rumbling, it was open. Poppy jumped off the recliner and closed the door. In *Love Actually*, which was actually too loud, Professor Snape was falling for his secretary and his wife knew it, which was not one of the stories her friends talked about. Charlotte had told her that by the time they were thirty years old, movies would not be on screens anymore, and if you wanted things to be quieter or louder you would just think it.

Poppy wasn't looking at the door, not at first. She heard the hinges squeak, just faintly, and thought she was imagining it. The only light came from the television screen, so it was difficult to say whether she was really seeing what she thought she was seeing. Poppy paused the movie and nothing happened. The door stopped opening and there were no sounds from the rec room.

"Hello?"

Apart from the old wood settling the house was silent. Poppy had already looked in the rec room, for her sister. Her voice would not work when she tried to speak again so she gave it a moment, breathed deeply, convinced herself it was nothing.

"Charlotte? You in there?"

Nothing.

Wind, maybe, or some other mechanical force she forgot a day after getting an A on the test. Poppy pressed play. The prime minister of Britain was off to find his chubby assistant. Poppy had sympathy for the assistant; they were about the same size. Not fat, if you asked Poppy or the prime minister, but on the way. The woman's dad called her Plumpy, and it was supposed to be a joke in that awkward British way. Her mom would never call her fat but she said it in other ways, encouraging her to exercise and to stop snacking after school.

The door kept opening. This time Poppy decided not to call her sister's name or pause the movie or even look. She would pretend not to see. But she saw.

The thin one came out of the room first, in a hospital gown that was only as long as a short skirt. She was covered in sores on her arms and legs, and old bandages, and her face was similarly blotchy. Though she wore glasses the thin woman acted as though she were blind, feeling around. If she was a ghost, she should not be able to touch anything. She should be vapour. But this woman touched the closest reclining leather chair and put her arms on it and looked at Poppy. That was when the door opened further and the big one crawled out in a terry cloth robe. "Where is that fucking nurse?"

Poppy wanted to scream, to get up and run, but she couldn't. Her brain and her body had trapped her.

"Aliya!" The big one used the side of the nearest recliner to try to lift herself up. "You again. What the *fuck* are you doing in my apartment? Aliya!"

Poppy screamed and cussed at them and called for her mom and dad and God and closed her eyes and put her fingers in her ears and screamed some more, so powerfully it hurt her head and neck. When she lowered her hands from her ears, she heard a noise at the side of the house: footsteps in the new snow. Then voices: her mother's voice. She could see her parents' feet through the window. When she looked to her left, to the intruders, they were gone. But the door to the storage room remained open.

She ran across the basement floor and up the stairs.

"Poppy?"

"Mommy!" She slammed into her mom in the middle of the living room. "Our house is haunted. I was trying to—"

"Sweetheart." Her mom spoke in her formal, frazzled voice. "Guess what? There's Indian food and we want to introduce you to someone."

It was a girl in an old parka with a crappy elf costume overtop. She smelled like campfire.

"I'm Poppy." Happy Poppy. Normal and friendly, question-asking Poppy who offers to help around the house, who can figure out how to get an A every time, who laughs when people make jokes that aren't funny because it makes those people feel good and worthy, who loves Christmas and cries about her dead sister and eats food and does not believe in ghosts and is not afraid to go to bed tonight. "Welcome to our home."

"Emma."

TWENTY-ONE

All it took to get Emma into their house was a thousand-dollar donation to the food bank. Emma had not understood who they were, not really, with the wind blowing. The blizzard was turning dangerous, they were hustling the animals of the manger into a van, and the food bank volunteers were beginning to dismantle everything for the night. Karen offered to order Emma's favourite food—butter chicken and naan bread.

The blizzard had made it a long and difficult drive across the city. As they pulled into the garage, she understood who they were. "Are you going to hurt me?"

"We would never hurt you." Karen checked her phone; dinner was about to arrive. When it did, Poppy transferred it into their best bowls and placed it on the middle of the dining room table: butter chicken, saag paneer, some kormas and dal in their best bowls, with plates of papadums and garlic naan bread.

Karen opened her second last bottle of white Burgundy. She would never drink wine this good again.

"You saw me, what, on your security cameras? It wasn't even me who planned it all. I got hardly any of the money. I was just like, 'I know a place,' and . . . "

"Did you . . . urinate in the car?"

"No. That was Skeezy."

Karen poured wine for Emma. "Skeezy did that?"

"Yeah."

"Who is Skeezy?"

Emma slouched in the dining room chair. She leaned over and her elbows were on her knees. Karen looked down at her.

"He's this loser guy from Red Deer."

Neither Benedict nor Poppy said a word. His phone was on the credenza, buzzing away.

"You broke into our garage and took our bikes and power tools and things."

"Skeezy's idea."

"And you knew of us because?"

"It's obvious I think."

"Tell us."

"I looked in your garage window. On Halloween night."

Karen glanced at Benedict, her lying husband, the founder of the feast. She didn't want to lead the woman in any direction. "What happened that night? Do you remember?"

Now Emma looked at Benedict.

He attacked me in the alley. He dragged me into your backyard and jumped on me.

"I was trying to break into houses. I was pretty high. I saw into your garage there and figured . . . Anyway, I ended up stabbing my crowbar into myself when . . . What's your name again?"

"Benedict."

"When Benedict rammed into me."

Karen took a long drink of her wine, which was a perfect match for the saag paneer. In the car, on the way home, Emma had sworn over and over again that she had never met a girl named Charlotte. Benedict had pulled a blown-up photograph of her out of his bag, and Emma declared she was damn pretty. But she hadn't seen her anywhere. She didn't hang out with teenagers, really, unless they were at the women's shelter or the camp. All four of them ate in silence for a few moments. The *Charlie Brown Christmas* soundtrack was playing and Emma bobbed her head in time to the soft jazz. "I fucking love this show, you guys."

"You know it?" said Poppy.

"My mom and I used to watch it when I was little. Last time I had Indian food I was working at the Fringe." Emma sniffed at the naan. "They made us volunteer for it, like they're making me volunteer for the food bank."

"You still live with your mom?" Poppy took Karen's glass of wine and sipped it before she could get it back from her.

"No. Well, sort of. We got kicked out of our place. Neither of us had a job and we hadn't been paying so . . . We're on a list. Right now I'm at the women's shelter sometimes but I usually just stay with her at the camp."

Poppy grabbed Benedict's hand. "The camp?"

"By the library."

For the next while, Emma told Poppy about her childhood—how she had ended up here at twenty-one. Her father was mean, abusive, and drunk. Her mother drank too much and took too many pills, had trouble keeping a job. She herself had dropped out of school in the eleventh grade and spent time on the streets in Vancouver, pretty strung out. When she came home, it was to get her shit together but she hadn't managed it yet. "So, yeah, I made some bad choices. Acted like a fucking orangutan, since we're being honest, and I'm learning not to blame anyone for it. It was me. I did it. So here I am. No big drama."

"Did you sneak in and write your name on the wall?" Poppy pointed above the mantel. "Did you pee on stuff?"

"My name? No. I've never been in here."

Poppy turned to Karen. "You see? It's the house, Mom. It wants us out. It took Charlotte."

Emma finished her glass of wine and picked up one of the flyers on the table. "I don't know Charlotte but maybe it's something like I did. I didn't *mean* to end up a goddamn mess. I've been good, real good, since the night Skeezy pissed in your car. But I own my bad choices. I know I'm just the Christmas Indian dinner guest but I bet the house didn't take your sister. I bet she took herself somewhere."

Karen sighed and lifted her wine glass, tapped Emma's wine glass. "We invited you here to meet you and to say sorry. It changed us, what we did to you. It's ruined our lives. To the extent our lives weren't already ruined." A glass and a half of wine made Karen more articulate, quicker, a better version of herself. Any more and all of the elegance would pass. She would begin slurring her words, losing track of things, forgetting. "We told ourselves we abandoned you that night, Emma, because if we told the truth it would get you in trouble. The break-in aspect. You're a thief after all, caught in the act. We thought you had died. Then I realized it was you, it was *all you*, and you took Charlotte."

"Let's settle this part. Number one I don't piss on things. That's a boy move and fucking gross. Number two I don't know shit about Charlotte. Sorry, Poppy."

Poppy had nearly finished all the food on her plate. She had looked pale earlier, paler than usual. But there was a new pinkness about her forehead and cheeks. "If it helps, I'll say it too. Shit. Piss. Fuck."

"Please don't." Karen pushed back her chair. "I think Poppy is right. The house is telling us something."

"You don't have a home," said Benedict.

Emma Scofield took a deep breath. "As long as I keep volunteering, and showing initiative, and if I stop backsliding into the kind of behaviour that got me into this . . . I mean, I was okay in school. I was just a regular kid. Not in a fancy place like this. We lived in an apartment on Fort Road. But I was regular!"

"What happened?" said Poppy.

"What do you mean what happened?"

"You were regular. And then what?"

Emma just looked at her. For a moment Karen thought the girl would say or do something scary, something wild or violent. "There's probably a reason. I don't know what it is. You talk to social workers and they want you to think a certain way, find the big cause of everything. What happened? Honestly I think it started at a school dance or something. I coulda turned left but I turned right. I couldn't find my way back."

"Back to what?"

"I don't know. My version of whatever this is. Jesus. Do you guys even know what this is? Poppy? You're sitting here in this . . . mansion eating Indian food with a mom and dad who love you, who're rich. I bet you're good in school and get whatever clothes you want. Let's see your phone."

Poppy's phone was always close. She lifted it on to the table. Karen couldn't keep track of the versions but it was the latest iPhone with the nicest camera.

"I know you're just a kid but don't you get it? What you have?"

"But my sister's not here."

Because of this Karen got up, when she heard the break in Poppy's voice, and kneeled on the floor next to her and hugged her.

"Sorry," said Emma. "I didn't mean to . . . "

"No," said Benedict. "It's okay."

When Poppy was finished wiping the tears and the makeup from her eyes with her serviette, she stood up from the table. "Can I show you around?"

Emma looked at Karen and then at Benedict. Her plate was empty and so was her glass of wine. "Yeah. Sure."

They started in the foyer. Then, in the living room, Poppy explained about seeing her name on the wall in red. Then she saw it at school, while she was dancing. "I floated in the air."

"What are you talking about?"

Poppy stuttered, as she tried to explain about Emma's name on the wall and the urine on the floor, looking back to her parents for confirmation. Emma turned to them as well.

"What the fuck is this?"

Karen shrugged. "We hoped you could tell us."

"What do you mean you floated? And what does this have to do with my name? Are you guys . . . religious people?"

"We like Christmas." Poppy led Emma through the dining room and into the grand kitchen.

With Vince Guaraldi jazz playing, Karen could no longer hear what they were talking about. Then they went downstairs. She did not want to be alone with her husband because she did not want to address what they had to address. Benedict spoke first. "Do you believe her?"

Karen did not have to think about it. "Yes."

"The wall?"

She shrugged. "There are more things in heaven and earth, Horatio."

"I painted over it that night and it came back." Benedict's phone hummed again. "I really did paint over it."

"Should you answer, one of these times?"

"It's Marie-Claude. I made the wizards sign a special NDA but I guess one of them broke it and told her."

"Why haven't you told her?"

"To protect her."

"Bullshit."

"Because I am a coward."

"Now you're talking."

Karen looked around. "Any sign of your ghost?"

"Not at the moment. But it's too big to fit in the house now."

"Like Pinocchio's nose."

Benedict nearly smiled. He tended not to drink but he reached for Karen's glass and tasted her wine.

"Will we have to give up the house?" Karen topped it up. "When all this comes out?"

"It's the one thing we don't have to give up. Bankruptcy legislation."

Karen looked around Finster House: the freshly painted white wall, the staircase, the new floors and ceilings they put in when they bought the place, and the scratches in various spots from Daphne's claws. Poppy led Emma back through the kitchen and toward the staircase. Emma was carrying two bags and cords popped out the top.

"You can leave those here for now," said Poppy.

Karen asked what was in the bags.

"I'm giving my stuff to Emma."

"What stuff?"

Poppy did not answer as she climbed the stairs with Emma, who shrugged at Karen. When she could hear their footsteps up there, Karen took the glass of wine back from Benedict. Before they became multimillionaires, less than a month ago, she had everything in place—at least psychologically—to leave him. Now there was an even better reason to abandon her husband to his failure, the best reason of all. He had lied to her and to everyone—to the *New York Times*. There would be a terrible reckoning, and he was right. The girls should become Sjöblads. They should run away from him the way Karen had tried to distance herself from her own father. "When did you say the number one wizard is coming to town, and all will be revealed?"

"Monday," said Benedict. "Gandalf comes Monday."

"So we have tomorrow. Twenty-four hours."

"When you signed on to this, when we married our fortunes together, I was a great prospect."

Karen decided not to disagree.

"I never made it real, that promise I showed back in school. I know you feel it was for nothing. I have stolen these years from you."

Not for nothing. But. She decided to let him talk.

"I lost one of our babies."

Karen was exhausted by thinking about all of this, for years and years and years. It was too late to go back and change a thing, and even if she could change something maybe she wouldn't. She didn't want other girls.

"All those nights in the painting bay of a car dealership, building nothing. Working against myself and my family, destroying Marie-Claude."

She wanted to shout it back at him. Yes! Building *nothing*! They went on holidays without him and ate hundreds of dinners without him. She made excuses for him to their own children. They never spoke, not about anything that mattered. The silence in their bedroom at night, when the girls were asleep, was actual torture. What was she to him? What did she *mean*? And here was Benedict, years too late, ignoring phone calls from his business partner and speaking about something that mattered—all that mattered.

"It's all gone."

But it wasn't all gone. They still had the house. Then again . . . Karen looked around and, admitting she had sipped three-quarters of a bottle of white Burgundy, she was not at all sure she wanted the house. It certainly did not want them. Their failure was total, and the only way to start over was to let it go. Not a little bit of it. All of it. The music had stopped. She could hear Poppy and Emma talking upstairs.

Her own childhood home, in Edgemont, had become dangerous nostalgia. Now that it was pissed on and gone, she was pleased to be free of the painting. The last time she and the girls went to Banff, in the summertime, she had taken them through her old neighbourhood in the Tesla and stopped in front of the house. Its current owners had updated the landscaping with attractive rocks, prairie grasses, and trembling aspen. A silver BMW sedan was parked in front. Through the massive front window, with its view of the mountains, Karen could see a piece of abstract art on the wall. Midcentury modern furniture. It was late in the morning. A woman in a white robe, a good thick one like they have at Fairmont hotels, walked past with a mug of coffee. It made her feel sick to see this woman, a podiatrist or the communications director for an oil company, in the house that would have been hers if her father had not done what he did.

Poppy could complete high school in New Westminster. Not just Poppy. Charlotte too. She was here somewhere, behind the walls. The house was holding her hostage, waiting for ransom.

"Why is Poppy doing that?" Benedict pointed to the shopping bags.

Karen took a final drink of the marvellous wine. "If we give it all up, Charlotte will come back."

"I have already given up. Like I told you—"

"No, Ben, give it *all* up. I wanted to be rich, and you knew I wanted to be rich, and fancy, and respected by . . . by these assholes in tuxedos and cocktail dresses. You know why? Because I'm ashamed. I figured you could fix it. And I think you knew that about me. I think it's why you did what you did, at least partly."

"I don't know."

"And you. The company, your parents . . . "

"I had a brother."

"What?"

"Mark. He had autism, the serious kind, far worse than me and Charlotte, and his epilepsy would come and go. He was violent, I guess . . . and he had this other disorder called fragile X syndrome. My parents couldn't handle it, couldn't handle him, so they gave him up. Foster parents took him in but they struggled too. My mother and father told themselves it was better for Mark to be with foster parents, with experts in care, but I looked into it. They weren't experts. There is no such thing. He died when he was a teenager. I didn't find out about all of this until after they were gone."

"Your hardcore born-again parents."

"They ran away. They ran all the way to Angola."

"Let's not run away." Karen took his hand. "Poppy's right. Let's give it up."

Poppy and Emma emerged again on the stairs, with two suitcases—Poppy's pink one and Charlotte's black one—stuffed and heavy.

"Poppy's helping me. I'm changing my life." Emma addressed Karen and Benedict as she carted Charlotte's black suitcase down the stairs. "I talk to a shitload of people who figure they can fix me. Poppy isn't like them. You should be real proud."

Benedict's phone was humming on the credenza again.

"You gonna get that?" Emma rolled the suitcase to the front door. "Guys, I should get back to the camp. My mom gets anxious about me, since . . . well, since our little accident. I'm off the drugs and I want her to know I'm staying off them. She won't believe tonight."

"Let me drive you." Benedict grabbed his keys from the Japanese bowl in the kitchen. It was one of a thousand gorgeous but entirely useless things Karen had purchased on her travels. She had bought the blue bowl in Osaka because it was lovely and because she could afford it. While she could not remember the exact price, it was one of a kind, the work of a ceramic artist named Akiko—enough to pay the rent in a two-bedroom apartment for three months.

Poppy said she wanted to go along and Karen did too, though the blizzard had turned nasty. She did not want to be alone in this house.

TWENTY-TWO

The camp was in the little park near the farmers' market and the old brick library. On the corner there was a gazebo where Poppy and Charlotte had done crafts when they were little, during the Fringe Festival, crayons and safety scissors and pipe cleaners, the smell of white glue and sunscreen. The festival happened at the end of summer when the nights got cold and the leaves started to change. Poppy would think about going back to school at that time, new clothes and a backpack, and Halloween, and Christmas.

Christmas lights hung from the gazebo. People wore serious parkas in there, and steam rose from huge vats. Soup.

Her dad opened the back of the Model X, where they had put Emma's things: video game consoles and an electric guitar that had only been played twice, two Bluetooth speakers and an iPhone that wasn't even old, a MacBook Air, a selfie stick, and all the stuff from her room Emma had thrown into the suitcases when Poppy had asked her to do it. Anything she wanted! Her fancy alarm

clock and hair dryer and curler, some books and board games and
DVDs and even a DVD player with a bunch of dust on it.

They were not allowed to hug Emma. They were not supposed
to have had her in the house either, but no one seemed to be following the rules in the city and that was why so many people were
getting sick.

Her dad's phone had been going nuts for the past while, but
he never paid attention. It was going off again, in his hand.

"I wish we had the money to set you and your mom up with
a place to live." He shrugged. "The truth is, Emma . . . "

Her dad hardly ever spoke when her mom was around. Her
mom was the talker. The camp was just a whole bunch of tents, put
up haphazardly, with a couple of teepees in the middle. It would
have been easier to navigate as a grid, with streets and avenues,
but that was the kind of thinking people didn't find too helpful
anymore. Poppy remembered the news. When the pandemic was
turning ugly, and summer was getting close, some people just
started putting tents up. It's a public park, so why not? The police
had taken the camp down a few times but then it was put up again,
and again. Some First Nations people made a pretty good point
about who *really* owned this land, and it was in the news and in the
end the mayor let it stay. The virus got worse, but even though
the old white guys on TV said the camp was a super-spreader,
they didn't smash the camp because churches and malls could still
have people and the schools were open. They talked about it in
social studies class, all this inconsistency and unfairness.

Smoke rose up from the middle of the camp, the only bit that
was protected from the wind, and over the hum of a big diesel
generator she could hear "It's Beginning to Look a Lot Like
Christmas." In a blizzard! Poppy moved away from the car while
her parents chatted with Emma and spotted carollers with masks
on. They were doing a performance for a big crowd on the other

side of a fire. It was hard to see with the snow so Poppy moved closer. The singers wore Santa hats and white T-shirts over their parkas that said Street Choir. On the days she walked home from school along Whyte Avenue, or when she was on the bus or the LRT, she saw people like this. If they looked at her, she looked away. They had different rules. But there was something about them, and Emma had a bit of it too. Was it something they were born with, something they inherited from their own parents or grandparents? What made her different—really?

Poppy was different. Whatever stuff she gave to Emma would come back to her, so she could give it all away and wish with all of her heart for Charlotte. The more she gave away, the easier it was for Charlotte to come home. The less she worried about herself, the more she could worry about Charlotte. She had not looked at her phone all day. She ate a normal amount of Indian food and chose not to hate herself for it, in case that is how she let the big woman and the little woman into her dreams. When you give it all away, Charlotte comes back. Poppy closed her eyes and did her little prayer again. *God protect me from the evil spirits I promise never to hurt people or animals or lie please God bring Charlotte home so I can love her better . . .*

Her mother was calling her back to the car. They would get back into it and drive home to a house of spirits, a house without Charlotte. Daphne would not bark when they came in, a silence that still broke her heart every time. A lot of her favourite things were with Emma now but not enough of them. Emma lived in a tent. She broke into garages in the night.

"It's Beginning to Look a Lot Like Christmas" ended and everyone clapped. She clapped too. Emma was still at the car, their hundred-thousand-dollar car, in her elf costume. At the fire, they were trying to figure out what song to do next, to do last. Then it would be quiet here too, apart from the generator and the awful wind, blowing in every direction at once, and everyone would wish they could start it all over again: come back, hopeful singers.

"Poppy!" There was frustration in her mom's voice now, the voice she used when Daphne was running after a jackrabbit. Poppy made her way back to the car. The storm was mean and it was getting meaner.

Snow had already gathered on the bags and suitcases, full of Emma's new things. Benedict wiped them off.

"Say goodbye," said her mom.

Poppy did not want to say it so she pulled her hand out of her pocket and smiled. She saw herself the way Emma saw her, the rich girl who was good in school and lived in a mansion with parents who loved her.

"It's all so nice." Emma grabbed the suitcases, one in each hand. Where was she going to put them? In her tent? "It's so nice to help me out like this. The butter chicken, the wine, all these cool things."

Poppy pulled her mother around the car. "Let's ask her to stay, her and her mom."

"Darling, we can't. The crisis team comes back in the morning."

"The crisis team can't help us, Mom. It's the house."

"It isn't the house, sweetie. It's us. It's me, and your dad, and—"

"You're getting a divorce."

Her mother shook her head. "In the next few days everything is going to—"

"Let's give it to Emma, Mommy."

"Give what to her? We already—"

"The house. I think we have to. If she didn't write her name on the wall . . . "

"Of course she did, Pop."

"She said she didn't and I believe her. You believe her too. Let's give her the house. I think we have to."

Her mother laughed.

"Mom. We *have to*."

There were times when Poppy knew she could turn her mother's initial *no* into a *yes*. No to a sleepover, a new iPhone, a donation to a girls' school in rural Kenya. There would be a moment of silence, as her mother considered it and saw there was a lesson here, or a night to herself, or however it felt to make her daughter happy. On the Saturday before Christmas, in the blizzard, this was not how her mother looked. She stared at the encampment. The smell of smoke crossed the avenue and her mother closed her eyes. Poppy tended not to notice the lines on her mother's face, her age, and now it frightened her. She would lose her mother one day, as her mother had lost her mother and her mother hers. It made the house, holding on to a house that did not want them, even more wrong. They would not be together forever. There was only so much time, and if you were careful, you could get it right. You could be proud of your different sister, of your body, of your father who never smiles. You could find a way to understand your mother's pain. They were wearing mittens but Poppy reached out and took her mother's hand because she seemed lost.

The wind pushed a new smell across the street. Soup. Her father joined them and seemed to understand something had changed.

"Poppy . . . Poppy thinks we should give it to Emma."

"We have already given her all of Poppy's consumer goods, anything that can be pawned. I have some money in my wallet."

"The house, Ben."

"Daddy, Emma didn't write her name on the wall."

Now he was quiet for a while. "Then . . . we would have nothing."

"Yes," said Poppy.

"Nothing," said her mother.

TWENTY-THREE

Karen had seen all the movies. She had heard all of the songs and she had read a lot of the books. At the dentist's and doctors' offices, whenever she spotted a ratty old December issue of decor or fashion magazines or *Reader's Digest*, she went straight to the Christmas bits. The fake tree of her childhood, balm for all horror. It was a soft-lighted marvel, not to mention the mantel scenes and nutcrackers and cool, Nordic carved wooden reindeer.

She had made lists and given presents according to some vague calculation of credit and closeness, but she never really *gave* anything. In recent years, it seemed the entire ritual had become a bloodless exchange of capital: your seventy-five dollars for my eighty-two. Karen had never sacrificed her happiness, her freedom, her comfort, or her wealth—not once, not for anything.

In the blizzard, for the second time in one night, she did not do what every instinct told her to do: argue against it. You couldn't *give your house away*, especially to someone like Emma. When Benedict's creditors came for him, in a couple of days, it would be their only asset. A repossession man would come into the house in a polyester suit, smelling of cigarette smoke and cologne, just like the one who had come into her childhood home in Edgemont. And then other men, his employees, would arrive to take it all away. They would live in an empty house that—they all felt it, even Benedict, who did not always feel—did not want them.

Now that she had lost her baby to despair and shame, the rest of it could go too. Karen had been blind, grasping, and proud. It took this culminating miracle of soup-scented loss to see it had to go too. And not to the bank. They had paid it off. It was theirs and not theirs. The house knew who it wanted.

Poppy watched her and so did Benedict. Karen was the one who made decisions about renovations and sleepovers and holidays and pizza and apps and clothes and donations to international charities.

Nothing.

Without another word, Karen walked around the Tesla to Emma, who stood shivering with the suitcases.

"Can you guys watch the bags? I'll bring the suitcases to my mom's tent and then I'll come back for them. Yeah?"

"Just leave it all for a moment."

Emma released them. "You changed your mind, Karen? Yeah, I figured. It's too much anyway. You know what the cops will do, when I try to sell this stuff? And what'll I say? 'No, no, really, they *gave* it to me.' Right."

"I'd like to meet your mom."

"What? Why? Did I do something wrong? You don't believe me about something?"

"I believe you about everything, Emma. We all do. And don't worry about the stuff. It's yours."

Emma crossed the snowy road a bit stiffly, mumbling to herself. Karen could not hear what she said, not over the generator and the carollers singing a sad and dissonant version of "O Holy Night."

They wove between tents, which was tricky business because boots and other items were piled outside the zip fronts, partially or fully hidden by snow. Street Choir. For a moment she stood and watched them, listened, and their lack of skill made the song and their performance of it sadder than usual. No, not sadder. That is not why she teared up at "O Holy Night." This feeling was not sadness.

"Karen!" Emma stood in front of a blue domed tent, holding up its protective front flap.

One of the singers, a woman with a crooked hat and mismatched mittens, placed her hands on her heart. She sang louder and more beautifully than the others. Karen whispered along. *Fall . . . on your knees. Hear . . . the angel voices.* When the singers were finished, Karen clapped along with everyone else and wiped the tears from her eyes with the back of her mitten and laughed at herself. "Coming."

Karen tried to figure out how to get inside the tent without carting a bunch of wet snow with her. Emma had unzipped it and held the flap opened. Karen took off her boots as she crawled in. Tents had never been her favourite. She hadn't slept in one since her teens. The space was lit by a faint orange lantern hanging by a hook from the ceiling. Emma's mother, Alice, was about Karen's age—maybe younger. She was thin-faced, wan and waxy, with teeth like her daughter's only worse, and she was wrapped in a number of blankets. The sleeping bags swished when Karen crawled over them to find a place to sit. It smelled like smoke and maybe mothballs, from the donated bed linen. There were so many blankets and a stuffed panda that had lost an eye, an empty bag of potato chips and two Diet Coke bottles squished and ready for recycling.

How to explain all of this? Emma introduced her and did a pretty good job of it, the attempted break-in, the blood, the proper break-in, Candy Cane Lane, Indian food, and all this stuff—two thousand dollars' worth, at least. A battered paperback copy of *Pride and Prejudice* sat next to Alice. She had a nose ring and a tattoo on her neck, some snaking design. If they were contemporaries, Alice would have been infinitely cooler than Karen in, say, 1995. She could see Alice in a Gastown pub, the bad girl, smoking and playing pool and wearing a white cotton singlet without a bra—everything Karen had wished she could be, if only for a night, during her bachelor of fine arts.

Once Emma finished explaining, Alice shook her head. "So what are you doing in here? Emma robbed your garage. Is there something you want me to do about it? I can't . . . Can't insurance cover whatever she stole? Sorry, I didn't dress for the occasion. Why didn't you call the cops? Please close the zipper."

"No, no, we did. The police came." Karen zipped the tent door shut, not that it would make one shred of difference. It was a tent. She wanted to tell Alice about Skeezy, who pissed in the car and was a garbage influence on Emma. "That doesn't matter. We just thought . . . You don't have a place to live. We'd like to give that to you."

Emma smiled and then covered her mouth with her hand.

"I don't understand." Alice looked at her daughter. "What is this?"

"They want to help us."

"Why?"

There was no short answer to this, but Karen had to say something. She should have prepared. "We have too much. That's why Emma tried to break in the first time, and why she and Skeezy . . . Listen, I have to tell you that Skeezy is not a good person. We have too much and you don't have enough."

"Is this a Christian thing? 'Cause we're not—"

"We've been doing it wrong for a long time."

"Doing what wrong?"

"Everything. Just every last damn thing. It was my daughter's idea to do this, just to give it away. *Give it all away* and start over."

Alice nodded. She wasn't the super-cool one in the bar in Gastown. She was the philosophical one who didn't lie or pretend, the one who could see the treachery and the weakness in the heart of someone like Karen. "You'll change your mind. Then what?"

"I married for money. I had experienced a reversal, when I was a bit younger than Emma, and I thought it would make me happy to marry a man with great promise."

"You don't love him?"

"I thought I didn't love him but I do. Like I said, I was just doing it wrong."

Emma put her arm around her mother.

"I struggle, Karen—it's Karen?—to understand." Alice sat up straight. "I don't understand what this has to do with me and Emma."

"We want to give it to you."

"Give us what?"

"Finster House. And everything else. It has to be everything or it's nothing."

"It's such a nice house, Mom. It's a frickin' mansion."

"You can't give a house to someone." Alice laughed. "You crazy bitch. What is this?"

"Mom!"

Karen realized she could not do this alone. "Will you come with me to the car? My daughter and husband are there, and together we can tell you what this is all about. Something has happened to us. Something we earned, something shameful. And there's only one way to get rid of it. When this thing is gone, our other daughter, the one who is missing, she'll come back to us."

Alice reached into the mess of blankets and pulled out a squished box of tissues. Karen took one, it was so cold, and touched her eyes with it.

"You're not gonna do something weird to us?"

"I wouldn't even know how, Alice."

"Let me get some decent pants on."

Karen thanked Alice for trusting her and unzipped the door. Emma thanked Karen for being understanding and apologized for her mom calling her a bitch, said she'd escort her mom to the car. The carollers were piling into a white van and the people in the gazebo were putting up thick tarps to protect the kitchen from the ravages of the blizzard. It was supposed to last all night. There would be deep quiet when the wind stopped, with the heavy snow and the new cold. Karen took the long way back to the car, weaving between the tents. A few people said hello to her. A man asked her to hold on to the fly of his tent while he fiddled with and cussed at a frozen zipper. He called it a horse's cunt, and it was the first time in all her life Karen had heard that one.

By the time she made it back to the car, Alice and Emma were already there. Both of them were tiny, Benedict was right, a couple of sparrows. The back of the car was open and the suitcases and bags were in there. Poppy pressed the button to close the hatch. Benedict was in the driver's seat of the car. Faintly Karen could see he was on the phone.

"Mom! I told them we're giving them the house, giving it to them for real."

"That's great, honey. You met Ms. Scofield?"

Alice crossed her arms and there was something between a frown and a smile on her face. "Yeah, we met. She's a real sweetie, Karen. I just don't know what to say about this. It's been the weirdest fucking fifteen minutes of my life and I've been through some things."

"When an opportunity comes along, Alice, you gotta learn to take it," said Poppy. "It's what the universe wants."

"All right then," said Alice. "Now what?"

Karen opened the passenger door of the car and Benedict was looking at his phone.

"Who were you talking to?"

"Marie-Claude." He did not look away from his phone. "I have to go downtown."

"Why?"

"She wants me to say goodbye to the wizards. They're having a party."

"I want you to meet Alice, Emma's mom. She's a bit concerned. She doesn't understand."

Benedict turned to Karen. "Do you understand?"

The wind was so strong it was pinning her foot in between the door and the jamb. That was just about enough blizzard for one night. Karen stepped back out of the car and shouted, though they were only a few feet away, "Hey. There's a party downtown, in my husband's factory. It'll be warm. Let's go there."

"Oh, I'm not big on parties anymore," said Alice.

Benedict stared straight ahead again. Karen got into the car and closed the door. She wanted to ask if his big and growing ghost was in front of them but she did not want to frighten Poppy or their guests so she removed her mitten and placed her cold hand on his wrist and squeezed.

"My husband's not big on parties either. I'm sure we won't stay long."

TWENTY-FOUR

From the vantage point of the pretty new bridge in the river valley, Karen Sjöblad's adopted city was a Christmas marvel— beautiful and deadly. The sports teams had terrible names and she had trouble living anywhere without either mountains or the ocean visible from a morning dog walk. But her daughters had been born here and this insignificant place had formed them, as much as that is possible. She wanted the city to know so she told it, out loud, that she appreciated how it had taken care of her.

She asked it to keep Charlotte safe in the blizzard.

"Mom? You okay? Just talking to yourself up there?"

Benedict adjusted the rear-view mirror so he could make eye contact with Poppy, as they climbed up the north side of the valley. "Your mom is okay," he said. "You don't have to worry."

Poppy made a sarcastic snort, and Karen was proud of her for it and said so. The capacity for sarcasm was a dark sort of cleverness, and Poppy would need it to get through the coming years. Her daughter was a blonde giant next to the Scofields in the backseat. The High Level Bridge was lit up red and green and the corny but wonderful Telus Tower had its blinking Christmas tree a-blinking. A big oil recession had turned into an even bigger one with the pandemic, but the blizzard-wrapped towers were slowly filling with artificial intelligence and video game companies. Karen still checked the price of West Texas Intermediate every day, hoping it was on its way toward profitability and therefore prosperity for her people, but it was over. All of the parties, the weekends at the Banff Springs Hotel paid for by Royal Dutch Shell, the feeling that she was at the centre of everything we needed to move and build, and that her father was simply well compensated for it, that he deserved it, that she deserved it, that she was *entitled to it*, all of those feelings she had grown up with were gone.

She tried to explain this to Poppy, as they reached Jasper Avenue and Benedict navigated toward 104th Street, but after the wine Karen couldn't fit her thoughts through the funnel. Judy Garland was singing "Have Yourself a Merry Little Christmas" on the radio. After her father disappeared, the song had become sad, a soft cry in the night, rather than simply nice. So many things were like that. Comedies turned melancholy on her, unless they had been melancholy all along and she had lacked the key to feel it. Karen kept her fingers on Benedict's wrist, as he steered with the other hand, and from time to time she squeezed in a manner she considered meaningful, to encourage him and to express her love.

The downtown decorations were modest and jolly. You could spend public money on beauty in this place but not much money. *Merry Christmas, you wonderful old Building and Loan!* She laughed at herself, for thinking this. Had she said it out loud? They parked in the lot next to the factory, in the spot reserved for the CEO, and it occurred to Karen that she had no idea why they had come. Marie-Claude was throwing a failure party? The music went silent, and the silence was sad. *Merry Christmas, you wonderful old factory of fraud.* Everything was warm in the car but she opened the door, and the chilly wind of the blizzard hit her in the face and took away her breath.

Emma linked arms with her mother, and Alice linked arms with Karen, and together they followed Benedict and Poppy to the door of the factory. She had forgotten that Emma was in an elf costume. She slipped in the elfin fabric that covered her boots but just for a moment, and the three of them remained on their feet. At the door, Alice asked whose party this was. And weren't parties against the law, during the pandemic?

"We're at Benedict's factory. There are legally exempt wizards inside, from around the world."

"Wizards and elves," said Alice.

Karen reminded them to put on their face masks.

There were two sets of doors to get into the warehouse. In the foyer they could already hear an orchestral version of "We Wish You a Merry Christmas" on the other side of the second door. When it opened, the song and the warmth hit them. There really was a party going on, with a gorgeously decorated Christmas tree and messed-up garland on the walls. There were five Kutisis, and Karen had not realized how big and beautiful they were. Two large men sat in front of one of the Kutisis, with its front panel off. The rest of the pretty silver boxes were intact and alight.

Marie-Claude was in the centre of the room at a table filled with snacks and cheeses and bottles of wine, singing along with two other men. This was in multiple ways a contravention of the pandemic rules, but they were already in such trouble. Poppy ran up to hug Marie-Claude and stopped herself.

"Almost forgot!" Poppy said, through her mask. She introduced Marie-Claude to Emma and Alice and they waved at one another.

Oh, bring us some figgy pudding!

Benedict stood several feet from Marie-Claude and the singing men. Marie-Claude pulled out her phone and removed her glasses and touched something. The music stopped and Benedict spun slowly about the space, his leather-soled shoes shuffling on the concrete. He had ruined his shoes in the snow tonight. Benedict put his hands over his face and slowly lowered himself to his knees. Karen was embarrassed and terrified for him, for them all.

The room was silent apart from the hum of the machines. In the corner, the two men inspecting the Kutisi turned around and the legs of their stools screeched on the concrete. Then they were silent too, looking at the floor, like they were hon-ouring the war dead.

Marie-Claude made her way toward Benedict and with the help of a stool lowered herself to her own knees, across from him, and whispered something Karen could not hear. It was so intimate and so quiet and Benedict was so moved, Karen had to look away. First he tried to stab her with a piece of wood, then they gave their home away, and now this. Actual mourning.

She considered these men, the wizards. One of the singers, an older gentleman, wore a tweed jacket. Tonight was their going-away party and it seemed the wine had gotten the better of them. Benedict said nothing. Was it not his job as CEO, his final job, to say something?

There was an open bottle of white wine on the centre table and several others chilling, and reds, and beer, and cognac. Karen grabbed a clean glass and offered one to Emma and to Alice. She preferred a wake to a funeral. "Here's to coal!"

Now the wizards turned to her like she was the one with the social ineptitudes. Scientists were so weird. It wasn't terribly funny, and her delivery wasn't good, but they didn't have to be offended. People took such enormous pleasure in being offended. She was tempted to ask the big men in front of the machine, whom she took to be the German wizards, if there was a word in their language for the ugly pleasure of feeling offended. Instead: "I'm sorry."

"No, no." Marie-Claude climbed up from her knees and grabbed a corkscrew from the table, eyeing Benedict. She opened a new bottle of white and filled Karen's glass, filled two more for Emma and Alice. "I've been trying to reach Ben. I must admit everything was a bit dreary, though I was not entirely sure why. Our Benedict, it turns out, had not told me everything—not that it would have made much of a difference. I slept some nights I shouldn't have, all things considered. And then Sir Walter . . . "

"Jarrow." The man in the tweed jacket extended his elbow. "Lovely to meet you. Ms. Sjöblad, I presume?"

So he was the British one, the haughty one. Fuck him. She bumped elbows with him. "Welcome to the colonies, belatedly."

"I leave tomorrow. Or that was the plan, anyway." He and Marie-Claude made eye contact that was not innocent of emotion.

Karen sipped the wine. It wasn't white Burgundy, by any means, but it was nice. A Pinot Gris from the Okanagan. She picked it up to read the back label. She really did not need another glass of wine.

"And then, just as we were finishing dinner, Sir Walter mentioned this *girl* who had been in the building," said Marie-Claude.

"What girl?"

"That's exactly what I said, Karen. Our security is rather tight, as you know. The notion of a girl wandering around at all hours, in what might be the most dangerous warehouse on the continent at the moment. Well." Marie-Claude turned to Benedict. "If things weren't bad enough with the company."

Just then Charlotte walked out of the kitchen, with a smoothie. Actual Charlotte, in her black jeans and black hoodie. Karen dropped her glass and the bottle of Okanagan Pinot Gris and it all shattered on the concrete floor. She did not stay to apologize to Sir Walter and Marie-Claude and Emma and Alice, who danced away from the wet explosion. She ran to her daughter.

"Mom, careful." Charlotte lifted her smoothie in warning, but Karen crashed into her with a huge hug anyway. She felt a cold blob of mushed fruit on her ear.

Poppy joined them, and the three of them hugged until Charlotte jostled out of it. There were so many questions Karen wanted to ask, and a bit of anger and panic mingled in with her joy at rediscovering her baby girl. Charlotte's hair smelled of cheap, apple-scented conditioner. Of all the issues that seemed crucial in this moment, was there a shower here? Who had stocked it with shampoo and conditioner?

Karen started blubbering these and other questions but Charlotte was making her way to her father. She held out her hand, not for a shake but to help him to his feet. Then she hugged him. Charlotte *initiated* a hug, the first in her life. Neither of them seemed in a hurry to end the hug, and in the midst of it they said things to one another. Secret words of love. Poppy grabbed Karen's hand and squeezed so hard it hurt. Poppy said she had never seen such a thing, her sister and her dad like this, and she audibly sobbed. When their embrace ended, Charlotte led her father across the room and through a set of doors. Karen knew these doors opened to the painting bay, though she had not been in the room since the day Benedict and his team moved in, and she and Poppy followed.

When the door closed behind them, the four members of the Ross-Sjöblad family were in the painting bay alone. On the other side of the door, "We Wish You a Merry Christmas" started anew and the drunk wizards resumed singing along.

Charlotte stood in the middle of the room, next to Benedict.

Poppy walked right up to the lone Kutisi in the corner, surrounded by benches and tools. "It's so silvery. I never saw one in person. Can I touch it?"

Benedict cleared his throat to speak. "Sure."

Karen put her hand on Charlotte's arm, just for an instant. "Darling, is this where you were the whole time?"

"I went to bed after going to the hospital, and I woke up in the middle of the night sick, and there was a ghost again, and I wondered . . . "

"You wondered?"

"It vibrates," said Poppy. "Just barely though."

The machine was the size of a compact car on its side, smooth metal with blue lights. Poppy placed her hand on a point where the blue light shone down on the logo Karen had designed.

"We really should find a way to repurpose them as art." Karen wanted to put her arm all the way around Charlotte, to hug her the way Benedict had hugged her. And not let her go. She'd have to call Carl to cancel the crisis team meeting. "Maybe one of the big New York galleries. That would be cool. Sell these last six as art, limited editions, once the madness dies down. You tried so hard. You could tell your side of the story."

Charlotte and Benedict looked at her like she had made another bad joke.

"Karen. Our Charlotte figured it out."

"What do you mean?"

"She made it work."

"The thing is making energy right now?"

Charlotte looked at her father and back to her mother. "You can't *make* energy, Mom. You transform it so you can use it, but in essence yes." She crossed her arms. "It's not yet plugged into the grid, but maybe we can get approval for that tomorrow."

"Probably not on a Sunday." Benedict approached the thing, removed the front panel, and took a step back. To Karen, it looked like the inside of a computer, with liquid. But somehow to Benedict . . . he wiped his eyes. Karen had never seen her husband cry. "I couldn't do it. The smartest nuclear minds in the world . . ."

"My sister did it," said Poppy.

Karen did not know what she was looking at, but she took a step closer. "But you said it was impossible."

"It *is* impossible," said Benedict.

Poppy clapped her hands. "Where did you sleep?"

Charlotte turned and pointed to an old couch at the back of the room, where a couple of blankets lay over a bald man.

Karen laughed. "And who's that? Just some dude?"

"His name is Dr. Darren," said Benedict. "He's the director of the Innovative Nuclear Power Reactors and Fuel Cycles program at the International Atomic Energy Agency."

Charlotte looked at him. "When I fixed his machine, he tried to kiss me and Sir Walter Jarrow punched his face."

Tried to kiss her! This was exactly why she wanted Charlotte to carry her iPhone at all times. She was the only fifteen-year-old girl in North America who did not want a phone. Even so, there was a surplus of communications technology in this building. She might have called. She might have checked in. Mom, Dad, I'm working on Kutisi. Don't worry about me. Karen told her so.

"I'm sorry to have worried you. The ghost, the woman from the future who lived in my closet, scared me. She told me what would happen if I didn't come here—to me, to us, to everyone. I did not trust her. But the more I thought about it, the more I knew I would not sleep until I tried. So I grabbed Dad's extra keys. I didn't sleep until today, after I figured it out. All I needed was a couple of blankets so I got them from Winners. Then I went to the factory kitchen, to get some food, and your scientists were there."

"A woman from the future." Benedict walked across the room and adjusted the blanket, which was falling off the sleeping wizard. "Who was she?"

Charlotte made eye contact with him and that was that.

Winners! She went to Winners in the mall instead of, you know, calling her mom and asking her to drop off a duvet. Or, better yet, *sleeping at home*. This would not, could not happen again. But. "Hold on. Ben, what does all this mean? The great wizard comes Monday to confirm that Kutisi doesn't work. Then the investors sue you and the bank takes everything from us and the police arrest you for fraud and misleading investors and various other malfeasance and you go to jail."

"Yes."

"But Kutisi *does* work."

"Yes."

"So . . . they *won't* sue you and bankrupt us and put you in jail?"

"I don't see why they would."

Karen kissed him and embraced him, and instead of stiffening he relaxed into it. "Benny, do you think the Hotel Macdonald has a nice big room for us, with a Christmas tree, so Emma and her mom can have the house to themselves tonight? There's that suite Queen Elizabeth stayed in."

Poppy tugged on Karen's sleeve. "We don't need to be fancy. At the camp, with the tents, I was thinking . . . "

"Thank you, Poppy." Benedict led his family through the heavy door and into the main hall of the factory. Sir Walter's bow tie hung unknotted around his neck and the two top buttons of his crisp white shirt were open. He stood close to Marie-Claude. Someone had swept up the broken glass but the smell of the wine hung in the room. Benedict made his way to the other wizards and bumped elbows with them, and though she could not hear what he said over the music he was clearly thanking them one by one. Like a leader. He put his hands together as in prayer, in spiritual gratitude. Her husband: hugging, crying, and experiencing spiritual gratitude.

Marie-Claude and Sir Walter made their way to Karen and all three of them watched Benedict. Just to make conversation, Karen was going to ask, *What's happened to him?* But she knew the answer.

Marie-Claude offered a fresh glass to Karen and reached for another bottle of Pinot Gris on the table.

"I never took him for a believer," said Sir Walter. "You Americans, how you can reconcile science and religion."

Marie-Claude laughed out loud.

"Last Christmas" started playing. Marie-Claude put down her wine and danced awkwardly with Sir Walter. Karen put her wine down too. She didn't want any more. While dancing, Poppy introduced Charlotte to Emma and Alice.

"We're giving Emma and her mom our house."

Charlotte took a step back. "Why?"

"To make the ghosts go away, and because it's Christmas."

Alice raised her right hand. "Wait, ghosts?"

"They're our ghosts, not yours." Karen encouraged Alice, the cool girl of the 1990s, to dance. "Come on. You know this one. You got a house today."

Alice danced. She was, as Karen had predicted, a cool dancer. The Germans sang along loudly with the ghost of George Michael, their accents sweetly ridiculous. Benedict had turned from one of the machines to watch them. The Kutisi factory no longer looked or felt like a car dealership because Benedict had installed blinds to hide what was happening inside. But the wall facing the alley was really just windows. Karen could feel the draft coming from them. She shouted at Benedict, over the music, if they could open the blinds and he pressed a button.

Karen left the dancers to dance and looked out on the alley, on the warehouse lofts and the towers above them, decorated for Christmas. An alley like this would be ugly in the day but at night, at Christmastime, there was a beauty in it Karen might never have recognized before this moment in her forty-fourth year. She could see into kitchens and living rooms and dining rooms, people with wine glasses, couples on couches and screens flaring in the dark. She had thought you could make energy. Benedict stood with her and then Charlotte joined them.

Karen took her husband's hand and again he did not pull it away.

"Ben, at Candy Cane Lane when I thought it was all gone: the business, the money, our reputation . . . " She reached out for Charlotte, on the other side of him, but did not touch her. Karen did not know how to say what she wanted to say to Benedict, and for now she hoped he knew.

"Last Christmas" ended and there was a long silence in the pause before whatever came next. One of the wizards cleared his throat.

"Another!" said one of the Germans.

Charlotte pointed up at the windows of the people in the lofts and apartments across the alley celebrating, cuddling, lying drowsily in front of screens. Even at this distance Charlotte smelled of apple-scented shampoo. "Poppy said this means the ghosts are gone. Are they?"

Benedict shrugged. "I have no evidence, darling, but not believing hasn't been terribly useful for me. So yes. I believe they're finished with us."

An orchestra began to play, with piano in the lead, Céline Dion's "O Holy Night." It was not Karen's favourite rendition but she would probably cry again tonight, at least once, and she did not care where her family slept as long as she could hear them breathe.

ACKNOWLEDGEMENTS

I am writing this in June, in the southern hemisphere, which feels a lot like December in Canada. There are Christmas in July dinners, in beautiful Tasmania, but they don't feel quite right.

This is not an autobiographical novel but we're about as religious as the Ross-Sjöblads. Even so, something is missing for my family and me, and we talk a lot about that magic. I suppose this novel is about feeling haunted by Christmas and by home at an exceedingly strange time.

Thank you to Gina, Avia, and Esmé for continuing to encourage me in these endeavours and for teaching me so much about what it feels like to be human in the 21st Century.

Thank you to Martha Webb for being my honest, kind, funny, and clever first-reader and friend. I am so lucky to work with Kelly Joseph, Jared Bland, and the brilliant team at McClelland & Stewart. Someday, I hope, we will be in the same city again and I can thank you all properly.

And thanks to you, for spending this time with me.

Cooper & O'Hara

TODD BABIAK's most recent novels are *The Empress of Idaho*, *Son of France*, and *Come Barbarians*, which was a *Globe and Mail* Book of the Year and a number one bestseller. His earlier work includes *The Garneau Block*, which was a national bestseller, a longlisted title for the Scotiabank Giller Prize, and the winner of the City of Edmonton Book Prize; *The Book of Stanley*; and *Toby: A Man*, which was shortlisted for the Stephen Leacock Medal and won the Alberta Book Award for Best Novel. Todd Babiak is the co-founder of Story Engine and CEO of Brand Tasmania. He currently lives with his family in Hobart.